W9-CEY-306

BENT GRASSES

BENT GRASSES

Frank Palmer

St. Martin's Press
New York

Though some locations are real, the East Midlands Combined Constabulary is fictional. So, too, are its cases, characters and the events portrayed in this story.

Library of Congress Cataloging-in-Publication Data

Palmer, Frank
Bent grasses : an Inspector "Jacko" Jackson mystery / Frank Palmer.
p.   cm.
ISBN 0-312-11752-3
I. Title.
PR6066.A438B46   1995
823'.914—dc20   94-36714   CIP

First published in Great Britain by Constable & Company Limited

First U.S. Edition: January 1995
10 9 8 7 6 5 4 3 2 1

For Richard and Penny

1

The Sport of Royals – Regina versus the rogues – was under starter's orders.

He read the list of cases in the glass notice-board as carefully as a punter studies the runners and riders. His name – Jackson J. – came third under 'Officer in Case'.

Ahead of him, a rapist had almost gone the full distance. The judge would finish summing up that trial first. A pre-trial review, which is a bit like a steward's inquiry, was fixed to follow. His fire bomber would lead half a dozen no-hopers bringing up the rear. Fridays in crown courts are often dustbin days – shovel up the debris and start with a clean sheet next week.

Swallowing a bored yawn, he stuffed his hands deep into the pockets of his grey trousers. He turned and gazed without interest round the crowded foyer, lifting his hazel eyes behind bifocals to readjust from close-range reading to longer distance viewing.

Barristers in their black colours sat at square tables taking last-minute instructions, like jockeys about to get mounted. Reporters hogged the two public phones shouting the odds. 'He'll get ten,' the evening girl was telling her office. 'He'll walk,' the agency man told his.

It's all a bloody lottery, Jacko grumbled to himself.

A hand waved at him above a sea of bobbing heads like a tic-tac man signalling a change of betting.

The heavy oak doors swung open, letting in a watery sun. A vintage black Rolls Royce drew up noiselessly in front of the worn stone steps. 'All rise,' shouted a woman usher in an astonishingly deep voice. Everyone stood.

Two judges – one in the blood-red robes of crime, the other

in the black and blue of personal injury – strolled sedately through a parting that appeared in the human sea. Slowly they climbed another set of stone steps, faced each other, bowed gravely and went into their chambers.

The crowd in the foyer thinned as the barristers straightened their wigs. Anxious relatives followed them into the two courtrooms.

He ambled across the sea-green carpet to the dark man in the dark suit who had waved. 'Hallo, Stan.'

'What are you doing here, Jacko?'

'Arsing about in court one.'

'If it wasn't for buggery, there'd be fuck all,' said Stan, with a solemn face.

Both chuckled briefly at what was an old CID joke.

'Nothing so romantic. Arson. Routine, really.' Jacko pulled a pained face. 'Time for a coffee?'

Detective Sergeant Stan Young seemed unsure. He turned to the woman usher about to sit down at the security desk by the side door. 'How much summing up's left in the rape?'

'About twenty minutes,' she said in a voice which had lost its depth.

'Give us a shout when the jury goes out.'

She nodded.

Young opened the side door and led the way down a cool cloister. To their right was a long, straight drive down which the judges had ridden in stately style. On each side were wide lawns, dampened by the morning's drizzle. At the edge of the southern lawn was an old red-brick jailhouse which served as magistrates' and coroner's courts. The north lawn ran into rougher grass dotted with majestic trees up to the high walls of the old castle.

Young lowered himself stiffly on to a green bench outside the opened door to the refreshment bar.

Jacko handed him a buff folder from under his arm and continued into the shaded room. He returned with two mugs of steaming coffee, handing Stan his as he sat beside him. 'What brings you here?'

'Hegan.' The name came out nervously, Young's eyes on the back of the woman usher's head, visible through the leaded windows of the side door.

Jacko's eyes were automatically drawn up the rain-blackened

asphalt drive to the arched gateway of the Norman castle. Beyond the gate was a cobbled square and another ancient arch. Behind that, and towering above, the mighty medieval Minster. All built from local limestone weathered the colour of honey. A mouthwatering sight; good enough to eat.

'Hegan?' Jacko repeated the name absent-mindedly, a little too loudly for Stan who shot him a silencing glance. So, quieter: 'I thought he'd joined the Foreign Legion.'

A throwaway line really, another joke detectives often make about wanted men they can't find, but Young looked startled. 'He made it as far as Morocco.'

Morocco, thought Jacko. Casablanca, Rick's Café, Ingrid Bergman – and no extradition. 'Why come back then?'

'For his loot. We never found the two million he pulled in that bank job, you know.'

Jacko yanked his head back towards the foyer. 'I didn't see his name on the crime judge's list.'

'He's charged under his real name.' Young glanced around to make sure he was not being overheard.

All clicked into place now. William Roberts. Second on the list, the pre-trial review. Everyone in East Midlands CID had heard of him, called him Orange Billy. Few ever talked about him. Fewer still knew he'd finally been caught. He was top secret. Cosmic top secret.

A Belfast terrorist who'd killed three times and got away with it. Eighteen months into an eighteen-year sentence for robbery, sang for his freedom. One of the biggest supergrasses ever on Loyalist para-military side. In return, a big bounty and his new identity as Michael Hegan. Bought a public house in the wilds of eastern England, a fenlands hamlet, a tiny peaceful place with a big bustling name – New York. Within two years his business was bust. He went back to the only trade he knew – armed robbery. Been on the run ever since.

Jacko knew this only from gossip in the Fairways, the HQ local. It had not been a squad job. Division had handled it. A start-to-finish cock-up, the gossipers had said. 'How was he caught?'

'An anonymous tipster told us he was back. Shook off one patrol car. The second got him.' A melancholic sigh. 'He's a sodding pyscho. He'd kill you as soon as look at you.'

'What was your involvement?'

9

Young glanced at the back of the woman usher's lowered head, talking in her direction. 'I was his bloody minder, wasn't I? I was even supposed to be with him on the day of the raid. Just my luck, eh?'

Jacko knew all about Stan Young's luck. They had started out together. Jacko had moved on and up twice since. Stan stayed on here, in their old home town.

Everyone had been certain he'd make inspector. Promotion never came, only tragedy. First his wife died. Then he injured his back. Nothing heroic like making an arrest or a sporting injury. He'd slipped on ice, well pissed, walking up his garden path after a CID party. Now he was on non-operational duties.

'Oh, Jesus,' said Jacko in genuine sympathy. He nudged Young gently with his right elbow when the usher beckoned through the door window.

Stan walked slowly and painfully like a crippled footballer about to leave the field of play. Jacko's own stride was slowed as he dug into his inside pocket to switch off his radio pager.

He loathed all new tech, bleepers especially. Once it had vibrated in his trouser pocket while he was giving evidence in a trial that followed a porn show raid, charging his groin with the sort of horny thrill the audience had been denied when they were arrested. Ever since he'd switched it off as he entered court.

They walked softly, almost on tiptoe, to a long bench in front of the public gallery which rose up in tiers to a deep red wall with a clock which showed ten fifty.

The judge, in his red robes and soiled wig, sat high in front of them, framed in oak, a carved canopy above him, solid walls of wood behind and at each side of him.

To the judge's right was the empty box which the rape trial jury had just vacated. To his left, a similar sized box with social workers and reporters in two rows. In front and below him on a sloping desk sat the clerk at the end of a horseshoe table packed tight with barristers.

Between Jacko and the judge was the dock where a tall, narrow-shouldered man, mid-thirties, stood with his back towards him, flanked by two prison guards, one handcuffed to him.

The black-gowned clerk stood, indictment in his hand. Oddly (in fact, uniquely, in Jacko's experience), he did not call the defendant's name before reading out the charge of armed robbery and asking how he pleaded.

'Not guilty.' A clear, firm reply. In his shiny grey mohair suit Roberts (aka Hegan) looked as calm and confident as he sounded.

A barrister rose from the leather-topped horseshoe and said that, as far as the prosecution was concerned, it was merely a matter of fixing a date for the trial, my lord.

'Not quite,' said a QC, who followed him to his feet. 'In the view of the defence, there is a far more important issue, though I hesitate to rehearse it without a direction to the press from me lud.'

The judge glowered at him. 'They know perfectly well that they cannot report legal submissions in the absence of a jury' – all a pretence of impatience which cleverly concealed a lecture to any reporter who had forgotten his law.

The fair-headed evening paper girl and the bespectacled agency man, both known to Jacko, took the hint and slid off the front row bound, he guessed, for the refreshment room. Behind them they left a heavy man, a stranger, who stopped making notes. Four social workers, three men and a woman, remained, too.

The QC talked for twenty minutes. To the sparsely filled public gallery, it must have been about as comprehensible as the Chancellor of the Exchequer's budget preamble before he sticks up the price of petrol, booze and cigarettes.

Having studied the papers, he began, the judge would be aware that the man in the dock – again, no name mentioned – had a background which could only be described as bizarre. 'He is denying the charge because, according to his instructions, he wasn't there. His behaviour in fleeing the country can only be explained by his background. He was, in effect, on the run from both sides of the law.'

Up jumped the prosecutor to argue that if the defendant (still, no name) was going to say he fled, leaving a police dog shot dead in his wake, because he felt his life was at risk, the jury would be entitled to know of his past.

Eventually the judge ruled that the accused man must be called Michael Hegan, not William Roberts, throughout his trial

11

and no mention made of any of Orange Billy's previous history which might prejudice a jury. It was up to his defence to decide how much of his background was to be revealed, he decreed, and the prosecution was not to go beyond the boundaries they set.

The case, he estimated, would last six to seven full working days. He fixed the trial to begin the first full week of the following month. 'Take him down,' he said without looking up from the notes he was making.

Jacko saw Michael Hegan's face in full as he stood, about-turned and walked to the top of the stairs which led to the cells below the court. A hard face, pale, almost white, neat gingery hair, and ice-blue eyes which fixed, unblinking and unsmiling, on Young until his head bobbed out of sight.

Young sighed softly as he slid sideways off the bench. He was so deep in thought he didn't even say goodbye.

'Put up Andrew Michael Heald,' said the clerk.

A slim, scruffily handsome young man bounded up the steps from the cells into view.

He wore a faded denim suit with ragged tears at the knees which pass for trendy. His black hair was shoulder-length now, hiding a gold stud in his left ear lobe. A guard tugged at his left hand to get it out of his trouser pocket as he lolled at the front rail of the dock.

Laid-back sod, thought Jacko with a smile. He quite liked Andy Heald.

The charge of arson was read to which he pleaded guilty. He cocked his head behind him as he sat to flash a confident smile at his parents in the public gallery.

The black stubble was still there, one day's growth on chin and cheeks that Jacko always associated with activists, worn as some sort of badge of defiance. He'd never worked out how they achieved it.

Surely they had to shave sometimes or their beards would be beyond their knees. Or maybe there was a new Remington out with blades that could be raised like a lawn mower's to leave one day's growth. Or maybe they shaved every other day and he only got to see them on non-shaving days.

Inconsequential things like this occasionally and unaccountably bothered Jacko, made him ponder, but he seldom came up with answers.

Heald was twenty-four, from a respectable family, the prosecutor began. He had a previous conviction for the minor matter of obstructing a public right of way during an animal rights demonstration.

'On the December night in question,' he went on fluently, 'he hurled a home-made bomb at the window of a shop which had coats from animal fur on display. The ensuing fire destroyed ten coats along with fixtures and fittings.

'Two days later listeners to a radio phone-in programme were debating animal experimentation when a call was received from a man who said he belonged to an organization known as Assisi's Army and claiming responsibility for the arson attack.

'The recorded voice was compared with tapes made of previous interviews with known animal rights activists and linked with Heald's.

'Initially he denied complicity but under questioning he finally admitted, "We have tried peaceful pickets. We have tried leaflet raids. Still the slaughter goes on. I decided on direct action."'

Heald's own barrister replaced the prosecutor on his feet. The defendant, he said, left school with triple As and went to university to gain honours in economics.

'There he had met a girl, a confirmed vegetarian. He became one, too. Once he stopped eating meat, he started to question how it was being produced on factory farms. He began signing petitions, then collecting them and marching to hand them in at Downing Street.'

This counsel was just as in command of his brief as the prosecutor but his droning delivery combined with the warmth of the court and the fact that Jacko knew the story anyway forced him to fight off sleep.

'He started standing vigil with like minded supporters,' the barrister droned on, 'with placards outside circuses, zoos, and on one occasion, a convent where the nuns kept battery hens, a demonstration which led to a fine for obstruction.

'He gave up accountancy in his last year of training to concentrate full-time on animal welfare activities. Unfortunately the media showed no interest in peaceful protest. Stupidly, he took the law into his own hands to try to create some attention.'

Criminal and dangerous though it was, the barrister expressed the half-hearted hope he could be dealt with by way of a suspended sentence.

The prosecutor rose again. 'I call the officer in the case.'

Jacko picked up the folder and slid off the bench. He walked swiftly down two steps, across a red carpet and up three steps into the witness box. He raised the bible and parroted the oath, feeling a hypocrite, wondering when, as an agnostic certainly, and an atheist probably, he would finally find the courage to affirm.

Yes, he agreed, the name was James Jackson, a detective inspector attached to the Major Crimes Squad and based at the headquarters of the East Midlands Combined Constabulary. And, yes, he confirmed, Heald did have an excellent family and academic background.

The droning defence counsel stood. A heavy-set man, he was an experienced advocate who had been for and against Jacko many times in their long careers, a sharp but fair operator. 'How long has he been in custody on remand?'

'Almost six months, sir.'

'His first taste of prison, is it?'

'Actually, no.'

'What do you mean?' interrupted the judge.

'Well,' said Jacko – the knot in his stomach that was always there when he gave evidence in the High Court tightened – 'the previous autumn Heald was the chief prosecution witness in an assault case. The defendant was a member of a hunt whose meet had been sabotaged by protestors laying aniseed trails and blowing horns to confuse the hounds. Heald complained he had been struck on the cheek by a riding crop and had the mark to prove it. The magistrates found the huntsman not guilty and decided to bind Heald over to be of good behaviour in view of his provocative conduct.'

All perfectly legal; all grossly unjust, in Jacko's opinion, which he decided against expressing. Instead he stuck to the facts. 'He went to jail for two weeks rather than sign the required recognizance.'

'I'll disregard that,' said the judge apparently as unimpressed with the magistrates' sense of fair play as Jacko had been. 'And indeed his fine for obstruction. I'll treat him as being of previous good character.'

The burly barrister beamed his thanks in the knowledge that he had already knocked a few months off the sentence to come. 'Apart from initial prevarication . . .' Lawyers love words like that. '. . . he was open and frank with you?'

'He was very co-operative.'

'Thank you, inspector. That will be all.'

The judge, smiling, added his thanks. Jacko picked up his folder from the ledge where it had rested alongside the bible and backed out of the witness box.

The barrister remained on his feet, pleading with increasing passion for the liberty of his client, describing him as 'a young man who committed one isolated act while suffering from a burning sense of injustice.'

Not the best phrase to use in mitigation of arson, mused Jacko, but lawyers are inclined to run away with themselves and their tongues.

The judge was not wholly swayed. 'No one doubts the sincerity of the views you hold,' he told Heald, on his feet for sentencing. 'But courts have a duty to protect legitimate commerce. Fifteen months.'

Heald turned from the railings, grinning at his parents, winking at Jacko. No hard feelings, he seemed to be saying. Jacko liked good losers. He winked back.

2

'Comfy, are we?' A mocking voice, polished by public school.

The squad room on a quiet Saturday morning was an unfamiliar setting for a personal appearance by Detective Chief Superintendent Richard Scott.

Jacko dropped the *Mirror* on the weekend duty DI's desk, pulled his legs off it and swung round on his swivel chair. 'Oh, come on, guv. I've worked my way down to the wire in the basket.'

Scott laughed briefly. They were good friends, Jacko and Scott, who was short and stout. He was called by everyone, though never to his face, the Little Fat Man. Splay-footed, he was approaching in long strides for a smallish man, business like.

Trouble, Jacko sensed. 'What brings you in?' He spoke carefully and eyed him cautiously. Apart from a grubby collar, he hadn't shaved and looked as though he'd been up all through a night that, according to everything in the wire basket, had been virtually crime-free.

'There's one I might like you to take a look at.' Scott dropped a pile of folders from under an arm on to the next desk. He sat down wearily. 'Sudden death from Lincoln nick.' He was making it sound like an everyday job for the coroner's department. 'A customer of yours, I'm afraid – Andrew Heald.'

Jacko felt as though he'd been winded and audibly sucked in air. 'Jesus.' His mouth sagged open to let the air out in a mournful sigh. 'When?'

'Rushed into hospital last evening. Suspected poisoning. Post-mortem's on now.'

'Not suicide, though.' Jacko shook his head firmly.

'Why so sure?'

'Spoke to his folks afterwards. He was expecting two or three years. Besides . . .'

His mind had drifted – to a background chat he'd had with Andy Heald's girl at their chaotic bedsit. She'd told him how six months on remand had given their lives a new radical purpose. 'Prison conditions are worse than a battery henhouse,' she'd complained. 'We're going to campaign for improvements.'

Scott broke into his thoughts. 'Besides what?'

Jacko told him of their chat. 'They've more or less dropped animal rights for prison reform. I got the impression he was looking forward to fresh research material.'

Scott nodded. 'Was he into drugs?'

'Dunno. I can soon find out. His lady will tell me.'

Another nod, only half interested.

'What have you got in mind – bad shit?' asked Jacko.

The question was ignored as Scott asked another, 'Any enemies?'

'Well, there's the owner of a fire-bombed shop, a whip-waving huntsman and the Mother Superior of a picketed convent, all likely to be miffed with him, but not that miffed . . .'

16

Scott was smiling, Jacko shaking his head. 'No, he's . . . was a helluva nice lad.'

Scott looked down at the files. 'You're only confirming my reading.'

His brown eyes, not a trace of tiredness in them, were up now, looking directly at him. 'We think he may have been murdered.' Pause. 'By mistake.'

Jacko frowned, said nothing.

'The real target, we think, was Orange Billy Roberts, alias Michael Hegan.' Scott chewed his top lip for a moment. 'And we're tipped that there's a bent policeman involved deep in the background on the bank job.'

Jacko wanted to stay silent but Scott awaited his reaction. His mind racing, all he could think of was: 'Who's we?'

'There's heavy input from the Yard, both Special Branch and the Anti-Terrorist Squad. Once you're in, you stay in. No backing out.' Pause. 'In or out?'

'Have I a choice?'

'It could be a dirty tricks operation. I know how sensitive you can be. Now . . .' He hung on to the word, rounding it out. 'In or out?'

Intriguing, thought Jacko. Better than pounding the beat which is where I'll be if I turn down this hard-nosed bastard. Besides, I locked up Andy Heald in a place where he should have been safe. I owe him. I liked him. 'In.'

Scott gave him a relieved smile which he switched off as he began his briefing.

'Some months ago the Met got a tip. Anonymous. All it said was that an attempt was going to be made involving Michael Hegan.' Scott nodded sharply. 'Note that. Hegan, his cover name, not Orange Billy, his Belfast name. So their thinking is that the call came from an underworld, not security, source who didn't know of his terrorist and supergrass background.'

Makes sense, thought Jacko.

'That info was bounced to Special Branch,' Scott went on. 'They couldn't be sure whether the tip meant an attempt on Hegan's life or an attempted jailbreak. They put an undercover officer into the jail to guard against both possibilities. Locally, only the prison governor and me know his identity.'

The way he hurried on told Jacko that he wasn't going to be in on it; made sense, too.

'Their undercover man in the jail alerted Special Branch last night to what had happened to Andy Heald and they phoned me. Their theory is that Hegan is being targeted by someone on the inside and your pal Heald copped it in error.'

'Who'd want Hegan dead?'

Scott shrugged, uncertain. 'The Republicans because he assassinated three of their men. The Loyalists because he shopped their bravest and best. But Intelligence want him alive. He claims to have more info.'

Christ, thought Jacko, angrily. They sprung him once before with a golden handshake and what did he do? A two million pound blagging on a bank with a shot-gun. Now they were planning another deal to free him. 'What's he got to trade this time?'

'He spent eighteen months on the Continent and in North Africa after fleeing from our armed police waiting for him at his pub. On his travels, he claims, he came across two Belfast men in the company of a go-between for an arms firm with South African connections. Could be true. They're desperate for technical know-how. The Loyalists are stock-piling in case we ever pull out the troops.'

'What's in it for Hegan?'

'His lawyer wanted us to drop the bank charge. Out of the question, we said. He'll have to take his chance in court. If he's found guilty it's a long stretch. He'll talk for some time off.'

'Jesus.' Jacko finally showed his disapproal with a sighing headshake. 'The RUC risked their lives to catch him. The government let him go. This force takes bloody months to track him down. Now they're about to let him out for a second time.'

Scott gave a tiny shrug, not dismissive, more disinterested in the politics of the situation, none of his business. 'Maybe the jury will let him out.'

He dipped into one of the folders on the desk. 'He fancies his chances in court. He's going to say, or at least infer, that his police minder fitted him up with fingerprints we found in the getaway van from the bank raid.'

Jacko sat upright, jolted. 'Stan Young? Never.'

Scott shook his head very slowly. 'Hegan's going to insist in evidence that the bank job wasn't down to him. His defence will be that he did a runner from his pub because he suspected he was walking into an ambush by terrorists who'd caught up with him. That, by the way, comes from his solicitor who's handling the plea-bargaining with Special Branch.'

'It's bullshit.' Jacko pulled a sour face. 'Stan's not bent.'

'Then you may have to prove it.' Pause. 'Hegan's solicitor says he's going to throw in the name of his police contact on this force as part of any deal.'

Scott shuffled three pink personnel folders to the top of the heap on his desk but didn't open any immediately. 'Know what puzzled me? How Hegan discovered there'd be such rich pickings at a small bank in a tiny market town in the first place. I've been up all night trying to work it out.'

'And?' asked Jacko.

'The answer, I'm sure, is that sleepy Sleaford, where the robbery happened, is at the centre of a vast agricultural area. The labour's casual, whole armies of them. Always want cash in hand. The bank informed us of this particular shipment because of its size. Guess whose desk that information passed over?'

Jacko groaned. 'Stan's.'

A curt nod.

Oh, shit, thought Jacko. And Stan said only yesterday he should have been minding Hegan on the day of the robbery.

'The money's never been found.'

'Didn't Hegan take any of it with him?'

'Only enough to last a few months. He was on his way back to collect the bulk of it when he was caught.'

'Who tipped us off he was back?'

Scott delved into the personnel files. He read from the top one. 'Marlowe, Frank, Detective Sergeant. Reports he took the call which gave the number of Hegan's new car. Says it was anonymous. Maybe there was no call. Maybe he wants Hegan out of circulation. Marlowe's got to be a suspect, too.'

A laugh, ridiculing. 'You're joking.' Jacko knew Frank Marlowe as well as he knew Stan Young. They had worked two vice killings together.

'Listen first.' Scott raised an admonishing eyebrow. 'Four days after the bank robbery, an alert went out for Hegan when his fingerprint was found on a map in the getaway van. Who was the armed stake-out at the pub, six hours on his own?'

19

Scott patted Marlowe's file.

'Hegan arrived by car but ran at the door. No cash was found at the pub. Why should Hegan go back if not to collect the cash? Who tipped him off to run?'

'But . . .' Jacko could think of no answers so he lapsed into a simmering silence. He'd allowed the Little Fat Man to trap him, con him into an internal affairs inquiry to investigate his workmates.

'One more suspect for you.' Scott opened another folder. 'Cross, Wayne, PC. After Marlowe reported Hegan had left without entering the pub, Cross was ordered into the search with his alsatian tracker dog. He radioed that he'd let his dog loose, heard a shot coming from a barn and seen a car driving away in the distance. He was ordered, in no uncertain terms, not to go it alone. He ignored that order, drove to the barn, found his dog shot dead. He was there for twenty minutes on his own.'

'So what?'

'If the money wasn't hidden at the pub it had to be hidden in the barn. It was found in neither.'

Jacko shrugged, unimpressed. 'He wouldn't shoot his own dog, would he?'

Scott tutted. 'Cross was transferred out of Dogs Section and into Traffic after Hegan's getaway. Months later he was put on alert for Hegan's car after Sergeant Marlowe reported the number. He radioed in that he was on its tail. Again he ignored an order to await back-up. He ran out of road in a chase. An armed response unit finally got Hegan at a road block. Either Cross is impetuous or he didn't want Hegan caught.'

Having twice been reprimanded for speaking his mind, Jacko maintained a brooding silence.

'And the bullet that killed the dog', Scott continued, 'came from a confiscated handgun missing from our armoury.' He cocked his head to one side, inviting comment.

'Surely . . .' A confused face. 'If either Young, Marlowe or Cross got their hands on two million, would they still be pissing about as serving policemen?'

Scott dropped the file on top of the pile, annoyed again. 'Would you double-cross a triple-killer? Or would you prefer him inside; better still, dead before he could shop you?'

'It sounds fucking complicated to me,' said Jacko huffily.

'Nothing could be more simple.' A patient smile, patently forced. 'We've got a terrorist hit man turned supergrass who's gone back to crime, aided and abetted by a corrupt cop. You're the logical choice to investigate Heald's death. He was your pinch. If you find it was an OD or bad shit, as you so eloquently put it, press on and find the missing two million and the bent bobby. None of the three suspects will even know you're looking. Now, what could be more simple than that?'

An evil smile, Scott finally enjoying himself. 'Aren't you glad you volunteered?'

3

At the top of a hill a road sign directed traffic left to the castle and cathedral.

Jacko forked right to the hospital. Tall extensions had been added to the red-brick original buildings where they had plastered up the hand he broke one New Year's Eve when he fell downstairs in pursuit of a burglar and was given a bollocking for letting him get away. Happy far-off days, he thought, parking outside the pathology laboratory.

A portly man dressed in a black crew-neck under a lemon V-necked sweater, looking as though he had been dragged from a Saturday lunchtime session in his country pub, sat at a desk, beaming.

'What's up, doc?' Jacko always gave him a Bugs Bunny greeting. He'd known the pathologist for twenty years.

The doctor glanced left to a uniformed constable with dishevelled red hair, who stood, helmet in hand. 'Do you know . . .' The doctor had forgotten his name.

'PC Cross, sir.'

One of Scott's trio of suspects, thought Jacko, surprised. A coincidence or had that crafty sod engineered it? He smiled, to himself really, extending his hand.

Cross fumbled to free his from the helmet which slipped from his grasp. 'Whoops.' He saved it from falling. 'Sorry.' He finally took the offered hand for a shy shake.

Jacko kept on smiling. 'Do his parents know?'

'Yes, sir. They were with him for the last hour or so but he didn't come to.'

'And his girl?' Cross gave a brisk shake of his head scattering his fine hair.

'She didn't make it in time.'

'But does she know he's dead?' Jacko spoke with emphasized patience.

'His folks broke the news when she arrived at the hospital.'

All three sat down. 'Can't help you too much yet,' said the doctor, on the defensive. 'Sent the stomach contents for analysis. Could take two or three weeks.'

'Anything would help,' Jacko said, sounding interested, not really too bothered.

'Well . . .' The doctor opened up guardedly. '. . . I think you can rule out food poisoning. Nor was it a bottleful of anything like aspirin or sleeping pills. The quantity wasn't right. The smell wasn't right for a killer like paraquat. And the symptoms weren't right for a killer like cyanide.'

'Was he a junkie?' Jacko asked.

'No puncture marks.'

'What's your money on?'

No response.

'Come on, doc,' said Jacko, smiling encouragement. 'Give us a clue.'

The pathologist ran his right thumb and index finger towards each other on his bottom lip, nipping it into a bulge. 'It's nothing you can buy over a chemist's counter. You need twenty or thirty times the therapeutic dose to get this result. Two or three tablets of an ultra-strong medicinal drug is my best guess right now.'

Jacko looked at Cross who shook his head. 'According to his parents he was as fit as a butcher's dog. He wasn't on any sort of medication.'

'What did his girl say?'

'Never got round to a chat.' Cross looked downcast.

'Did anyone give any indication that he might have been depressed?'

A firmer shake. 'None at all, sir. In fact, his folks said he was expecting three years.'

Jacko nodded, satisfied, the opinion he'd expressed to his chief confirmed. He turned back to the doctor. 'No chance, is there, that he swallowed, say, a condom packed with drugs which burst before nature took its course?' He knew it was a dangerous, sometimes used, method of smuggling dope into jails.

'You can rule that out,' said the doctor definitely.

'Had he eaten?'

'Not recently.'

'A couple of sandwiches at court at lunchtime,' said Cross, butting in, 'but he skipped tea when he arrived at prison.'

Jacko began to get up out of his chair. 'Let's hope it wasn't those courthouse sarnies. I had one, too.'

'I'd better keep my knives sharp,' said the pathologist with a happy chuckle.

Jacko pushed open a set of swing doors, stepping on to the footpath outside the path lab. 'I think I'll stroll round to the nick.' Cross, pale and drawn, fell into step beside him. 'What time did you start?'

'When I came on at ten, sir.'

'Last night?'

Cross gave a tired nod.

He'd already done more than a double shift, Jacko realized. I should send him home. No, he corrected himself. He's knackered. He might make a mistake, trip himself up. Keep walking and talking. 'Your first post-mortem, was it?'

Cross nodded again, holding his helmet in place. As they walked, he said he had bagged and labelled the prison clothing Heald had been wearing, sealed the prison bus and asked forensics to look at them as well as the leftover food he had taken from the refreshment room at the castle.

'Busy boy.' Jacko tried to make it sound admiring.

He'd already decided that the three officers Scott had named as suspects would have to be pumped individually, and casually over pints in pubs, perhaps, when they were off guard. He began to probe very gently. 'Been in the mob long?'

'Six years.'

Cross spoke with the nasal accent of Merseyside. He spent most of his school years in Africa, he replied, where his father worked as an engineer for a rubber firm.

Because he lived so long in Zimbabwe, which used to be

Southern Rhodesia, his mates called him Ridgeback after the brave hunting dog native to that country.

Studying him with sideways glances, Jacko detected some of the characteristics of the breed in him. His brown eyes had a sharpness undimmed by the loss of a night's sleep. His physique was firm and lean. He had a reservoir of energy which made him walk fast on the damp footpath beneath a line of lime trees.

'Slow down, for christsake,' pleaded Jacko, wanting to make the walk last. 'No one is running away from where we're going.'

He'd joined the force at twenty, Cross continued. After training he'd been posted to Dogs Section where they gave him an alsatian.

His dog Winston had shared his home with his mother when they were off duty until he was killed. 'Two years ago on the 23rd of next month.' His face seemed etched with genuine pain.

They rounded a corner, walking on the pavement across the road from the red prison walls topped with purple bricks.

'The bastard who shot him is in there.' Cross flicked his head left towards the prison.

'Who?'

'Hegan. Know him?'

'Saw him in court yesterday when the judge weighed off Heald.' Jacko let out a little of his cover story. 'Andy was my case. That's why I've got this job.'

Without much prompting, Cross continued with his story. 'I couldn't face being assigned to another dog so I switched to Traffic. Now I'm back on the beat.'

'Why?' asked Jacko as casually as he could.

'Wrote off a car in a chase.'

'Chasing who?'

Another angry lick of his head across the road. 'Hegan. Six months ago. After he'd sneaked back into the country to collect his money. And if I'd have caught up with him I'd have killed him.' His brown eyes hardened and filled with hate.

Looking into them, Jacko wondered anxiously if he'd botched an attempt last night. But he wouldn't be admitting motive now, would he? If he's cunning enough, maybe. He needed time to think, to check. He changed the subject. 'Bored on the beat, are you?'

Cross made no reply, lost in his murderous thoughts, so Jacko tried again. 'Thought about CID?'

'Superintendent Upjohn, my commander, rejected my application. Know him?'

'Oh, yes,' said Jacko very casually.

Who on the force didn't know Superintendent Clive Upjohn? One apocryphal story, twenty years old, just about summed him up. At the time Upjohn was a traffic patrolman who operated a policy of the more you booked, the better your promotion chances.

He pulled up a speeder who pleaded, 'Give me a break, officer. I've got the golden squitters and I'm desperate to find a shithouse.'

Upjohn took out his notebook and pencil, gave the lead a lick and said, 'You've found one. Name and address.'

He knew Upjohn all right. He, Stan Young and Jacko had joined the force the same year.

Most people Jacko could take or leave. A handful, the Little Fat Man and an American police buddy among them, who had entered his heart, enhancing and enriching his life, would remain there for ever.

Some he would see only a couple of times a year or so; some, like the New York detective, much longer. That never mattered. They knew where each other would be when they were wanted and, when they were wanted, he knew, just knew without question, that they'd be there, at his side. There were six or seven of them at the most, two women among them. He regarded himself as the world's luckiest man to be blessed by their friendship.

And then there were people like Upjohn, only half a dozen of them, who he loathed. A shithouse and a creep; much worse, a credit-claimer, a police plagiarist, who made a habit of turning up at the end of an inquiry, barging off the team who had carried the ball, so he could score the glory goal and give the interview and have his photo in the papers.

It wasn't jealousy, envy at being outranked by him. He didn't want to shuffle paper as a superintendent in charge of a subdivision, thanks very much. He'd found that rare combination of challenge and contentment working for the Little Fat Man.

In a sense, Stan and Jacko had courted the hatred Upjohn undoubtedly held for them. It was the booze, guv. Stan had been well pissed that night when the very sober superintendent approached him at a party and said, 'Lend me ten pence. I want to phone a friend.'

Stan tossed him twenty pence and said, 'Here. Phone 'em all.'

And Jacko had been well pissed, too, that party night when he phoned Upjohn and asked, 'Are you Upjohn?' Might have been funny but not, perhaps, at three in the morning.

Oh, yes, he knew Clive Upjohn all right.

He chided himself for a wasted moment on a trip down memory lane when there was work still to do. 'What about the armed response unit?'

Cross shook his head. 'My super turned me down for that, too.'

'Ever had a look round the armoury?'

'Don't know one end of a gun from the other.'

Then how the hell could Cross have got hold of the gun from the armoury that killed his dog on the night Hegan made his getaway? Jacko was asking himself.

'Who assigned you to this Heald job?' They were crossing the road to the main prison gates, fortified like a Boer War barracks.

'Mr Upjohn, sir.'

Not Scott then. All this walking had done was tire him and waste his time. He'd got nowhere. Not true, he decided. The beginnings of a plan of action were taking shape, an undercover operation stunning in its simplicity. 'Want to stay on this inquiry?'

'Oh, yes, sir.' Cross answered with obvious enthusiasm.

'I'll get my chief to fix it with your commander.'

He rang the bell. The wicket gate opened.

A bearded man in Saturday casuals rose from behind a green steel desk and introduced himself as the acting governor. 'Sorry the old man isn't here to greet you. He's away on an inquiry into a riot down south.'

He motioned to a woman with close-cropped fair hair who

was sitting in a chair beside the desk. 'Shirley Thomas. Our deputy head of security.'

They smiled and nodded.

'She's handling our internal inquiry.' He sat down again, waving towards two chairs in front of him.

Jacko asked for a timetable of the previous day's events. Shirley Thomas took over. She was in her mid-thirties. She wore a royal blue suit, slightly creased, and a loose polka-dot blouse that could not hide the size of her full bosom.

Andy Heald and his fellow prisoners, she said, had their cells in the remand wing unlocked at seven, half an hour earlier than usual. 'They needed no waking,' she said, rather languidly. 'Prisoners never do on judgement day.'

The acting governor shot her a sharp glance which she totally ignored. A mind of her own, thought Jacko, warming to her.

'Those without in-cell toilets had to empty their plastic chamber pots,' she continued, disgust on a pale, shiny face that bore no trace of make-up.

Jacko imagined the smell and his top lip curled involuntarily.

'Razors were handed out with hot water.'

'Not Heald though,' said Jacko.

'He took a day off from shaving.'

Observant and accurate, Jacko decided. She could come in useful.

'Remand prisoners are allowed to wear their own clothes. Those who had opted for prison uniform were handed theirs. No one likes to appear in the dock in jail garb.'

She gave him a cynical little smile and her acting boss a slight shudder at her frankness.

'They collected their breakfast from hotplates and were locked back in their cells to eat. They missed their hour's exercise in the yard. The bus left at nine for the ten-minute drive to the crown court in the castle.'

Shirley Thomas looked away from him, for the first time, down at wads of notes on a clipboard which rested on her knee. 'Four guards were on the bus which was driven by a civilian. Hegan and the rapist had been handcuffed together and then to a guard each.'

'The jury convicted him then?' Jacko asked, trying to get her to look up at him again.

She nodded, head still down. 'Twelve years. Both were

regarded as category A, high risk, potential escapers. All four sat in their chains on the bench at the back of the bus.

'Andy Heald and a dope dealer were handcuffed together and a lager lout to a bungling hold-up man. A child abuser sat alone and unchained.'

She looked up at last, just for a sad second. 'He's terminally ill.'

Her head went down again. She unclipped a sketch plan, handed it to Jacko, gave him time to study it, then continued, 'On the journey there'd been a police car at the front and behind the bus. They entered the cellblock beneath the court through barred gates in the far corner of the sunken car-park at the foot of the bank which leads up to the castle wall.'

She stopped again to pass over a second sketch. 'Inside are ten cells. Each man was locked in individually. At nine thirty a baby-battering mother and a wife-battering pensioner surrendered to their bail and were put in unlocked cells.'

She leant across towards him to point out on the plan which prisoner had been in which cell. He caught a fragrance which was disappointingly earthy, rather than stimulatingly sexy.

'In the hour before business began upstairs, all had visits from their lawyers. The mother and the pensioner had walked free from the dock upstairs. The rest returned to their cells after sentencing.

'At lunchtime the refreshment room staff delivered sandwiches for eleven, the four guards and seven of the prisoners.'

She looked up suddenly and intently, a point to make. 'Michael Hegan declined. He had sandwichs sent in – smoked salmon, in fact.'

'How come?' asked Jacko with a puzzled frown.

'Remand prisoners are permitted a take-out.'

Jacko nodded, smiling bitterly.

'After sentencing came visits from social workers. Heald, the dope pedlar and the lager lout were visited by relatives, too. Healey's parents were a bit down, apparently, but he was full of himself. He was a bright likeable lad, you know.'

The woman's bloody brilliant, Jacko thought.

'The bus picked them up just after four thirty. They returned in the same formation. In reception Hegan and the bungling hold-up man were escorted back to the remand wing wearing their own clothes. The rest had to strip off their civilian clothes which we box and store away.

'The rapist was offered solitary for his own protection under rule 43. It means being locked up in a cell twenty-three hours a day with just an hour's exercise. He accepted. The child abuser was offered the hospital wing. He accepted.'

Heald and the dope pedlar, who was called Carl Marsh, were briefed on the regime, and Shirley Thomas briefed Jacko, sparing nothing between the 7.30 a.m. slopping out their plastic pots and 9.30 p.m. lights out.

It sounded more Victorian than the jail buildings that housed them; all the more so because of the disdainful Home Counties accent in which she delivered her lecture.

The acting governor seemed to squirm in his seat from embarrassment.

No wonder they riot now and then, thought Jacko.

She had reached the last sheet in her thick bundle and read from it.

'Heald and Marsh were escorted to the cell they were to share on the first-floor landing of A Block. They made up their beds. Tea and cakes were brought to them. The door was unlocked at seven. Heald stayed in his cell lying on his bunk. Marsh went out to scout round the recreation facilities. He returned at eight with two cups of tea.

'Heald appeared to be asleep. Marsh woke him. His hands shook and he spilt his tea as he tried to drink it. Sickness struck so quickly he had no time to make it to the plastic pot in the corner and vomited over the cell floor.

'Marsh pressed the alarm bell to summon the warder. The MO took one look and ordered his removal to the emergency department of the County Hospital round the corner. They didn't wait for an ambulance. They took him in a van. Casualty doctors worked on him till past midnight when he died.'

Shirley Thomas smoothed the papers flat and looked back at Jacko, her blue eyes exhausted. Another one who has missed a night's sleep and her morning shower, Jacko thought guiltily.

It had been a briefing which had saved him a full day's work. He wanted to enthuse, say 'Terrific' or something. Something held him back. He merely nodded.

'I don't think anyone can point the finger at delays here,' said the acting governor. Jacko, who had almost forgotten he was there, recognized a middle-rank civil servant's instinct for survival.

'PC Cross . . .' Jacko flicked his head towards the silent, fast-wilting constable. '. . . has got Heald's prison clothes from the hospital. We'd like Marsh's, too, and the civvy gear both wore in court.'

Shirley Thomas lifted a black dustbin liner, fastened with plastic-coated wire, from the fawn polished linoleum by her chair. 'We gave Marsh a complete change. The stuff he was wearing last night is in here.'

She handed it to Cross who nursed it on his knees.

'We also gave the cell a strip search,' she went on. Jacko eyed her expectantly. She gave her head a slight shake. 'Nothing.'

He pursed his lips, disappointed. She smiled at him. 'We've got Marsh on hold across the corridor if you want to talk to him.'

Both stood. Jacko reached the door first. He opened it and half stood back to make way for her. 'Go for it,' she said.

Now he knew why he'd held back from gushing his thanks. She's a feminist, he decided, who doesn't like doors opened for her or, I bet, her coat held, or condescending men.

He made two mental notes. First, not to chat her up. Second, to ask Scott to fix it with the Home Office for her to join his investigation team.

It was a decision which was to save his life.

'Stand 159,' bellowed the warder, opening the door for her. 'Lady present.'

The peak of his cap rested on his eyebrows, in the way of army drill sergeants, so he had to crane his neck up to see.

Jacko rejoiced in the look of irritation on Shirley Thomas's face which supported his view of her sexual politics.

Marsh was standing when they entered the interview room, which had a big barred window and a plain desk in the centre with four black plastic moulded chairs scattered around it. The smell of cheap disinfectant and polish reminded Jacko of his army days.

Marsh was tall, very slim, athletically handsome, despite his sullen look. His hair was shaved from his ears half-way up his head to a skull cap of tight, dull black hair.

'Sit down, please.' Jacko put on his friendly smile. The warder backed against the door, clanking it shut, and remained there. The other three sat round the table.

'I'm sorry about your mate Andy,' said Jacko as sincerely as he could.

Marsh's eyes locked on him. 'Sorry, my arse. You suspect me of giving him bad shit.'

'Watch yourself, sunshine,' said the guard, belligerently. 'You'll be on report.'

Shirley fixed an annoyed look on him. 'In the circumstances, I think you had better wait outside.'

'But Miss Thomas – '

'I have a big, strong, strapping detective to look after me.'

Jacko grinned. He regarded himself as a man without much muscle beneath the black leather coat, his weekend duty dress, which hung loose on his shoulders, a size too big. He'd scraped into the service at minimum height – five feet ten in those days. His weight fluctuated wildly between eleven and twelve stones, depending on how hard he was working and how much he was worrying about that work. In mirrors, his brow looked permanently furrowed and deep creases darted from sallow cheeks towards always weary, hazel eyes behind steel-framed bifocals.

The guard visibly bristled at his dismissal as he closed the door. Marsh unwound himself in his chair.

'Listen.' Jacko rested his elbows on the table, putting his hands in the prayer position and rubbing his nose up and down with index fingers. 'It's a fact that you were handcuffed to him on the bus there and back and were in the same cell here. Apart from when you were both in the dock, you were together all day. You're central to the inquiry.'

No response.

Shirley took out a packet of Bensons and a lighter from a huge blue canvas bag she eased off her shoulder and rested on the table.

'Don't smoke,' said Marsh when she offered him one. 'I'm no mug, man.'

Jacko longed for one. He'd given them up. Yet again. A year before, during a crucial interview on the killing of a private detective, he had absent-mindedly taken and smoked one and finished up on thirty a day. It had taken him months to kick them. Yet again.

31

He had rumbled now what was odd about Marsh. He was white but talked black, as if determined to fit the media sterotype of a dope dealer.

Jacko asked him to begin at the beginning, the easy part. Soon Marsh lengthened yes, no and don't know answers into sentences. He and Andy, he said, had not shared the same cell in the remand wing. Andy was with the hold-up man and he was with the lager lout. But they had been in custody together for five months and become good pals.

'Everyone liked him. I mean . . .' He looked away. '. . . Not everyone has had his schooling, you know. He helped with letters. He knew the rules. He was very brainy, no bullshit.'

On the bus, he went on, Andy had been very chatty. 'Reckoned he'd get two to three. Fifteen months didn't bother him. He knew his way round. He was into prisoners' rights.

'He gave the thumbs up when he came down the dock steps. His parents visited him in the cell and stayed ten minutes. His mother kissed him goodbye. Then a social worker popped by.'

Jacko accepted that Marsh, in the next cell, had noticed all of this, not because he was nosy: he had nothing better to do.

Back in prison, climbing the stairs to the first-floor landing, Andy lagged behind. Once they'd made up their beds he flopped on his and said, 'I feel shattered.'

When the cell door was unlocked for evening recreation, he turned down Carl Marsh's suggestion that they should suss out the recreation facilities together.

'Too groggy,' he said.

Marsh repeated this quote and added, 'He was certainly sweating. I asked if he wanted the MO but he said he'd sleep it off. When I got back he was so ill I hit the bell.'

'Was he on drugs?' Jacko asked.

'In here? Come on!' Carl pulled his head back in feigned surprise.

'We all know they get in,' said Shirley, quickly, smiling. 'We're not asking how.'

An easy shrug. 'A joint now and then, perhaps.'

'Pills?' asked Jacko.

'Don't mess with them.'

'Did he?' A slightly raised voice.

'Outside he may have popped now and then. Who knows?' An apprehensive look.

'Inside?' Jacko used his low voice, impatient.

Carl shook his head, looking down. 'Not that I know of.'

'Did he ever ask you for any stuff?'

'Shit, no.' He raised his voice and gave Jacko a harsh glare. Shirley resumed. 'Syringes and things?'

They were, Jacko knew, a constant worry in prisons. The few that did get in were widely shared, running a frightening risk of Aids.

A sincere headshake. 'Nope. He wasn't into that.'

Jacko believed him, in view of the doctor's findings, even if he didn't believe the rest of what he'd said. He had used Shirley's intervention as thinking time and took over again. 'Did he have any enemies?'

'Connelly didn't like him.'

Jacko looked for guidance at Shirley.

'The hold-up man, his cellmate on remand,' she explained.

'They had a big shouting match one night,' Carl continued. 'I heard Andy calling him a bigoted bastard. But Connelly wouldn't dare harm him. A lot of people in here owed Andy.'

'Did you see him pop anything yesterday?'

'Told you that already.' An emphatic pause. 'No.'

'Did you give him anything yesterday?'

Carl closed his eyes tightly, giving his head a hard shake. 'How many more times?' A low grumbling voice, almost a growl. 'You are trying to stick this on me. I said no. No. *No.*'

'OK, Carl,' said Jacko, happy for the time being with what he'd got. 'See you soon, no doubt.'

'I'll be here,' he said, glumly.

4

Most women of her age, Maureen Beckby supposed, fantasize about a month of unlimited, uninhibited sex. She longed for a month without. Now her wish was to be fulfilled.

She must have loved him once, surely? She wasn't sure. All she knew for certain was that she hated him now and his pathetic do-gooding; loathed sharing his bed, his touch.

He wouldn't be touching her for a week or two. Not with his

ailment, as he pompously called it. An abscess on the arse, he means. A pain, like him.

Her bitter smile sweetened with memories of her real love that two years apart could never dim. Soon they'd be together for ever.

Maureen Beckby pictured herself with him, the holding, the hugging. She never pictured the actual sex act, the heaving, the humping. She wasn't sure if she was good at it, had no yardstick for comparison. All but one of the men she had known weren't that experienced, either. The exception was her police lover. He'd been around, demanded rough foreplay.

She glanced up at the driving mirror; at glistening blonde hair that set off a deep tan, blue eyes, white teeth and the little scar at the side of her chin, the result of a childhood fall.

There'd always been a man in Maureen's life. Not for the sex. For romance; the needing, the wanting. Sometimes more than one at the same time. Nowadays, three. Her live-in lover, twenty years older than her, a man she had come to hate. Her police lover, useful once, a major problem now. Her real love for whom she was chancing everything.

All had started in the usual way. Drinks with a crowd, private looks exchanged, an agonizing few days wondering if he'd make the call, or if he'd surrender to an inner voice warning him it was dangerous and daft, grinning like a schoolgirl into the mouthpiece at his casual invitation to lunch and hearing herself saying, 'Oh, how nice.'

She liked lunch first, didn't like being rushed, needed time to make up her mind, adored the slow build-up.

Lunch, when he passed the test, was followed by dinner and a quick peck in the car outside her place. The next date ended with cuddles on the doorstep. The time after that, inside for coffee and heavy petting and, though not always, bed.

Her live-in lover hadn't used that old line, 'My wife doesn't understand me.' When she'd asked point-blank, 'Do you love her?' he'd looked away; for her, answer enough.

He'd left his family for her, a flattering commitment. They'd moved into a country cottage close to the hamlet of New York. Idyllic in that first year when she'd been turning down dates from lawyers she'd met in her job.

Through him she'd found her real love; zapped from heaven, she'd been, never experienced such a yearning before. In his company, in the pub, she'd been shy, overawed by his reputation.

She knew all about the Irish connection. Her live-in lover had told her. To warn her off? Maybe. If it mattered at all, it only added to the buzz.

She plucked up courage and gave him that head-slightly-down, sidelong look through wispy strands of blonde hair. Next day he phoned for lunch. A fortnight later, after the usual slow build-up, they were in bed; her teaching him. A virgin at thirty? He'd said so and he'd been so inexperienced, not a man of the world at all, that she believed him.

He wouldn't hear of her leaving her live-in lover. 'Could affect my parole,' he'd said. So she'd stayed at the cottage, a slum in her eyes now, and slept with that body, wrinkled and aged compared with her Michael. She repeated the name to herself, adored saying it to herself. My M-i-c-h-a-e-l. A quiver ran right through her.

Without qualms, she'd slept with two police officers to get the information he needed to plan the bank robbery to finance their new life together. Willingly she'd run risks, more for love than money, and was running them still. Now. Today.

Apart from the live-in lover and duty sex with the rougher of the policemen, she'd been faithful while her Michael had been on the run in North Africa.

Maureen Beckby switched off her bitter-sweet thoughts as she turned off the north end of a bridge by a big public house and drove down the embankment.

The man in the rugger blazer, open-neck white shirt and grey slacks, was waiting where he'd said he'd be – outside the imposing gateway, with curved wings and tall columns in white stone which looked like a picture postcard from Rome.

She parked her little white Peugeot 205, nearly new, very dirty, and got out, feeling scruffy in jeans and a baggy black sweater. She walked up to him. No sway today. Not fizzing or flirting. Strictly business. 'Sorry I'm late, Mr Layton.'

'Just got here myself.'

Business like, too; good, she thought. 'Let's walk.'

They turned their backs on the pillared gateway to the garden of remembrance overlooking playing fields on which Sunday afternoon cricket games were about to begin.

In silence they crossed a road lined on each side with high plane trees, their upper branches touching in the middle. A stiff breeze rustled the heart-shaped leaves above them. They came out of the shade into bright sunshine which glittered on the ruffled surface of a wide, fast-flowing river.

'Sorry to drag you this distance,' she said. 'I thought Nottingham would be more secure than Lincoln.'

Layton showed no interest in small talk. Suited her, too. 'How much in advance?'

'Eighty thousand.'

A short brittle laugh, shocked. 'It would be cheaper to hijack a helicopter.'

'They're wise to that after the Gartree bust. Anyway, it didn't work. They were only airborne for five minutes and then they landed in the wrong spot.' Layton looked down at her. 'Lincoln is criss-crossed with radar from RAF stations. They'd pick us up in ten seconds flat.'

He spoke with the rhythm of south-east London. Thin strands of fair hair straggled across a peeling bald patch. He had a Desperate-Dan jaw which made his head seem too big for his broad body.

'Over the wall then?' she asked, fishing.

'No chance. They'll keep him on the move from cell to cell in solitary and you've no one permanent on the inside to feed us info. Right?'

None of his business, she decided. 'What's the plan then?'

'Snatch him from court.' He made it sound very melodramatic.

Done three recces, he went on, the last one on Friday after he'd been in court, sitting in the press box, posing as an out-of-town freelance journalist. 'The bus leaves twenty to thirty minutes after the judge in his Rolls. There are always one or two police cars as escorts. You're sure the lead one is a rapid armed response vehicle?'

'Certain.' Maureen was under strict instructions from her police lover not to tell him how she knew.

'Two handguns will be locked in a steel box in the boot,' he said, untroubled. 'So it will take a team of eight. Me and my partner have to get cracking with the trial only three weeks away. We'll buy a little terraced house in a back street behind the castle. Plenty for sale. A major outlay but we must buy, not rent.'

Loose change, she thought, with almost two million awaiting collection.

'A van, hard cash, and stencil the name of a paint firm on the sides. We must be established as residents coming and going to work in white overalls within a fortnight.'

On the shopping list, too, a window cleaners' cradle on pulleys and eight pairs of blue overalls bought well away from the city.

He paused. A pretence for dramatic effect, Maureen guessed. For this was a man who'd already thought everything through.

'Friday, the 8th of July, is D-day.' Layton made it sound like an historic announcement, a declaration of war.

'We can't assume the trial will go into a second week. Sometimes they zip through the evidence. Once your fella is weighed off he'll be out of Lincoln nick and into one of a dozen top security places.

'The decorators' van won't go near the castle. It will be left downhill on the old racecourse. Another van will be in the castle car-park. Three men to that. It will be parked in a position to block off the narrow exit.'

Maureen visualized the scene, knew the castle well.

'The driver will stay in the van,' Layton went on. 'Two will take a police car apiece, covering the crews with sawn-off shot-guns.

'Me and my partner will be raised up the outer wall on the cradle with two more men operating the pulleys and another at the wheel of the second van. My partner'll get a shooter, an automatic. I'll have a revolver and bolt cutters to snap through the handcuffs.

'Hegan and me will go up a ladder while my mate covers our retreat. The three of us will come down the cradle and off to the van. The boys in the car-park will shoot out the tyres of the police patrols and take off.'

Maureen had listened wide-eyed, wordless, gripped with admiration – and a trickle of fear – for his meticulous pro-fessionalism, his single-minded ruthlessness.

Layton had paused again, inviting questions. 'What then?' she asked, indulging him.

'At the racecourse, Hegan, me and my partner'll change into white overalls in the waiting painters' van.

'And here's the beauty of it all.' Very proud. 'We drive back uphill. Road blocks won't be expecting that. They'll only be stopping traffic heading away from the scene. We hole up in the house for a week or two until the tracker dogs are called off.'

In the stolen car, also parked near the racecourse, he went on, would be golf bags, fishing tackle and sporty clothing. 'There's a course next to the race track and a river behind that. Those three can leave whenever they like.'

'What about the three in the car-park?' she asked, just to show him she had followed him thoroughly.

'They'll look like male models under their boiler-suits. They'll dump the van and walk to the White Hart where they'll be booked in for the weekend.' A cheerful chuckle. 'Who's going to look in a four-star hotel for a jailbreak gang?'

'Won't they be spotted hanging about the car-park?'

'Stonemasons, they'll be. They're always working on the castle wall. Restoration is never-ending. Like painting the Forth Bridge.'

He looked down at her, full of himself, all but saying: Better that.

She nodded, deeply impressed.

They fell into strolling silence. The footpath followed a sharp curve in the river and a bridge came into view, flat as a fenland field, its railings painted in olive green and gold above three arches through which the Trent flowed up to Newark and beyond, into the Humber and the North Sea. Across the river stood municipal buildings with copper roofs weathered bright green.

'Why eighty?' she asked.

'Say, thirty for the house. Two-up, two-down are dirt cheap up here. But the deal has got to be legit. Cash down – like the van. We don't want rent or remittance men knocking. We could be in hiding for a couple of weeks after the break. With equipment and wages, we can't do it for less.'

'Can we talk money?'

'Half and half, you said.'

'Of what's left?'

'Of the total haul – two mil.'

'Does that include your partner's £100,000?'

'Listen, lady. He earned that riding shot-gun on the bank raid.'

'It isn't Michael's fault he's had to wait.' She spoke hurriedly, annoyed. 'There's another hundred thou due to the informant who tipped him about the bank.' No need to tell him about her police source, she decided.

'Not our problem. Take it or leave it.' Layton made it sound very final. To confirm there'd be no debate, he added, 'Any loose ends?'

'A passport. Michael wants it before he takes you to the money.'

She reached into her back pocket and handed him a brown envelope. He slid out two identical photos of Hegan, more than two years old, and studied them. 'No problem.'

She smiled brightly at him. 'Sounds fine. I'll get the money to you. And I'll get the message to Michael. Friday July the 8th.'

'After the court rises,' he added.

They turned and walked back.

At the car, she said, 'Phone me only in an emergency. Just say . . .' Silence, thinking. '. . . say you're Olive's Malc. Remember that, Olive's Malc and you've had a breakdown. Give a location and I'll come to you.' A wide, white smile. 'Thanks.'

Just for the hell of it, couldn't help herself really, Maureen Beckby gave him that sidelong look through strands of blonde hair.

On the way back she was beset with the problem of how to handle her live-in lover. He'd have to pass the message. The police lover wouldn't. Too dangerous.

How could she talk him into it? She set up many scenes in her mind and finally decided to get it over with that night.

'Darling,' she'd say. 'I need a huge favour. I want you to visit Hegan and simply say, "Friday the 8th July, after court."'

He was bound to ask why. Judging his reaction was guess-work. Most likely he'd accuse her again of having had an affair with him. With enough drink inside him, he'd slap her. Like he'd done when he found out about her other police lover, the first one. And harder still when he'd overheard Michael making contact, after all those months away, to arrange a rendezvous his arrest had stopped him keeping.

She wouldn't resist, she decided. Through her tears she'd say, 'I have been indiscreet over Hegan' (she wouldn't use his first name) 'but not in that way. I've not been unfaithful. Some of the things that policeman told me about money movements I passed on to him one night in his pub when I'd had too much to drink. That implicates me in the bank robbery, accessory before the fact. That's why he phoned me just before his arrest. Now he is threatening to inform on me unless I help him escape. You know what a rat he is. He informed for his freedom in Belfast. Now it's my turn. We both know with our experience of courts what I will get for that. Five years minimum.'

Yes, she thought, a good script that, a bit like an old Joan Crawford black and white. Needs a little polishing.

And what then, just to apply that polish? Say something like, 'There's £25,000 in it . . .' No, double it. He won't get it anyway. 'There's £50,000 in it for our help. We could get a place, away from here. And he'll be out of our lives for ever. Just you and me, darling. Together. For ever.' A lot like Joan Crawford, that.

And she'd sob a little and shake her shoulders, then sigh dramatically and raise her bosom. And, yes, she thought, satisfied at last, something like that ought to work just fine.

Maureen Beckby transferred her thoughts to her police lover. He was panicking, no doubt about it, over that death in prison. Strange that Layton had not mentioned it. Maybe he didn't know about it. Only made a paragraph in last night's *Echo*. Or maybe he wasn't bothered about it, too professional.

Her police lover bothered about it, though, worked himself into a lather when he called. 'They've put a detective inspector on it,' he'd said. 'He's like a rat up a drainpipe.'

'Can't you buy us a little time, darling?' she'd said, apprehensively. 'Just muddy the waters a bit for him.'

'He's a hard, mean bastard. It will take more than that.' Heavy menace in his tone. 'I shall have to put him out of action.'

He'd think of something, she was sure of that. He had covered all their tracks before.

Amazing. Him a police officer. And they'd had the gall to lock up her Michael.

The mental mention of his name calmed her. She thought of him now, and only him, for the rest of the way home.

Maureen Beckby wore a sugary smile; a lover's smile.

5

They'd been a perfect pair, Andy Heald and Tina Beaver. A partnership made in heaven, Jacko concluded, if that's what you want to believe in.

He and his Jackie were like that. They were more than man and wife. They were friends as well as lovers. They came alive together, making fun of each other, making each other laugh. He often kidded and chatted up women workmates but the thought of bedding one never entered his mind.

(Oh, come on. It's tell-the-truth time. OK, then. Started to cross his mind but never reached the other side. That better?)

Freely, but privately, he acknowledged that he wasn't smart intellectually or in the way he dressed. His annual new suit, once worn, looked slept-in. His thoughts were frequently flawed. Without his wife and his workmates, he'd be in deep cold trouble. Recognizing this and accepting it had made him half-way to being a decent detective.

Tina Beaver had been Andy Heald's Jackie. Lover, friend and workmate, Jacko realized, listening and sitting on a white basket chair shaped like a satellite dish in the cluttered bedsit they had shared.

With their degrees, they could have lived in one of those riverside executive houses with a roof garden near Trent Bridge instead of this placarded squalor.

All four pale emulsioned walls, tanned by nicotine, were covered with horror posters. The centre piece on one was a black and white picture of hens, packed like sardines, row upon row, their heads poking over a horizontal steel bar. 'A Price That's Too Painful To Pay,' said the caption.

The wall opposite was plastered with posters from the prison reform lobby. The most vivid, again in brooding black and white, was a picture of a prisoner, back to the camera. A guard knelt before him, feeling with both hands behind his knees. A tiny barred window was set high in a painted brick wall. A narrow, metal-framed bed was to the prisoner's right; a filthy wooden cabinet with a plastic bucket on top was to his left. The inmate had both arms outstretched. His fingertips were touching the walls on either side of him.

Every night for almost six months, while her Andy was locked up on remand, Tina had gone to sleep with that picture hanging over her.

Jacko wished, oh, how he wished, that he'd never caught him. It was a pinch that wasn't worth a pinch of shit to him now.

She sat on a crumpled blue duvet on a double bed. Her bare feet, soles soiled by walking on the worn floral carpet, were tucked beneath her. She wore a billowing pleated skirt, black with tiny blue flowers, which she tugged beneath her knees. Her shirt was of unironed denim blue. For a veggie, she was a big-boned, hefty woman, a year older than Andy.

There was a good reason, Tina was saying, why she had not been in court to see Andy sentenced. An engagement both thought more important. She'd been to a prison reform meeting in Sheffield.

A police car was waiting for her when she got back to the three-storey Victorian house, two bedsits, one shared bathroom per floor, on a busy bus route leading east out of Nottingham. They covered the thirty-six miles to the hospital in Lincoln in forty minutes.

'Fifteen minutes too late,' she added with a bleak little smile.

She followed his eyes to the prison poster and he sat through a long diatribe on jail conditions and regulations, patiently waiting for an opening to discuss drugs.

Two or three times a week she'd visited him in the remand wing. Two buses and one train each way; four hours door to door. All for fifteen minutes together.

'No handbags or shopping baskets in the visiting room,' she went on. 'I was always searched. All the food I took in, supposedly a privilege on remand, was picked over. We weren't even allowed a hug in case I passed on any drugs. People like us are automatically pigeon-holed as users.'

His patience had paid off. He pounced. 'Was he?'

She replied without thought, with honesty. 'Cannabis, yes.

Since our university days in Manchester. It's cheaper than booze and the effect's the same. Ever tried it?'

'No.' Jacko shook his head slowly. Then he decided to relax her a little by telling her why, to share a confidence. 'That's not on moral grounds. I've got this great mate, a detective in New York. We met on hols in Italy. When I went over to see him, almost ten years ago now, he took me to listen to some blue grass. Best fiddle-playing I ever heard. There was plenty of grass around, too.'

She laughed, lightly, for the first time.

'He rolled up and kept offering it to me. I was too scared to try it, but only because I thought I might get to like it.'

Her exhausted smile vanished when he asked, 'Did you pass him anything on those visits?'

'No.' She shook her head, unoffended. 'He could take it or leave it.'

'What about hard stuff?'

Her reply was a hard stare.

'I need to know if I'm going to find out what happened.'

'Never.' She raised her voice harshly. 'That's like pumping steroids into capons or artificial insemination. Not natural.'

'LSD?'

She shook her head, very firmly. 'Not for years. One trip made him ill.'

'Pills?'

She shrugged, less sure, and hesitated. 'Now and then. If they were on offer, yes. The odd pep pill. Gee-ups, he called them.'

'So,' said Jacko slowly, concentrating, 'if he was offered one in the cells or on the bus from court to prison, he might have popped it?'

'Suppose so.'

'I've told my boss I'm ruling out suicide. Am I right?'

'Absolutely.' The very notion shocked her and it registered in her face and voice. 'I'm surprised it's occurred to anyone. He wasn't worried about prison. He regarded it as . . .' She was struggling for the right phrase and clutched at one from university days. '. . . source material. He was full of plans. He was even talking of . . .' a smile for herself '. . . looking round for a newsy by-election to stand as an independent on prison reform.'

He'd have lost his deposit, thought Jacko. There are no votes in prison reform.

'Can I rule out murder?' he asked.

'Good lord.' For just a second Tina closed her eyes. 'He hasn't an enemy in the world.'

'Is it possible he picked up something sensitive on the prison grapevine?'

She gave it a thought, deep and genuine. 'He knew everybody's business, if that's what you mean. He helped them with correspondence, censored, naturally.' A smirk, unnatural on her face. 'He didn't tell me some of the things they talked about. Many of them are illiterate. Never known a loving home or a caring school, most of them.'

More campaigning spiel now. 'One in every five are inside for not paying fines . . . Their crime is being poor . . . Afro-Caribbeans have seven times more chance of ending up in jail . . . Their real crime is being black.'

Jacko let his mind meander.

'He'd never break a confidence.' She paused and fixed him with a challenging look. 'He never told you I was on that petrol bomb raid with him, now did he?'

Jacko shook his head sadly. 'Promise me you won't say that to any other copper or we'll both be in trouble.' She smiled, eyes down, conspiratorially.

'Did he have a view on euthanasia?'

Tina jolted her head up.

'You see.' Jacko paused, tentative. 'There was a man in court and on the bus who's dying of cancer. He's a child abuser, fiftyish, who won't see the outside again. Is there a chance, you know . . . as an act of mercy, I mean . . .' Difficult, this, he realized. '. . . that he was helping to get something to him to end it?' Another pause. 'And it went wrong?'

She furrowed her brow in profound thought. Her answer came slowly. 'We are both in favour of abortion, of course, and the woman's right to choose, but I don't think we ever thought it through from the cradle to the grave, so to speak. I'm sure he'd be against that.'

'Why?' To Jacko it had seemed a logical extension to their radical views.

More deep thought. Then, 'We had this cat. Took her in when we were in Manchester. Old even then. Here, when she

44

was on her last legs, I mentioned taking her to the vet. "No," he said, "animals know when their time has come. She'll just curl up in her favourite place. We'll get up one morning and she'll have gone peacefully." And that's what happened.'

A tear slipped from the corner of her left eye which she brushed away with her forefinger, sniffing.

Jacko waited for her.

'So,' she continued, in control again, 'though we never discussed it, his view would be that, while it's wrong to prolong life artificially, it isn't right to take life. These things should be left to happen naturally. I know that's what he would have said.'

Jacko remained silent. He knew that she knew. She knew Andy's thought processes as well as Jackie knew his. A long pause, poignant. He cleared a catch at the back of his throat. 'We know he didn't kill himself and we can't believe anyone would want to kill him. Right?'

She nodded.

He looked away, talking, in effect, to himself. 'So let's work it out. Someone gave him something he thought was safe?' He let the question hang. 'But someone fouled up and gave him something deadly?'

'Must be.' Barely audibly.

'By mistake?'

'Must be.'

'Or, alternatively, someone planted something fatal with another victim in mind and Andy took it accidentally?'

'It's possible,' she said doubtfully.

Jacko took a pen and book from his inside pocket. 'Mind if I take that down?'

She watched him writing, read his summary of their conversation and signed it.

He climbed out of the basket chair, hands on his knees, pushing himself upright, feeling drained, He looked at the dresser, its top ringed in white where hot mugs had stood, its mirror cracked and blackened at one corner. On it, a portable typewriter, at least thirty years old. In a tray, drafts of the pamphlets she was pecking out, a jar of Body Shop handcream acting as a paperweight.

Next to it was a small desk, more scarred than the dresser. On it, a dainty flower vase, colourfully striped porcelain, filled with brushes, pens and pencils. The cat's old blanket was on the carpet beneath the desk, ginger hairs clinging to the fabric.

Lying flat on the desk was a large sheet of thick white paper on which she had pencilled the outline of a poster. Structurally, she had based it on the battery henhouse placard but she had converted the bars from horizontal to upright. The prisoners still had the bodies of poultry but their faces were human, though their noses had been extended to give the illusion of beaks.

She slipped off the bed and stood at his shoulder, looking down at it. One face had become Andy's, framed for ever as a campaigner.

'I'll finish it when I've got myself together,' she said very softly.

'What are you going to call it?' He spoke in a church whisper.

'Something simple like "Doing Bird".'

'How about "Caged"?'

They smiled at each other and he squeezed her ice-cold hand.

Well, he thought, driving home over Trent Bridge, not looking sideways at the river, I've got what I went for. A signed witness statement suggesting murder-by-mistake. Now he could break more cover without mentioning Scott's suspicions.

The plan that had begun to occur to him at the jail yesterday was fully formed now. He could treat Andy Heald's death as a murder investigation. He could pick his own squad to work with. He'd already commandeered Cross, the constable who'd twice missed out on arresting Hegan. Now he'd ask for Detective Sergeant Frank Marlowe, the armed stake-out at Hegan's pub, the officer who had taken the supposed tip-off that he was back, and for Detective Sergeant Stan Young, the officer who'd minded Hegan and had no alibi for the day of the big bank robbery.

All three targets in the same incident room. Cunning, that. He could monitor their every move. Inspired, too. All would think they were probing Heald's poisoning. None would be aware of Scott's real motive to unmask the corrupt cop among them with the key to the missing two millions.

He would worm his way into their confidence, use their nicknames, have fun together, the way he always worked. He'd defend them against outside interference, jolly them along. All for one, one for all. The Four Musketeers. The perfect set-up.

6

'It's cor blimey time,' Jacko announced as they sat round a block of five pushed-together desks, a lime-green phone on each.

'What's that?' asked Cross, with the pale, tense look of a new boy at school. He was wearing a greeny-grey jacket with a brown leather button missing and gaudily striped tie, his idea of plainclothes.

Sergeant Frank Marlowe stretched his long legs beneath his desk and leaned back in his chair. He was not yet thirty but had many world-weary mannerisms.

In front of them were the buff files of statements they had taken in the last couple of days from prisoners and guards in the court cellblock and on the bus. Next to them were the red dossiers of inmates' criminal records and the pink personnel folders of the staff.

'We all read each other's statements. Follow?' Marlowe spoke schoolmaster-style. 'When you got something that sends a tingle down your spine, you jump out of your seat and declaim, "Cor blimey. Listen to this." You then read aloud what has sparked your interest and we bounce it round the table.' He moved his body as though operating an invisible hula-hoop so that his head circled round his audience.

Shirley Thomas, her pale blue blouse tucked in at the waist of her dark blue skirt, smiled. Stan Young rested his dark chin on a hand, eyes down already.

'Now,' said Marlowe, hands cupped together on the back of his neck, 'it's possible one of us will think of a logical explanation. If not . . .' He pulled himself upright and pitched himself forward. '. . . you may have uncovered what is known to us seasoned detectives as . . .' He paused, theatrically. '. . . a clue.'

Anyone, he went on, who came up with a proven cor blimey was excused putting their hand in their pocket that lunchtime. A false cor blimey meant the first round was on him or her.

'Thanks, sergeant,' said Cross politely.

'Philippe.' Marlowe rolled his nickname lovingly off his tongue. 'Everyone calls me Philippe. I am an amalgam of my revered namesake and Maigret.'

Liar, thought Jacko. Marlowe had got his nickname because the black beret he wore for weapon training made him look like a French onion seller.

Philippe lit up a cigarette. Jacko watched with almost unbearable yearning as he drew in deeply. Withdrawal pangs overwhelmed him. He would have preferred him to have been smoking Maigret's pipe filled with dung; anything but that seductive white cylinder with that soothing smell.

He lifted his legs on to the top of his desk, his reading position. 'The trick, Ridgeback . . .' He craned his neck in no particular direction. '. . . everyone calls him Ridgeback, by the way. The trick is not to be shy. Shout out. Remember, villains get away with it when detectives are frightened of making fools of themselves. No matter how many mistakes you make, you will never replace Philippe as the village idiot.'

All five looked down with smiles that soon faded. Four of them because their reading was depressing and disturbing; Jacko because his private thoughts were. The only person in the room he could trust was the only civvy – Shirley Thomas. The Home Office had agreed to her joining his team with such speed that he was beginning to fret about just how high up in Whitehall the decisions on this case were being made.

He looked up again, furtively studying Marlowe. He was fun to work with, a fair detective, but a bit of a Jack-the-lad, a spendthrift with a fast car and a taste for exotic holidays. Or had the Little Fat Man poisoned his mind?

Scott, pulling strings behind the scenes, had established that Marlowe was on leave on the day of the robbery and could have had a sight of the memo about the movement of the bank's money.

Cross, too, had been off on the day of the robbery but had no access to the memo that Scott could discover.

In his mind, Jacko was drawing up a chart with opportunity and inside knowledge down the left-hand side and the names of the suspects across the top. Marlowe already had two ticks under his name; Cross a tick and a question mark. When Jacko had a complete line of ticks, he'd got his man.

He started his reading. The rapist had told Philippe in his statement that he was so shocked by his twelve-year sentence that he was in a daze in the cells and on the bus and saw nothing. An answer to sex offending seemed as far away as a cure for cancer, Jacko brooded.

The child abuser was beginning to curl up on his bunk in the hospital wing in the way that Tina's cat had lain down to die. Friday was his day for his once-a-week pill which supplemented his four-times-a-day painkillers. Officer Haywood had given it to him after breakfast. It always made him drowsy, he told Shirley. The day had just drifted by. Another no-no.

Michael Hegan (aka Orange Billy) had declined to see Stan Young. Jacko stopped reading. Interesting that, he told himself. Stan was the man who had nursed him on and off in the time he had spent between payroll robberies in bomb-blasted Belfast and sleepy Sleaford. He was about to be accused (though he didn't know it yet) of planting the fingerprint evidence.

'Stan.' Very casual. 'When you left me in court on Friday, did you visit the cells?'

'Went straight back to the station.'

'Pity.'

'Why?'

'You might have been able to corroborate some of this stuff.' He nodded at the sheaf of statements. 'Get up to the prison much these days?'

'Upjohn assigned me to talk to Hegan; you know, all pally-pally, off-the-record. His brief banned me. The only police officers he'll talk to are Upjohn or his DI.'

Jacko resumed his reading. Shirley had been fielded as Stan's substitute. Hegan asked for Officer Haywood (him again, Jacko noted; check on him) to witness their interview.

Apart from lunch, when he ate his smoked salmon sandwich alone, Hegan had spent most of the day in his cell with his London-based solicitor who took down a long proof of evidence he was to give at his trial next month.

'Nothing untoward happened within my sight or hearing,' he said in the legal lingo of a man who had made many statements in his supergrass days.

The trial of Connelly, the bungling hold-up man, had been put back when he unexpectedly changed his plea of guilty to not guilty. He obscenely denied to Ridgeback ever quarrelling with Andy Heald when they shared a cell on remand. 'I'm being setup, scapegoated.'

He insisted on being transferred to the segregated section that houses informers, sex offenders and other prisoners at risk from attack. Does he protesteth too much? Jacko mused.

'Sound statement, this.' Jacko waved it. 'Do you get to do many prisoner interviews these days?'

Cross blushed. 'I was up there a fortnight ago taking TICs from a TWOC.'

Shirley didn't query the jargon of a service that adores reducing everything to initials. Jacko assumed she'd know Cross meant additional offences a joyrider wanted the court to take into consideration of taking without owners' consent.

He didn't translate. Instead: 'How about you, Philippe?'

He shook his head in a cloud of smoke. 'Once I've banged 'em away, I don't go visiting.'

Two crosses and a tick went under their names alongside a new column headed: 'Access to potential middleman in jail.'

Jacko himself had made a seventy-mile round trip (it was good mileage and he was, after all, the boss) through the Fens the day before to see a youth called Rod Daniels, starting a nine-month term in a desolate young offenders' institution for battering a policeman.

'Andy was a good mate,' he said, friendly without ten pints of lager inside him.

His own weeping mother had kissed him goodbye before lunchtime when sandwiches were served, Daniels said. Andy had been in the cell opposite. He ate his two. The guard opened them up for a peek first. 'I had exactly the same. D'yer think it's salmonella?'

'Hope not,' said Jacko. 'I had the same.'

He told him a joke. About a prisoner who queued for half an hour for his plate of food. When he sat down in the packed dining hall he realized he had forgotten his knife and fork. Frightened that a famished inmate would steal his meal, he wrote out a note which he stuck with a toothpick on his boiled potato: 'I have spat on this.' When he got back with his eating irons someone had added underneath: 'So have I.'

The tale didn't cheer up Rod Daniels, though.

According to him, Andy Heald's parents had spent ten

minutes with him inside the cell, then a social worker chatted to him for a few seconds through the bars.

On his worry list Jacko made a note to find out which social worker.

The statement ended. 'Him, me and Carl Marsh were all muckers in the remand wing. Andy never spent any time with his cellmate Connelly. He thought he was a religious nut.'

Another name was added to Jacko's jobs-to-do list.

They broke off for lunch and walked from the city's main police station, a modernish building, near the bottom of one of two steep hills that led to the cobbled castle square.

It was sunny and very warm, a beautiful June day. Jacko took them to a bar opposite a tiny theatre which was advertising a page three girl as a forthcoming attraction in *In One Bed . . . and Out the Other* – a thespian treat that reminded him of his schooldays.

They sat at a table in the corner of the bar which had signed photos of stars hanging on panelled walls. Without a cor blimey between them, they kittied up for a huge plateful of sandwiches and three rounds – beer for Philippe, Stan and Ridgeback, dry white wine for Shirley and Coke for Jacko, who seldom drank at lunchtime.

He didn't want to talk shop, needed to yarn, to relax them, looking for that opening, that slip-up.

Across the road, he told them when they had settled, he'd seen his first nude woman. 'Or part of her,' he added moodily.

Everyone apart from the back wooden row of the gods where he and his mate were sitting got a view of her, completely naked and still, standing on a plaster pedestal shaped like a Roman column.

'The trouble was the fire curtain. It was half-way down and, with her standing on her bloody pedestal, I never saw anything above her thighs.'

He gave his happy audience his mournful look. 'It took me four more years and half a week's army pay to make that discovery. My mate kept saying afterwards, "She shaves. I'm sure she shaves." He was making it up. He couldn't see any better than me.'

Philippe gleefully suggested that he should potter across the road to the box office and, more than thirty years on, demand his money back.

Shirley, tears in her eyes, turned to listen to Stan. He had dark, bushy eyebrows and lines etched deep into his forehead. Jacko's first marriage had finished in divorce when his wife left him for a married sergeant, but Stan's had ended in far greater tragedy. His wife died in a car crash. He brought up their two children with his mother's help. The youngest left home for university last autumn. Now he was on his own with a worsening back injury and a bullshit boss, Upjohn, who liked his men able-bodied, brawny and brainless.

'They all shaved in Health and Efficiency, right, Jacko?' he said with a nostalgic smile.

Jacko nodded glumly. 'Those bodies glistening with sun lotion weren't half erotic.'

'Johnson's Baby Oil is best,' said Shirley, knowledgeably. 'Don't you find?' She looked mischievously at Jacko.

'Not really.' He was still affecting his air of despondency. 'It clogs up my string vest.'

There was long happy laughter and, in the dressing-room style of camaraderie he was seeking to promote, they swapped holiday stories.

Stan hadn't been away. Ridgeback had been fishing in Scotland and had never been back to his native Africa.

'Took my lady to the Gambia last year,' said Philippe in his world-weary way.

(Jacko made a mental note to look up where it was. When he thumbed through his atlas, he found it on the same page as Morocco and perked with interest. His wife Jackie worked out it was 1,600 miles from Casablanca – 'as the vulture flies'. A long way for a day trip to see Hegan, he agreed, and he lost interest in this line of inquiry.)

Brief biographies were soon being exchanged.

Shirley, he was surprised to learn, was nearer forty than thirty. A long affair with a married barrister in London had recently ended. She'd been a senior probation officer before joining the prison service.

She hated security. Her ambition was to shake up the workshops and start proper training, wanted fewer prisons, not more. 'Most are filled with harmless inadequates.'

She didn't want to become the governor (not governess, Jacko noted). She wanted to go to the Home Office where the policy was made and the real power lay.

A radical, pioneering, careerist feminist, a frightening combination, he thought.

'Which is why,' she went on, 'a good result on this inquiry will do me no harm.' She fixed Jacko with a look that told him it was time to go.

He led the way, Shirley following. Only Stan's sharp reflexes stopped the door from snapping back into her face.

Back to the station, back to the reading.

Senior Officer Downes had stated that he examined all the sandwiches taken into the cells that lunchtime. They included the smoked salmon sandwich sent in for Hegan from the White Hart hotel where his high-powered solicitor was staying. Nothing suspicious was found.

Not bad, mused Jacko, breaking off for a moment. Smoked salmon on legal aid while we've just had chicken and ham out of our own pockets.

The rest of the guards saw nothing as far as Andy Heald was concerned. They regarded him as a barrack room lawyer but no danger. Their brief had been to watch the two high-risk prisoners, Hegan and the rapist.

Somewhere in that reading were clues, Jacko realized, but no call of cor blimey meant none had been spotted yet.

The phone rang. 'What the devil's going on?' A strident voice he recognized from way back.

'Oh, hallo, sir.' Jacko forced himself to sound respectful.

'I've just got back from weapon training . . .'

Jacko had a mind's-eye view of the caller, Superintendent Clive Upjohn, sitting behind his desk, bandoleer strapped across his broad chest and a Viva Zapata hat with scrambled egg on the rim to denote his much-prized rank.

'. . . and what do I find? First, you press-gang Cross, now Young for this tuppenny-hapenny inquiry.'

'You assigned PC Cross on Friday night.'

'For the weekend at your chief's request. Not for the duration.'

'Mr Scott wants PC Cross for continuity and Sergeant Young for background.'

Both stopped reading at the mention of their names.

'What background?' Upjohn chuntered on.

'On Hegan. He was his minder.'

'What's Hegan got to do with it?'

'One theory is that an attempt was being made on him and Heald accidentally got in the way.'

From the silence it was obvious that Scott had not briefed Upjohn.

'So,' Jacko went on, wondering whether he should be telling him this, 'Stan's knowledge on him's very useful.'

'Useless, you mean.'

'I don't follow,' said Jacko guardedly.

'Not a very good job he did on him, did he, hanging about in Sleaford waiting to meet Hegan when he was robbing a bank down the road?'

Jacko bit his bottom lip, said nothing.

'Now look here.' Upjohn seemed to have recovered. 'I was in charge of that operation. If you want background you come to me. Meantime I want Young back.'

'Mr Scott OK-ed it.'

'He's not running a big patch and the armed response unit, is he? I want him back tomorrow. Hear me?' The phone was slammed down.

Young and Cross viewed him with anxious eyes. 'Trouble?' asked Stan.

Jacko rubbed his chin. 'Nothing we can't handle.' Feeling more of a hypocrite than when he took the oath in court on a bible, he added, 'Together.'

7

Jacko drove up the hill, taking a hairpin at a crawl.

'Christ,' said Philippe, sitting behind him with Ridgeback, as everyone was now calling Cross, 'it's like a mountain rally.'

He'd begged a lift for Ridgeback and himself. Both were bound for the castle to question court ushers and refreshment room staff.

They were discussing cars, of no interest to Jacko who didn't know one make from another.

'Mine's in dock,' Philippe was explaining.

'Always service my own,' said Ridgeback, rather smugly.

'I'm a detective,' snapped Philippe, 'not a fucking motor mechanic.'

The tyres of Jacko's white Montego buzzed angrily over the cobbles in the castle square and hummed happily on a narrow track behind the old jailhouse which widened into the car-park.

They climbed the stone steps just before the barred entrance to the cellblock. The grounds of the sun-trap castle were busy with people dressed with the indifference of travellers well into their see-Europe-in-three-weeks tour.

They parted at the top of the steps. Philippe and Ridgeback headed for the crown court buildings, covered with shiny ivy. Jacko walked towards the old red-brick jailhouse, where the inquest on Andy Heald was to be opened.

Tina Beaver was standing on a flagstoned terrace, shaded from the sun. She wore the same gypsy skirt and Jacko the same grey suit and same tie. Only their shirts had changed. Both wore white.

The man standing next to her was Jacko's age. Grief had added ten years. Mr Heald was in a deep navy-blue suit in mourning for his only son. His handshake had the chill of a mortuary. 'How's Mrs Heald?' The answer was a sad headshake from both.

Jacko slipped the statement Ridgeback had taken at the hospital from a buff file he carried. He ran through it rapidly with Mr Heald. He asked no questions. He'd got all he needed on his son's drugs background from Tina, whose still-exhausted eyes pleaded with him to seek no more.

They stood in awkward silence looking across the lawns where two sightseers had closed their eyes on too many sights and gone to sleep beneath a huge copper beech.

Less than a hundred yards away Philippe stepped out of the refreshment room and started walking in a gangling sort of gait down the driveway towards them. Quite suddenly, he turned on to the grass, head down.

The sneaky bastard's off on a skive but spotted me, thought Jacko, amused.

His eyes went left, along the courthouse, and stopped at the top of the steps from the car-park. Upjohn rose regally into view, then marched, military-style, steps measured out by a swagger stick, towards the crown court entrance. A tall, handsome figure of a man in full uniform; the last one Jacko wanted to see at any time, particularly now when he was about to stitch him up.

He looked round, desperate for escape. The coroner's officer, a young uniformed sergeant, beckoned. He scurried inside, Tina and Mr Heald hurrying behind.

The courtroom was as cosy as the crown court was imposing. The walls were lime-green and the railings of the small, empty public gallery were painted a glossy deeper green. A young girl reporter sat on the press bench.

The only other person in the room was the coroner, Major William Jarman, MC, tall, slim with a straight back and a full head of silver hair. The only concession to his seventy-plus years was half-moon spectacles.

He never elevated himself to the bench where the magistrates sat in the mornings. He preferred the sloping desk in front of the bench, where he sat now, eyes down, signing papers. He was wearing a rusty tweed suit and a brown and cream bow-tie.

He peered over his gold-framed half-moons and nodded to his officer who, with a bored voice, intoned, 'All persons having anything to do at this inquest, touching the death of Andrew Michael Healey, draw near and give your attendance.'

His experienced eye immediately sought out the grieving next-of-kin. 'Step into the box.'

Jacko and Tina sat down as Mr Heald walked to the witness box where he stood and, bible in hand, repeated the oath. He gave his name and address, his son's date of birth, confirmed he was with him when he died in hospital and gave formal evidence of identification.

The coroner studied the statement Ridgeback had taken. 'A fit young man with no illness?'

'Yes, sir,' replied Mr Heald huskily.

'No addiction to drugs, not under medication?'

'No, sir.'

These questions and answers he turned into a deposition which he typed out himself on a battered white portable. He shared Jacko's hatred of new tech. Tapes were not allowed in his court. If a bleep went off during a hearing, an embarrassed reporter would be threatened with being held in contempt.

He was high Tory and an awesome autocrat, feared by everyone except people like Jacko who had once served as his officer. Upon them he bestowed loyalty without question, a loyalty Jacko was inexplicably beginning to feel he might need on this inquiry with its terrorist and political undertones.

Such style, thought Jacko, watching him at work. Such class, and he realized with regret that men like him were fast disappearing from public life.

The typing completed, Major Jarman looked up. 'Hmmmm.' A thoughtful moment. 'A mystery, in fact.'

He glanced at the girl reporter to make sure she had got her headline. He was publicity-conscious, but not for ego's sake. He saw no use in conducting inquiries into deaths unless the living learned from them.

He'd discovered long ago what his current subject, Andy Heald, had found out. To ensure headlines, to get your point across, you had to say things out of the ordinary. He added for good measure, 'Any death in custody is a matter of grave public concern.'

He rummaged into his files to extract the pathologist's preliminary report. 'I see the doctor has taken all the samples he needs.'

He looked at Jacko without a trace of recognition. 'There's no need, is there, to delay the funeral arrangements?'

Jacko shook his head.

'Very well. I'll issue a certificate.'

He signed a paper his officer placed before him in an ink pen and dried it on a blotting pad. 'And I adjourn these proceedings to a date to be fixed, same venue, pending further police inquiries.' He gave Mr Heald a solemn look. 'You have my condolences.'

The coroner stood without warning, slid from behind his desk, skipped lightly up two steps at the end of the bench and vanished into the justices' retiring room. He always adjourned between cases, no matter how short, for a cigarette. He was a fifty-a-day man with no time for health fads.

Tina and Jacko stood after him. Mr Heald joined Tina. He was holding the death certificate the officer had given him. His hand trembled. The paper rustled. His son's death was official now, registered. So had delayed shock. Jacko's heart ached for him. He promised to keep in touch and watched them shuffle, weighed down by grief, arm-in-arm out of the court.

He turned to the sergeant and nodded towards the closed door. 'Can I have a word with the old man?'

The officer climbed the steps, tapped on and opened the door, mumbled something. He motioned Jacko up.

'Young fellow-me-lad,' said the major through stained teeth. Jacko felt ten years younger; about the time they last worked together.

He was sitting in a square maroon leather chair with a crystal glass brimful of Tio Pepe held between thumb and forefinger. Between the middle fingers was a black cigarette holder. A woman wrapped round his little finger would have given him a handful of everything doctors warn against, thought Jacko, grinning, happy to see him.

The coroner sipped and tipped the glass towards him. 'Fancy one?'

Jacko shook his head. Sherry always made him fart.

'What's been happening to you?' he asked.

'Promotion, transfer, marriage and fatherhood,' Jacko answered.

'Now, Mr Jackson.' He always addressed him as he would his warrant officer in the desert where he won his medal. 'What's this one about?'

'You're right. It's a mystery.' Jacko went on to brief him fully.

Major Jarman grasped all the implications immediately. 'It's possible, isn't it, that young Heald's death has nothing whatever to do with Hegan and his activities? They could be entirely unconnected.'

Jacko nodded. 'It's only a theory right now.'

'I don't have to tell you, Mr Jackson, that my sole role as coroner is to establish how, when and by what means young Heald died.'

A second nod.

'Naturally you have my blessing to use this inquiry as a subterfuge to root out corruption in your force, but, if it's not connected, we still have that separate duty to perform, you know. We owe that to the boy's family.'

A third nod. Jacko knew. He felt torn two ways. The coroner was telling him he wanted Heald's case solved whether it

58

involved Hegan or not. His chief wanted the police villain exposed and, in truth, didn't give a shit how Heald died. Jacko would have to decide on priorities, play politics between two men he admired and respected. On top of all my other worries, he groaned inwardly.

The coroner interrupted his gloomy thoughts. 'How long will you and the doctor need?'

'About a month, to be on the safe side.'

He pulled a brown leather diary from his pocket and flicked through to the page he needed.

'How about, provisionally, Friday p.m., 8th of July?'

'Fine,' said Jacko.

'Pop up with a progress report, meantime.' The coroner made a note and looked up. 'Anything you need from me to oil the wheels?'

'Well, sir,' Jacko began, 'this could be a long, hard inquiry and I do have a small personnel problem over Sergeant Young, one of our team . . .'

When he left, Major Jarman was on the phone to the crown court offices barking at someone he kept calling Superintendent Jumped-up John and threatening to order an autopsy on him, notwithstanding the fact that he was still alive, if he dared to interfere with an investigation ordered by Her Majesty's coroner.

8

A scribbled note on the back of a brown bill envelope was pinned to the windscreen of his Montego by a wiper blade. 'Delayed,' it said. 'Don't wait. We'll walk.' It was signed, 'Philippe.'

Still skiving, thought Jacko, stuffing it into a pocket.

He climbed in, belted and started up, wound his window down half-way. He drove at less than five miles an hour out of the car-park and round the back of the old jailhouse and the entrance to its chapel, a tourist attraction now.

The left front wheel caught a pot-hole. The car jolted. He heard a metallic sound. Cautiously, concentrating, he turned right under the archway. The tyres rumbled lazily over the cobbles in the square.

Opposite the elegant pillared judges' lodgings he turned right into the hill which soon swung right again, a short, not-too-steep gradient, like a beginner's ski-slope. He stayed in second gear.

Priorities, he instructed himself. Let's think. He did a lot of his thinking on his travels. Now then. If . . .

Automatically, he touched the foot-brake as the high-walled corner to the hairpin appeared. Left in a second and down a longer, steeper stretch, an advanced ski-slope.

He tugged down the steering wheel with his left hand.

Nothing.

Shit. I'm missing the turning. Concentrate.

He pushed up the wheel with his right hand.

Still nothing. He was going straight on towards a narrow street that flattened out ahead.

Holy Christ. He felt as though he was skidding on ice. Something up front seemed to have a mind of its own. Straighten it, for fuck's sake. He waggled both hands, suddenly clammy. The steering wheel felt impossibly light.

Nothing. Straight on towards an approaching van.

You're out of control. Panic shot through him. Pump your foot.

He pumped. The car slowed.

Pull up the handbrake.

He hesitated.

The steering's gone, you berk. The brakes seem OK. Pull. *Pull.*

His left hand dropped to the brake. He pulled it up.

Tyres whinnied, like a pair of spooked horses, his Montego's and those of the approaching van's which veered violently to his right.

His head was thrown back against its rest as the car's off-side mounted the footpath. His body jumped out the seat, lifting his right foot off the brake. He contorted himself to stamp down again. His left hand was gripping the brake so tightly that it came up even higher, as high as it could.

The car stopped, straggling the gutter, ten to twelve yards past his turning and just a couple of yards short of a lamp standard, engine sounding normal beneath the bonnet.

He stared, unseeing, through the windscreen, right hand still holding the wayward wheel.

His body was rigid. Only his stomach moved, rumbling. Involuntarily he passed its winds, rasping.

'You OK?' A man's voice through the window.

He couldn't speak.

'You ran me off the road. Look.'

He couldn't turn.

'You been drinking?'

He gathered himself. 'Not even a sherry, mate,' Jacko said in a quavering voice.

'Look.'

Jacko ducked under his car. He followed the force's senior vehicle examiner's oily finger pointing at a grimy bracket above the left front wheel lolling at a crazy angle, tyre flat and ripped.

He looked but didn't really see. 'What is it?'

'Tract rod end. The thread's exposed. The nut's gone.'

His car was six feet in the air on a four-poster lift in a white-tiled inspection bay. The place smelt of grease, detergent and fuel, an explosive mix, finally ending a vein-enlarging craving for a cigarette which had lasted throughout the tedious process of getting his car to a garage and calling out the chief inspector.

'Someone loosened it.'

'Couldn't it have been normal wear and tear?' asked Jacko, not fully comprehending.

'I've been on to your garage. They visually checked it on your last service last month. Sound as a pound. You've never reported steering difficulties, have you?'

'She always handles well.'

A severe headshake. 'You've been sabotaged, Jacko.'

'When?'

The chief inspector closed an eye, thoughtfully, cautious not a man to be rushed. He was short and stocky with crinkly hair, greying here and there. His stained boiler-suit did not bear his rank.

'Where?' asked Jacko, urging him on.

'Not in your own driveway. You wouldn't have made it thirty miles here. Could have been outside the station, but making it up the hill without mishap means the castle is more likely.'

'Could it have been loosened with fingers?'

The chief inspector's bright, alert eyes dropped down to a blackened bench with tools hanging from nails round three edges. 'He'd have needed a 19-mil spanner.'

'Would he have had to go under the car?'

'Just squat down beside the wheel.'

'Christ,' said Jacko softly.

'He could have killed you, you know.'

Jacko didn't need telling. In that split-second of shock, he'd panicked. Hadn't put his brain into gear, didn't work out quickly enough what was wrong, didn't realize he still had his brakes. The road ahead from the hairpin had been his escape route, pure luck. Without it, he would have run out of road, into a wall, an emerging vehicle, anything. He'd never been in Traffic, wasn't an advanced driver, hadn't got the training or experience for that sort of emergency. He felt foolish, incompetent.

'If you'd made that bend and got on to the steep stretch with traffic coming up . . .' A mournful shrug, no need to say more.

Jacko could picture the scene without him completing it. He felt sick.

'I'll whack in a report.'

'No.' Jacko raised his voice, shut both eyes for a moment.

'I've got to.' Startled, disbelieving. 'This is attempted murder.'

'No.' Jacko paused. 'Wait.' Another pause, thinking at last. 'Right.' He'd collected up his fragmented thoughts, began to speak normally again. 'Yes of course. But do me a favour, Ron. One copy only for Chief Superintendent Scott's eyes only. I don't want anyone else to know.' He briefly explained why. 'Seriously, I could turn it to my advantage.' He smiled, appealingly. 'Please.'

The chief inspector gave him a sad look. 'OK then. I'll give you a pool car while it's off the road. I'll change it every day. You can't be too careful, Jacko. Someone wants you dead.'

Four faces rose from reading to greet Jacko when he walked into the incident room. Only Shirley Thomas's showed genuine concern, he judged without real reason.

She spoke first. 'All right?'

'Fine,' he lied. 'They've loaned me a pool car.'

'I mean . . .' Her face shadowed, displeased. '. . . are you all right?'

'Yeah,' he replied, over-casual. 'Thanks.'

'What happened?' asked Philippe.

'A broken tract rod.' Jacko repeated the cover story the chief inspector had given him.

'Much damage?'

'Buggered tyre, distorted rim.'

'Not a suspension failure then?' asked Stan.

Mechanical know-how, Jacko noted. That had been the break-down man's original diagnosis. Another tick went under a new column in his mind.

He sat down, making a washing motion with newly scrubbed hands. 'How are we getting on?'

Ridgeback nodded to a new file in his in-tray. 'All done.'

Jacko opened it and flicked through six more statements. Philippe had taken only one. He looked at him. 'See Upjohn at the castle?'

'Not half.' He chortled. 'He almost caught me nipping off to the barber's.'

Jacko tried an old routine, playing them along. 'In the firm's time?'

'It grows in the firm's time,' said Stan, catching on.

'Not all of it.'

'He hasn't had all of it cut off.'

It was new to the other three and they laughed. Philippe smoothed the back of his neck where the hair was short and neat. Even so, Jacko ticked his name under another new column headed: Opportunity.

All the time his eyes darted round the desks, inspecting their hands. None looked any dirtier than his own.

They settled on Ridgeback. 'You should have gone to the barber's with him.'

'Too busy.'

Jacko thumbed the statements again, conceded he might have been, decided he could have still found time to slip out to the car-park in Philippe's absence, had the mechanical knowledge, and put two ticks next to his name. He wondered where either could have got hold of the necessary spanner since neither was in his own car. He changed two ticks to question marks.

'How did you two get on?'

Stan answered for Shirley. 'She did the solicitors' firms with staff up there on Friday . . .'

'Nothing new,' Shirley broke in, despondently.

'. . . and I manned the office,' Stan continued. 'Messages are there.' He nodded to a pad beside Jacko's phone. 'Nothing important.'

The phone rang.

'Hi.' His Jackie's voice, southern, cultured and (to him) sexy. 'Busy?'

He told her what had happened, scaling it right down. She asked lots of anxious questions, which he made light of.

'That explains it,' she said, finally.

'Explains what?'

'I tried to phone you earlier. I wanted you to pick up a bag of potatoes from that farm shop. But there was no reply.'

So Stan had sneaked away from the office, he concluded darkly. He'd have tools in his car boot, too. Two more ticks went against Young's name.

9

Maureen Beckby nonchalantly swung her still-grubby Peugeot into the car-park of a modern, soulless hotel where neither was known and where they sometimes had dinner and took a room for an hour or two. 'For afters,' her police lover always called it.

He was waiting in his car, got out before she'd pulled up and tapped on the off-side window when she came to a halt.

The seat belt was pulled taut across her body as she leaned sideways to release the passenger door. A quick thrill for him, she thought, maliciously.

He got in, face set, unthrilled. 'Let's talk here.'

'Aren't we going to eat?' she asked, puzzled.

'No.'

'There's time. He's busy tonight. The coast is clear.' She giggled.

'That's not the point,' he said, acidly.

She felt a surge of annoyance. The after-dinner sex she

wouldn't miss. The meal, she would. She was hungry. 'What's the matter?'

'We can't see each other for a while.'

She masked her relief. 'Why ever not, darling?'

'It's getting heavy.'

'Why?'

He shook his head, distractedly. She noticed how washed out he looked.

'What's gone wrong?' She failed to keep the alarm out of her tone.

'Nothing.'

He was lying and she knew it.

'This inspector is making a lot of waves,' he said. 'It's too dangerous. That's all.'

'What's his name?'

'Jackson. If he calls . . .'

'Why should he call?' she snapped. 'There's nothing . . .'

'I said, if he calls,' he snapped back, very edgily, 'watch your step.' He drew in breath, steadying himself. 'Meantime, it's wiser not to meet. And, for God's sake, don't phone me.'

She said nothing, stunned.

'There's no need, is there?' he hurried on. 'The plan's in place.'

'What about your share?' She knew he'd never get it but mentioned it anyway to try to find out what had so frightened him.

'We'll fix a meet afterwards.'

'But how? Where? They're keeping him holed up for a week or two before he collects the money. I don't know where . . .'

'I don't want to know. When you've collected, phone me.'

'No.' Firmly. 'You phone me. Around two weeks after Hegan's free.' She always called him by his surname, pretended to hate him. 'Just say that Malc's Olive wants to see me. Give a time and place.'

She lent across towards him, the seat belt tightening a pink cotton dress across her high, round bosom.

He didn't look down or turn his lips towards her, just straight ahead, so she planted their goodbye kiss, their last kiss, on his cheek.

10

'Gawfuckme.' Ridgeback jumped to his feet amid laughter, hooting, howling. The triumphant look on his face dissolved into flushed embarrassment. 'Shit.' His outdoor complexion went a deeper red. 'Sorry.' A hapless glance at Shirley.

'Quite all right,' she managed to splutter.

He looked at the convulsed Jacko. 'Sorry, sir. I meant cor blimey.'

'I think I like that better.' The laughter died. 'What you got?'

Ridgeback sat, picking up a paper from a pink folder with personnel details on prison staff. 'I've been checking on Officer Haywood, sir, like you said. His career doesn't add up.'

He gave his head a single shake so his ginger hair scattered and settled again. 'An inspector in the British Transport Police at twenty-eight. A year ago, he quits to become a warder.'

'I changed services.' Shirley's careless shrug disclosed she hadn't given the point much thought.

'And did your salary go up or down?' Jacko asked bluntly.

She dodged it. 'Maybe he's a late graduate entrant getting operational experience.'

'A Salisbury comprehensive,' Ridgeback read aloud from a form.

Jacko pulled his legs off the desk and straightened himself in his chair. 'How long's he been here?'

'Five months, after six months' initial training at Brixton, it says here,' said Ridgeback slowly, still reading.

Within a few weeks of Hegan's arrest and remand in custody, Jacko reckoned rapidly. 'What's his religion?' Only when working round the edges of the Irish question does a police officer ask that.

'Catholic.'

Shirley was thinking now. 'It's unthinkable.'

'Why?' asked Jacko sharply. 'We have the occasional bent police officer. Why not a bent prison officer?'

Shirley sat back in a sulking silence.

Philippe sought to relieve the tension. 'It's easily checked.'

He put in a call to a contact with British Transport police. Shirley phoned her opposite number at Brixton prison in London.

Jacko sorted through his files to find the dossier on the child abuser. He re-read how Officer Haywood had given him his weekly pill on the day that Andy Heald died. He asked Shirley to find out its name from the prison medical officer in the hospital wing. His answer was immediate.

'Turnotoxin,' Shirley repeated.

Jacko phoned the pathologist in his laboratory. 'It's a slow release painkiller, limited dosage, only used in controlled conditions,' he explained.

'Which means?'

'It should only be administered no more than weekly by a qualified person, a district nurse, say, visiting a cancer patient.'

'Could it have killed our boy?'

'I'll run some tests. Everything else has proved negative so far.'

Within a few minutes, Philippe's and Shirley's contacts had reported back. Neither could find any record of a Roger Haywood with the same date and place of birth on his personnel record.

Jacko's hazel eyes toured the faces turned towards him and rested on Shirley's. She stirred nervously in her chair. 'You ought to know that, while nearly every officer wears summer shirt-sleeve order, he's never without his tunic top.'

He's armed, she was saying, and everyone knew it.

'Shall I get on to Jumped-up John for authority to draw a couple of guns?' asked Philippe, paling.

'You'd need back-up,' said Jacko.

'I'm not weapon-trained,' said Ridgeback.

'I'm out of date,' said Stan. 'Upjohn dropped me when I did my back in.'

So, thought Jacko, at the time he would have had access to the armoury and the gun that killed Ridgeback's dog when Hegan made his escape. Another tick against his name.

A small, clever smile played at his lips as he dialled HQ and waited until Scott answered. 'Morning, Richard. This undercover Met man Haywood . . .'

He held the phone away from his ear and the room filled with a mumbled torrent of abuse coming from it.

He put the phone back to his ear, smiling wickedly. 'You can't blame me.' More muffled obscenities and he talked over them. 'It's your fault for not sharing your Special Branch secrets.' He was laughing out loud now. 'I've got a terrific team here. We were bound to find out.'

Four pairs of eyes shone warmly at him when he replaced the phone. He told them Haywood's true identity and his undercover assignment. He repeated Scott's dire, almost hysterical, warning that if it went outside the room they'd all be charged with breaching the Official Secrets Act.

He knew for certain that he had captured all their hearts. He had shared a huge confidence with them. They trusted him completely. Now he could turn the screw, without them even knowing, to find out which of them was Hegan's inside man.

That lunchtime Jacko bought Ridgeback a gawfuckme pint and sarnie. 'For a near miss,' he said. That night on the way home he had two more pints with Philippe at a roadside pub.

Casually he coaxed out of them the parts each had played in the bungled attempt to capture Hegan at his pub after the bank robbery.

Almost two years had gone by but their stories seemed so vivid, attention to detail so great, that, aided by the scenes-of-crime photos, Jacko imagined himself a part of it, witnessing the drama personally.

Philippe had staked out several domestic sieges and played his part in ambushing a gang of armed robbers. 'But a terrorist hit man those Whitehall wankers had set free?' He pulled an agonised face and shook his head, angrily. 'Sweet Jesus.'

All afternoon and evening he'd lain in wait inside Hegan's pub, which was called Michael's Pub, beyond the crossroads in New York village. Just before dusk he heard an approaching car.

He withdrew a .38 pistol from a holster in a blue webbing belt round the waist, silently dropping to the floor beneath the curtained window. One glance told him this was not the car he expected. Mentally he repeated the index number he had read from the plate, committing it to memory.

He lay on his stomach, elbows on the worn carpet, gun in both hands, pointing at the door. It had been a long watch, plenty of time to think and plan. Only when the target was inside, closing that door, back to him, would he shout the obligatory warning: 'Armed Police.'

'I was hoping to Christ nothing silly or sudden was about to happen, specially if he was the wrong man.'

All police marksmen, Jacko knew, live in fear of this moment, in dread of mistakes. One second's delay and you could be dead. One misread sign and someone else is, someone innocent. A hiding to nothing.

Philippe heard the car skid to a halt on the gravel and footsteps grinding the loose pebbles. They stopped at the door. Footsteps again, faster and departing, an engine restarting, tyres speeding away.

He rose to his knees and peered through a gap in the net curtains drawn across the window. The car was going through the 'Out' gap in an evergreen hedge.

He switched on the radio. 'Just had a visitor in a maroon Cortina.' He repeated the memorized number. 'Now heading south towards Boston.'

'Hold one,' said a youthful voice. An older, deeper voice came on, Superintendent Clive Upjohn, controlling the operation from an RAF base just outside the hamlet. 'Did you get a look at the driver?' he asked.

'Only the back of his head. I didn't break cover.'

'Mmmmm.'

Philippe, adrenalin racing, sensed implied criticism. 'He could have been a passing customer.'

'Mmmmm.' Upjohn sounded unimpressed. Then he heard him issuing the order: 'Get dogs down both those side roads.'

A few minutes later Philippe saw two blue vans passing the pub in convoy. Each had a uniformed constable at the wheel. Behind a steel grill in both vehicles sat alert alsatians.

At a crossroads, the second van swung to the west. Within a hundred yards of the junction it pulled on to the grass verge. Ridgeback recounted walking round the back and opening the door. 'Come, Winnie.'

The dog jumped lightly on to the verge. He reached into the van and took out a soiled sweat-shirt which he had brought from the living quarters above the pub when he dropped off Philippe almost seven hours earlier.

'Here, boy.' The alsatian sniffed the shirt, wagging his tail.

'Seek then,' Ridgeback watched the dog disappear into a field of high golden corn which rustled when he entered.

A flock of crows rose high, angry, protesting, in the darkening sky as a bird-scarer exploded a triple report. He looked across the field but failed to locate the hidden gas cylinder which had fired off its warning every few minutes. 'I knew it would not disturb Win. We had trained together in mock gun battles.' The dog, he said firmly, was without fear.

'Here, boy.' He listened in the fast-gathering gloom for the rustle of corn which would tell him of his return. None came.

'Win.' He raised his voice and lengthened the name. 'Winnie.' Nothing. 'Winston.' Sharper now. He heard another single report that echoed across the fields from a collection of farm buildings down a grass track. Rooks and pigeons flew up, squawking, from the crops.

'*Winston*'. He shouted loudly, an impatient parent calling in a reluctant child from play.

A car started up near the distant buildings, just a black outline behind full headlights, and headed away from him down a lane that joined a road running parallel to the Boston road.

'*Winston*'. He was flushed, despite a night that was chilly and grey for midsummer. 'Winnie.' A pleading voice. 'Win.' He ran forward, sweating, flushed again. 'Win.'

Ridgeback was panicking now. '*Winston*. Please, Winnie. Come, son. Come. Here, boy. Here.' Nothing.

He stopped at the entrance to the track leading to the buildings, barely visible in the gloom. He wrenched at the radio at his unbuttoned breast pocket. 'My dog may have picked up a scent. Headed for some outhouses. Not returned. Heard a sound like a single shot. Seen a car.'

'Hold,' said a calm voice, quickly replaced by the more urgent one of Superintendent Upjohn. He gave his location and the direction the car was going.

'Make and colour?'

'Dark, that's all I can tell you in this light, sir.'

A two-second pause. 'Stay where you are. On no account go down that lane.'

Ridgeback ran to the van, started it, drove to the end of the lane and turned in. His speed was so fast, the track so rutted that his head hit the roof, knocking off his cap. He wound down his window. 'Win.' He fought to hold on to the wheel.

He reached the farm buildings, leapt from his vehicle, grabbing a powerful torch from the passenger seat, and ran to the nearest, a decaying shed. He burst through the door so fast that dust from empty fertilizer bags scattered on the earth floor rose in a white cloud. Nothing. He raced to the next, a clapboard barn big enough to house a combined harvester.

He peered through a gap at the side where a plank of wood had been prised away from rusting nails. He could just make out the outline of a car. He shone the torch in. A deep red Cortina.

Then he heard him. Just that frightened little whimper he sometimes gave when his sleep on the mat in front of the fire had been disturbed by a bad dream.

He ran down the side of the barn through the opened doors. The beam from the torch picked him out straight away. He was lying on his side, black back towards him. He lifted his neck back and up in an attempt to welcome him.

Ridgeback knelt, catching the dog's head, cradling it on his knees. He bent and spoke softly into his ear. 'It's all right, son. All right.'

His long straight tail gave one thump on the hard, dry earth. A shudder ran through his lean, firm body. Then the dog lay silent and still in an expanding pool of blood.

Philippe was ordered out of the pub and found him there, still kneeling, holding Winston's head in his hands. Gently, he took the dog's head in both his hands as another officer helped Ridgeback to his feet and walked him outside, hand gripped tightly to his elbow.

Within minutes the derelict land on which the buildings stood was filled with cars, men, lights and noise, so much noise.

Only vaguely did Ridgeback hear what was being said. 'Get scenes of crime . . . Widen the cordon . . . Cancel the Cortina . . . Stop and check everything . . . Get Constable Cross back to base.'

Each was asked individually and obliquely what they noticed about the other. Neither saw any sign of any bags big enough to hold two million pounds.

Ridgeback was driven back to the pub. Everything, he insisted, was just the same as when he'd dropped off Philippe hours earlier.

Jacko smoothly moved both conversations on eighteen

months to Hegan's eventual arrest after his return from North Africa.

Philippe recalled picking up the phone and saying, 'CID.'

A man's voice said, 'If you still want Michael Hegan, look for this car.' He gave a make and a number and rang off.

'Did he ask for you by name?'

'No – and I didn't give it. Just CID. There was no conversation. Just that. I reported it straight on.'

Ridgeback had been on solo patrol on the A1 when all cars were alerted. He spotted the wanted car heading north. 'Control told me to trail, not intercept. He ran me off a country lane on a tight bend.'

'Were you trying to overtake?' asked Jacko quietly.

A defiant nod. 'I'll catch up with the bastard yet.'

Jacko sat back in silence.

So they alibi-ed each other in stories, movingly told, thought Jacko. If you want to believe them, that is.

Ridgeback seemed as wholesomely naïve as Roddy McDowall, the child actor, from that Hollywood era of Lassie films but, Jacko reminded himself, McDowall grew up to play lots of heavies.

Maybe Ridgeback and Philippe were in it together, covering for each other. The idea was so fanciful that he dismissed it almost immediately.

Over the next couple of days, Jacko bumped up the station's phone bill with long calls to Belfast and his own out-of-pocket expenses drinking with Stan Young and Haywood, the Met undercover man.

He didn't know the solution to Ireland's ills, but he did know the answer would never come from men like Michael Hegan.

At school he was carrying parts of guns in his flute case. Soon he was a look-out when the mob went collecting protection money from shops and building firms. A lot of practice joy riding in stolen cars was followed by promotion to getaway driver from robberies.

'Not all the proceeds went to the fighting fund, of course,' said a war-weary detective in the RUC intelligence. 'Part of it went on sharp suits and drinks. A month's trip to America, too. They said he was fund-raising but he spent more than he raised.

'Next came graduation to sectarian killing. There's little doubt he did at least three. His victims were snatched and shot, once was enough, behind the right ear.'

God in heaven, thought Jacko, almost numbed, how could anyone do that to a human being? Close enough to hear his last mumbled prayer, to see his begging, pleading eyes, to smell the sweat and the urine of fear.

'Never worked, never went to church, never had a steady woman, 'the RUC man continued. 'I think he gets off on a gun. He was pulled in many times. No questioning ever broke him. No forensic evidence ever tied him to anything.'

It came to an end when he and two robbers ran into an army/ RUC road block after a robbery. The unarmed postmaster put up a brave fight so he was shot in both legs. Hegan fired one shot as he tried to escape, wounding a soldier. It was returned with a fusillade.

'He wasn't used to having people fire back. No surrender, my arse. He surrendered, hands high in the air.'

He got eighteen years on two charges of attempted murder. He stuck it for eighteen months. 'Just couldn't hack it,' said an assistant governor from the Crumlin Road jail. 'Never been inside before. Couldn't handle the sounds, the smells, the threat of the place. The real politicos inside regarded him as a toe-rag. He may have been Bertie Bigtime in his own street but he was nothing in here. He was going mental.'

He asked to see the governor. He wanted to be placed in the secure unit for his own protection. Then he wanted to talk to Special Branch. He talked and talked. His evidence smashed a gang in the outlawed Ulster Volunteer Force.

Now grasses, Jacko reflected, have been around since Judas. Cops need and use them. He had often traded a few quid here or a blind eye there for something bigger and better. Supergrasses, though, blossomed in Ulster. They were men who would shop wholesale for their freedom and a reward.

They kept him in mainland jails or military guardrooms, flying him in and out of Aldergrove to give his evidence in a series of trials.

On one such trip he landed in Lincolnshire, an isolated part of the world, the perfect place for a man with a price on his head to start a new life.

He'd picked his new name with care. Hegan had a religious,

transatlantic neutrality about it. He retained a smattering of Americanisms from his stay to soften his harsh Belfast accent and give credence to his cover story that he'd been working as a bartender in New York, New York, until he ran into difficulties with his green card.

He found what he was looking for just outside the crossroads hamlet of New York, Lincs, which got its name from the workers who drained the surrounding fens. They brought it with them as returning soldiers from the American War of Independence.

He sank his bounty into a rundown country inn on a minor road out towards Boston, Americanized it with bar stools, a foot rail and baseball posters on the wall. And he hung up a swinging sign: MICHAEL'S PUB – a name that seemed to please him enormously, but he never explained why.

Special Branch asked the East Midlands Combined Constabulary to babysit Hegan. Headquarters asked Division who passed it on to Superintendent Upjohn. He set the operation up, then assigned Stan Young.

'Business was good for a while,' said Stan. 'Buds and burgers; it was different. Made enough to build a single-storey extension.'

Stan's job had been to check out anyone who was getting too close to Hegan. At first he popped in once a week. Gradually it tailed off into monthly visits. Panic buttons linked to the sub-division HQ were fitted behind the bar and in the upstairs flat, but there were never any alarm bells.

The Home Office asked a senior social worker called Bryan Holden to advise on more personal problems – National Insurance, HP, tax, setting up a home, hiring part-time staff, things he'd never learnt.

'Sometimes,' Stan went on, 'you can hardly move for Americans in Lincoln Cathedral and Boston's Stump but Michael's Pub didn't exactly feature on the Pilgrim Trail. It was just a trendy fad that didn't last long. He was a hopeless businessman. Spent too much time on the customers' side of the bar drinking the profits.'

Out of the blue Hegan's social worker phoned Young one summer's morning two years earlier. Hegan wanted to see them both urgently. A meeting was fixed for noon in a hotel car-park in Sleaford, the small market town where Hegan collected provisions.

No one turned up. Young waited an hour. Then he drove to the pub, found it closed, the only regular part-time helper left on the payroll laid off.

He checked with the social worker, who apologized for pulling out of the appointment at the last minute because his mother was taken ill. 'We both thought he'd gone bust and done a runner from his creditors.'

While Young had been waiting alone in the car-park, two men, wearing crash helmets, were holding up the bank wagon in a shopping precinct a mile away. The raid was carried out with swift brutality. A sawn-off shot-gun was fired into the vehicle's roof, the crew threatened by a man with an Ulster accent who fired again to kill a schoolgirl's barking dog. His partner ran with a pronounced limp. The haul was two million pounds, never recovered.

Young reported Hegan's disappearance to Superintendent Upjohn who linked it to the robbery. A few days later a stolen van was found in a lock-up garage in Sleaford. Inside was a road map covered in Hegan's fingerprints.

Young had been on a day off, collecting one of his children from university in Bristol. An inspector tried to contact him at lunchtime to call him in. There was no reply at his home.

That afternoon Upjohn launched his big operation and Jacko knew the rest from Philippe and Ridgeback.

'Look, Stan,' said Jacko, probing, 'Philippe is sure something scared him or tipped him off at the pub. He must have driven straight to the barn to a fresh car and a change of clothes. Any ideas?'

Upjohn, Stan said, had asked the same question when he carpeted him next day. 'You were in Sleaford, unalibi-ed when the raid happened,' the superintendent said. 'You've got a limp like the second man.'

Stan gave an easy-going shrug as he recounted his interrogation. 'He thought I might have used my association with Hegan to go out and boost my pending pension.'

He was able to prove he couldn't have tipped Hegan that he was walking into a police trap. He'd given the mother of another student a lift to collect their children. He was alibi-ed throughout the day of the stake-out and getaway.

'I was set up by Hegan and nearly walked into it. Upjohn still has this lingering doubt about me.'

Which he passed on to the Little Fat Man, Jacko suspected.

Upjohn maintained the watch at Michael's Pub until another stolen vehicle with Hegan's prints was found at Heathrow airport. Eighteen months later the search was resumed after Philippe had taken his anonymous call. Hegan was captured at a road block within an hour of Ridgeback's crash.

Next night Inspector Roger Haywood turned up for a private drink and a chat in the theatre bar. Yer, he said in a faint West Country accent, he'd been keeping watch over Hegan for five of the six months he'd been held in the remand wing.

'He made contact with the Branch via his brief saying he was prepared to talk about what he'd learned in Africa. He's having a bad time in the nick. On tranquillizers.'

Jacko pricked his ears. 'Does anyone know that?'

'Only me.'

So, thought Jacko, puzzled, why should anyone give Heald a pill to pass on to Hegan if nobody knew he was on them?

'Who visits him in nick?'

'His solicitor and assistant often. Holden, his social worker, occasionally.'

'Sergeant Stan Young ever?'

'Never. That super now and then but he's never said much to him. Why?'

Jacko shrugged and changed the subject. 'Is Hegan worth all of this?'

'Honest answer. I don't know. His life in the long term isn't worth a light. His brief has given the Branch a taster of what he claims to know and intelligence seems to rate it.'

Out of his bogus uniform, Haywood was a casually smart dresser – beige slacks and dark brown shirt that made his face look pasty.

He'd found protection detail boring, his off-duty hours lonely. Detectives, Jacko knew, are gregarious. They like to be out and about with the boys and girls. They are ordinary people from ordinary families whose job sets them apart. Only fellow officers seem to understand the isolation they suffer and most understanding of all are policewomen.

Sometimes, at parties, he had difficulty in remembering who was living with who. At one he'd walked up to Upjohn. Years before, Jacko had introduced him to a pretty WPC, a good chum, at Lincoln races. 'How's my little Wendy?' he'd asked.

'She was two marriages ago,' Upjohn had replied, stiffly.

Jacko told the story to Haywood who laughed, then, demonstrating that he missed nothing, he said, 'He certainly doesn't like your mate Stan Young.'

'Why do you say that?'

'I overheard Upjohn bad-mouthing him when he was talking to Hegan at one interview.' A playful smile. 'Is that why you were asking about Young?'

Jacko came clean then but Haywood had no knowledge of the name of the police source Hegan was going to trade in as part of any freedom deal.

'Source, singular?' asked Jacko, double-checking.

Haywood nodded.

'Who's after him?'

'All the tip said was, "an attempt involving Hegan". Our guess is the Prods. Some of his old gang are doing thirty.' Haywood seemed suddenly unsure. 'Then again, the IRA have at least three scores to settle.'

'Why did he blow a perfectly good cover to go back to crime?'

'Here's a guy who's lived his life by crime. He knows no other way. You want money, you go out and get it. He's a nutter; no guilt or remorse over the people he's killed, robbed or shopped.'

Christ, thought Jacko, and Andy Heald who wouldn't put a dying old cat to sleep was killed in his place. Or was he?

The words of the coroner came back to him. Maybe he's right and the Little Fat Man wrong. Maybe there's no connection between Hegan and Heald's death. In which case he had two separate mysteries to solve. He hadn't got a lead on either.

11

'Chat up those four social workers who were on court duty,' Jacko told Shirley. 'Don't pump or push. Sniff around, see if anything odd, anything different, happened in the cellblock.'

She spent all morning taking statements from the three men

and the woman worker who had sat together across the well of the court from the jury box.

And what was odd and different about senior social worker Bryan Holden was that he sat there and he lied to her. She was sure of it.

Carl Marsh, the dope dealer, and Rod Daniels, the lager lout, had given detailed descriptions of the social worker who'd spoken briefly to Andy Heald through the bars of his cell below court after his parents had left. Mid-forties, tall, thin, fair receding hair, gold-framed spectacles, brown suit with a faint blue stripe, both said.

She could see at a glance that the other two didn't fit. One was much younger; the other bald. It was made-to-measure for Holden. Yet, according to court records, he was the social worker assigned to Hegan. Heald was not one of his cases.

Shirley spoke to all four separately, sitting at a polished oak table in the almost-deserted foyer. 'Yes,' said Holden, 'I went down to the cellblock two or three times. I wanted to see Hegan to sort out a few personal loose ends. Every time I looked in, he was engaged with his solicitor taking a deposition for his trial.' He never got his quick word, he claimed. In the end he gave up, but he had since seen Hegan in the remand wing.

'See or talk to anyone else down there?' she asked, pushing just a little.

'No.' A firm reply. 'I wanted to get away. I had a basketful of paper to shift at the office before the weekend.'

Shirley wore a look of numbed disbelief when she reported all this back to Jacko. 'He just sat there and lied.'

He clucked his tongue, disapprovingly. 'Well, well. If you can't trust a welfare worker, who can you trust?'

'Shall I pull him in?' asked Ridgeback, whose confidence was maturing ahead of his dress sense. His latest outfit was a chocolate cotton suit with outdated flares.

'Research first,' ruled Jacko.

If ever a social worker was in need of the care of social services, it was Bryan Holden, Jacko decided, feet on his desk, studying the team's background file a couple of days later.

He'd been among the hordes of welfare state whizz-kids who poured out of the campuses in the sixties as bachelors in the art of half-baked bullshit, masters in the science of pseudo-do-gooding, clamouring on council estates and in courthouses, interacting and interfacing in alternative advice centres. In inner cities they created a new addiction: social service dependency. If, like Jacko, you didn't have your own personal counsellor, you regarded yourself as under-privileged.

Nowadays social workers were suffering the sort of press that comes the way of all meddlers. Miss a tiny tell-tale sign of potential baby-battering and the headlines scream: *Scandal*. Play safe and take a baby into care only to discover the parents had never laid a finger on their offspring and the headlines scream: *Scandal*.

Holden, a careful, conscientious plodder, had avoided professional scandal. He'd married a biology graduate who gave up a career in public health. They had three daughters.

The scandal had come in his private life. Three years earlier he had walked out on his family for a woman almost twenty years younger; a girl who worked for a local law firm.

'What's this bird's name, Stan?' asked Jacko.

'Maureen Beckby,' he answered, not looking up from his reading.

'Met her?'

Stan seemed to swallow. 'A few times, at Hegan's pub, with Holden.'

'What's she like?'

'Not a bad looker. Long blonde hair, blue eyes. A bit of a scar there . . .' he touched the right-hand side of his chin. 'But . . . well . . .' He was looking up now but away in thought. '. . . Her mum was also in the pub one lunchtime. A bit heavy and frumpy. Off-putting somehow. Know what I mean?'

Jacko knew. A beauty that wouldn't last. Hips and a waist and legs that would lose their trimness, like her mother's.

Holden and his lover rented a small cottage, rose-covered, near Woodhall, a spa town. Michael's Pub was only a few miles away down the road to Boston.

'That's why Holden got the job, I expect,' Stan went on. 'I only saw him in the pub three or four times. Maureen was always with him. An odd pair. She was lively and looking for discos. He was intense and ill at ease. He hits the booze a bit.'

'Was Hegan giving her one?' asked Jacko, trawling for a motive. Shirley gritted her teeth.

'Never any indication of it,' said Stan.

'A classic case', Philippe declared, with a grand wave of a hand, 'of male menopause.'

'Rubbish,' snapped Shirley. 'That's an insult to women. They don't leap into toy boys' beds. He cynically traded his wife in for a fresh, new model. He's just a selfish, bored, dirty old man.'

'Middle-aged man, if you don't mind.' Jacko corrected her with a caustic smile.

He could well understand a man in his forties and fifties asking himself: What have I achieved? What will I leave behind? He'd soon have to face up to that question. He wouldn't go chasing sex in discos, he'd vowed. It would interfere with his sleep pattern. He rather fancied a shot at writing – nothing too deep with his limited intellect; detective yarns with a touch of realism and social comment. He couldn't type, couldn't spell, but someone somewhere would knock it into shape.

He went back to his reading. Holden had done what he must have cautioned all his clients never to do – fallen behind with agreed maintenance.

In the background file, it was easy to see why. He finished up in hospital after a car crash with two broken legs which saved him from being breath-tested. Maureen had given up work but still dressed expensively. Only a legacy that came with the death of his widowed mother a year before, after a long illness, got him out of debt.

'Cancer,' said Shirley, looking at her notes. 'And, yes, she was on Turnotoxin.'

'OK,' said Jacko to Ridgeback. 'You can fetch him in now.'

'I'm Detective Inspector Jackson.' He didn't rise from behind the green steel desk on which stood a dual tape recorder. 'Thanks for coming in.'

'Wasn't given much choice, was I?' Holden hesitated at the door of the interview room. He was in his brown suit, which shone with age. 'Hope this isn't going to take long.' He looked more impatient than annoyed.

Jacko nodded to a chair opposite him and Holden lowered himself in very slowly. Ridgeback sat between them, a yard or so from the desk.

'Depends on you,' Jacko said, expressionless.

'What do you mean?' A worried look. 'What's it about?'

'You know that we're inquiring into the death of Andrew Heald . . .'

'So he told me.' Holden interrupted, flicking his head towards Ridgeback.

'. . . and it's my duty to caution you . . .' which Jacko did, viewing him intently, watching his dull eyes behind his spectacles, detecting alarm.

'What's this all about?' His speech had tightened, went up a pitch.

'About this.' Jacko withdrew the statement he had given to Shirley from a manila folder on the desk, holding it towards him. 'Recognize this?' He jabbed at the signature with his index finger.

'Of course.' The beginnings of a bluster.

'Why did you withhold from Miss Thomas the fact that you spoke to Heald in his cell?'

'I don't know what you mean.' Annoyance now, anger almost.

Jacko pulled out two more statements from Carl Marsh and Rod Daniels. He read extracts, describing Andy's visitor in the cellblock. 'That was you, wasn't it?'

A nod, slightly contrite. 'I forgot.'

'Forgot?' Jacko's turn to bluster. 'You, an officer of the court, the last person to see him alive, apart from prisoners and staff, and you forgot?'

'I'm sorry.' He looked very apologetic.

'Let's go through it again, shall we?' His baleful glare.

Holden said he had left his place on the bench when the judge rose for a break. He went through the dock and down the steps to try to talk to Hegan. 'He was in a huddle with his solicitor. I was walking out the way I came when a young man, the fire bomber I saw in court, called through the bars of the end cell. He just wanted me to pass a message to his own social worker who hadn't turned up to see him.'

Jacko leaned forward in his seat. 'You knew this young man had died in what the coroner has publicly called mysterious circumstances; yet, you mentioned none of this in here.' He slapped his statement. 'Why?'

Holden gave his head a single shake. 'Miss Thomas caught me at a busy time. If she'd have asked, I would have told her.'

'What was the message?'

A thoughtful silence.

'Well?'

'Confidential, I'm afraid.' Holden's face looked more at ease but he still sat uncomfortably.

'Why? He's not a client of yours.'

'I was a sort of stand-in.'

Jacko switched suddenly to Hegan. Yes, Holden confirmed, eyes alert, he had been his social work contact during the eighteen months he had been at Michael's Pub which he regularly visited.

'Socially, occasionally, with your lady, I understand.'

'What the hell's Hegan got to do with this?' With some difficulty, Holden sat upright, real anger on his face now.

'Because we suspect he may have been the target of a murder plot and Andy Heald was an innocent victim.'

His chin sagged, mouth opened, shocked. 'I see.'

'So naturally we're looking at Hegan's activities and associates.'

Picking his words carefully, Holden recalled the day of the robbery. 'Hegan phoned my office and asked me to contact Sergeant Young as he wanted to see us both urgently in Sleaford that lunchtime. Wouldn't say why over the phone. I passed on the message to Young.'

'But you didn't keep that appointment yourself?'

A sad headshake. 'Soon afterwards I got a call to say that my mother had been found by her daily help in a collapsed state and put to bed. I went straight there. I tried to call Hegan and Young to explain. Neither was in.'

'When did you become aware that Hegan was involved in the bank robbery?'

'An inspector phoned me a few days later. I was out at lunch.' Relief flickered across his face. 'You can check this. I returned his call when I got back. He asked if Hegan had been in contact since his disappearance or if I had any clue to his whereabouts.'

'And did you?'

'No. He'd vanished.' A questioning look, suspicious. 'Why are you asking me all of this after two years?' Pause. 'Why am I under caution?'

'Because his accomplice on that raid had a limp and at the time you were recovering from your car crash injuries.'

Holden gasped. 'Are you real?' He turned to Ridgeback, appealingly. 'Is he real?' Back to Jacko, speaking slowly, hurt. 'I was with my mother that lunchtime.'

'Alone?'

Holden nodded absently.

'And, sadly, she's since died.' Jacko looked down at his files, then up. 'From cancer, I see, for which she had been receiving Turnotoxin.'

Holden lent forward, eyes meeting Jacko's. 'What are you saying?'

'That there's a possibility that Andy Heald died from Turnotoxin.'

He slumped back. 'I see. I . . . er . . . I didn't . . .' He was visibly fighting to take control of himself. 'I really don't know what she was taking, except that they were powerful pain-killers. They were administered by the district nurse. I can't recall even handling them.'

Jacko maintained silence.

'I do assure you, inspector, that I had nothing to do with that robbery or that youth's death.'

'We'll see,' said Jacko, unassured.

'Let me tell you . . .' He was in control now. 'I take great exception to being dragged down here, cautioned and having to sit here, listening to your allegations. Your Sergeant Young knows Hegan. He walks with a limp. He was in Sleaford that day – and he was in court.'

Ridgeback looked anxiously at Jacko who said nothing through several seconds of thought. Is this a rat in a corner? Or is he trying to tell me something? 'Why do you say that?'

'Only, well . . .' A regretful face. 'I mean, this is so unfair. I know no more than Sergeant Young. Less, in fact. That's all I'm saying.'

Jacko needed time to work that out so he went back. 'That message Andy gave you – did you pass it on to his social worker?'

'No point, was there? He was dead.'

Jacko allowed a look of surprise to fill his face. 'You knew he was dead but you never bothered to tell Miss Thomas you spoke to him? Now, what was the message?'

'I don't see how that helps.'

83

'The coroner will be the judge of that.' A stiff voice, formal.

'Look.' Holden attempted conciliation. 'I'm unclear about the ethics on this. I don't want to break a confidence. I'd like to check with my boss before answering that.'

Jacko eyed him sternly. 'Then answer this. Did you hand any pills or tablets to Heald with a request that he should pass them on to Hegan?'

Holden's reply came out as a splutter. 'That's an outrageous suggestion.'

'Have you ever had any Turnotoxin tablets in your possession?'

'I've never touched them. Don't even know what they look like.' Holden gave a halt sign with a hand and shook his head firmly. 'In view of your line of questioning, I'd like to consult my director before I say any more.'

Jacko didn't stand when Holden, greyish-faced, got up painfully. His eyes followed him out of the door. He walked slowly, dragging his feet, like a condemned man on his way to the gallows.

He'd got a lead now. More. He'd got a suspect.

12

'*Gawfuckme*.' Philippe was on his size eleven feet before he had replaced the receiver on its cradle. He danced a lumbering lap of honour round the pushed-together, file-strewn desks. Beaming, he sat down and theatrically picked up the buff dossier on Stewart Connelly, Andy Heald's cellmate in the remand wing.

'Listen to this. Twenty-seven, Glasgow-born and raised, with a record from his juvenile days – probation for gang shoplifting, Borstal for shop burglary with five similar offences taken into consideration, three years for a masked, armed off-licence job with two TIC-ed. Always a series, mob-handed; nothing south of the border.'

He looked up. 'So what, I ask myself, was he doing making such a hash of a petrol station hold-up on the A1 miles from home on his own?'

He read on rapidly, 'No mask or gloves, carried a crowbar

but no gun, accepted less than a ton from the till when there was a safe at the back, picked up by a patrol car within half an hour thumbing a lift in a lay-by.'

Philippe read from the arrest report. 'No sign of drink, no resistance, an immediate confession.' And from the court reports. 'No application for bail.'

He spread his hands. 'It's almost as though he had wanted to be nicked.'

He recapped on the dates. He'd been on remand six weeks shorter than Hegan. He went back to the last court entry, 'A sudden change of plea on a confessed open-and-shutter. Why?'

'You tell us,' said Jacko, humouring him.

'Maybe because Hegan's trial had been put back and an adjournment in his case would keep them together in the remand wing.'

Philippe opened the prison file. 'Along with Hegan, he is on Rule 43 at his own request for his own protection. Why? Only because he . . .' He nodded at Ridgeback, debonair in a brand new black blazer. '. . . put to him the statements of Carl Marsh and Rod Daniels in which they suggested he didn't get on with his old cellmate Andy Heald. What had Andy called him? Not a fur-wearing meat-eater, but a bigoted bastard, a religious nut. What is his religion?'

He paused teasingly and let his own answer come slowly. 'Protestant.'

Mmmm, mulled Jacko, and who did Special Branch suspect was after Hegan?

Philippe had not finished yet. He'd called Strathclyde police headquarters, he went on, and quoted their reply word for word, 'Suspected UVF activist, pal. We've had him in under the Prevention of Terrorism Act but nothing stuck. A fund-raiser, certainly, maybe more."

'So I asked them if Connelly had any friends or relations sold up the river by an informer known in Belfast as Orange Billy. Know what they just said?'

Philippe smiled gleefully down at the phone. 'Only a step-brother doing thirty.'

'Gawfuckme,' said Jacko, admiringly. 'Let's go.'

*

A guard opened the wicket gate, supervised the signing-in at the reception window, infuriatingly slowly, and led the way out of the echoing archway. Barred gates rattled open ahead of them and clanged closed behind them.

They walked alongside the purple brick topped wall, a drizzle-dampened strip of grass at its base, the graveyard of the executed.

A working party in drab grey brushed a wet concrete path lethargically, plenty of time. They looked up, inquisitive smiles mixed with sullen stares.

Another door rattled open when they reached a red-brick block with a church-style window without stained glass. They stepped inside the building. Anti-suicide safety nets were strong across the gaps between two railed landings above. Smells of body fluids that recent disinfectant couldn't mask made Jacko's nose wrinkle.

'Where's Connelly?' asked the escort.

'Exercise,' said a bored warder on a stool at a desk just inside the door.

'Who with?'

'Hegan.'

Shit, thought Jacko.

The guard caught his anxious look. 'Who's supervising?'

'Officer Haywood,' said the warder.

The escort turned and opened up the door. He went first again, Jacko, Philippe and Ridgeback walking so close and fast behind that he had to quicken his step to stop them treading on his heels. Involuntarily he broke into a trot, his followers keeping pace.

The sound of their fast footsteps faded when they reached the corner of the block. An expanse of open ground stretched out before them, a sizeable sports field, grass worn thin by teams that never played away games.

No one walked on the cracked path round the outer edges, flanked by beds of sturdy multi-coloured summer flowers, immaculately weeded.

To their left, a cage with high wire mesh, twice the size of a tennis court. Inside the cage, alongside the wires, prisoners from solitary had worn a path like padding zoo lions.

On the path walking towards them was Hegan, dressed

touristy in a light blue shirt, cuffs rolled back and stone-grey slacks tight to his slim hips.

Six paces behind came Connelly, shorter, broader and darker. He was in a tartan short-sleeved shirt and black cords wearing silver at baggy knees.

At a wire gate stood Haywood, in full, thick uniform, looking every inch a genuine prison officer. All three stared at the four men running in their direction.

'Stop,' called Haywood.

Hegan stopped. Connelly took two more paces before he halted. His eyes fixed on Ridgeback, whose own concentrated on Hegan.

Haywood turned his back on the prisoners. 'Trouble?' he said through the mesh.

'Could be,' said Jacko quietly.

Haywood pulled a bunch of keys from a trouser pocket and fingered one free. Four pairs of eyes outside the fence followed it urgently to the gate's rusting lock, then looked up again at the sudden scraping sound of heavy footsteps on bare, hard earth. Like a runner out of his block, Connelly reached Hegan in two long strides.

'Fokker,' shouted Hegan, head half-turned.

Connelly had landed cowboy-style on his back, forcing a forward stumble under his weight. An arm hooked under Hegan's chin and across his throat, yanking his head back.

'*Fokker*.' A scream, panicked.

Haywood, confused, looked over his right shoulder.

'Open it,' shouted Philippe, fingers curled on the gate's mesh.

Jacko saw Connelly's free hand jabbing furiously into Hegan's kidneys. His eyes screwed shut in agony and fear. '*Fokker. Fokker*,' he cried as Connelly slavered obscenities into his left ear.

Hegan bucked forward and back, trying to shake free. Connelly rodeo-rode him, wrapping his legs round his hips, kicking his heels into his groin.

Haywood pulled and Philippe pushed open the gate. Both ran forward shouting as Hegan fell face first on the path.

Ridgeback, behind Philippe through the gate, overtook him, arms piston-pumping, Jacko trailing both. Four yards from the two men, wrestling, groaning, swearing in a heap, Ridgeback took off into a long jump, screwing his body to his right, stretching his legs forward, a land-to-air missile.

He hit Connelly, shoe soles first, on his left shoulder, unseating him from the back of Hegan, who was lying with his head on one side on the path.

'Bastard,' Connelly gasped, breathless, as he was knocked backwards.

Ridgeback rolled, ripping his new blazer at the shoulder, on and over Hegan's body, covering the back of his sandy hair with his hands, pressing his face down.

Philippe ran round them. Haywood jumped them. They swept up Connelly, an arm each, and dragged him on the seat of his cords through the wet grass. At the fence, Haywood pulled handcuffs from his back trouser pocket. He hooked one end on to the wire, the other to Connelly's right wrist. Philippe's hands made a rough, rapid body search.

'Is he OK?' he called to Ridgeback without looking up.

Ridgeback bent forward as Jacko reached them in time to hear him almost whisper in Hegan's right ear. 'You OK?'

'No.' He spat on the ground. 'No. I'm fokking not OK.'

Ridgeback pulled his face off the ground with a handful of hair and ran his other hand round Hegan's neck, chin and mouth. Sweat, snot and saliva smeared his palm.

He could kill him now, Jacko realized with frightening clarity. In revenge for his dog. Or to silence him. It mattered not. He could kill him now and get away with it. Just one quick tug.

Jacko put a hand on his shoulder. 'Easy.'

Ridgeback let the clump of hair go. Hegan's face fell back with a thud on the path. Ridgeback wiped his hand clean on the blue shirt as felt round his kidneys. 'No blood.'

Jacko knelt down and rolled Hegan over. His eyes were shut. His face was snow-white. His whole body shivered.

A damp patch was slowly spreading outward from the zip of his grey slacks.

The killer who had shot without mercy three men in Belfast and two dogs in Lincolnshire was pissing himself with fright.

I should have let Ridgeback have him, Jacko thought, disgustedly.

*

88

Till midnight they questioned him in pairs. Hours of nothing but Glaswegian abuse every other word with 'No surrender' in between.

It was Stan Young who finally cracked Connelly's resistance. 'We'll be transferring you out of here, of course. We'll tell your family where you are and why. I doubt whether there'll be any proceedings over this bit of bother. He wasn't injured and we gather he's a bit of a . . .' He raised a buttock from his chair and tapped it lightly.

'Whatdyemean?' growled Connelly.

Stan gave him a leer and Connelly suddenly realized he was saying that Hegan was a bumboy.

His mouth dropped in dismay at the thought of the word going round the clubs where they wave orange lilies that their hit man had got close enough to be importuned, to climb aboard, but still failed to even hurt his target.

'He's a paid informer, worse than a Fienian,' said Connelly, almost spitting it.

It came out then, or at least part of it – how he'd got himself arrested, to get alongside Hegan (who he kept calling Billy Roberts). He became boastful. 'I'd have killed him if you 'ad no stopped me.' Then cautious, 'It was my idea. No one else was in it.'

'Have you tried to kill him before?' asked Jacko.

'Never the chance.'

'Have you made a previous attempt involving drugs?'

Connelly looked astonished. 'Whatdyemean?'

'Did you try to give him drugs?'

'Git awar.'

'Did you give Andy Heald any drugs to pass on to Hegan?'

'Never.'

'Did you hide any drugs in your cell or clothing which Andy might have found and taken by mistake?'

'Never had drugs. Never touch them.'

'Do you know anything about the manner in which Andy died?'

'As Elizabeth is ma Queen, no. Never.'

'So we're no nearer?' said Scott, disappointed.

'I'm bloody well trying hard enough.' Jacko raised his voice, rare when he was talking to the Little Fat Man.

Normally they were at ease with each other in the knowledge that confidences were kept. Tense moments only occurred when Jacko was tired and despondent. That morning he had a double dose of both.

'OK,' said Scott soothingly. 'OK.' He held up both hands in mock surrender. A capricious smile spread over his round, polished face. 'All I'm saying is that the hard work has been done for you. It must be the only case in the annals of crime where all the suspects were in court or jail and you still can't catch him.'

Jacko laughed. It was impossible to stay angry with him for long.

A humid morning, thunder clouds gathering, rain about to freshen the waters of a marina, and they strolled by bobbing swans, black barges and white boats, talking through the previous day's events which ended in Connelly's 2 a.m. transfer to a top security jail fifty miles away.

'The Yard are mightily pleased.' Scott looked mightily pleased. 'They'll keep their man Haywood on as insurance till his trial, but they're sure we've eliminated the threat.'

Finally he said what he'd come to say. 'Well done.'

Jacko knew he'd played a minor role in it. Philippe had made the connection, Ridgeback rescued Hegan, Stan got Connelly to talk. But he accepted the credit for his subordinates' work the way Scott would have done from the Yard, the way it is in police service. 'Thanks.' Guiltily he added, 'It was a team job.'

'Are you going to charge Connelly?' asked Scott, coolly colonial in an oatmeal cotton suit.

With what? Jacko asked himself. He was hot under yesterday's grimy collar after sleeping for what was left of the night on a couch at Shirley's flat. 'He had no offensive weapon, apart from his foul mouth. His cell was strip searched. Nothing. Hegan wasn't harmed, apart from his inflated pride.'

He speculated hesitantly. 'Connelly was planted by the UVF, with orders to kill, but we can't prove conspiracy. He'd never got that close to Hegan before. When he saw us he knew we had dug into his background and rumbled him. He could hardly let the grapevine get back to family in Glasgow and Belfast that he had been shipped out of Lincoln nick without some attempt. It was just a token.' He decided to pass the buck. 'It's up to you.'

They slowed in thought as they walked up stone steps beside the bridge which had a white-plaster and black-beamed Tudor café sitting incongruously on it.

'Your mate Upjohn's been on to HQ, complaining about lack of co-operation and courtesy, wanting you off the job. He says Hegan is his case.'

That was brave, thought Jacko, after the ear-bashing the coroner gave him. 'What did you tell him?'

'To get knotted and you're to do the same. That's an order. He fouled up the job first time round.'

Jacko gave him a with-pleasure smile.

'So,' Scott asked as they emerged into a crowded High Street, 'we're still short of answers on Heald's death, Hegan's source and the missing money.'

Jacko talked as he walked – slowly. 'We can't rule out Holden. He had the opportunity to slip Andy something. Maybe he asked him to pass it on to Hegan but Andy, thinking they were pep pills, popped them himself. Holden is hiding something.'

'Was he in on the bank raid, do you think?'

'He's no alibi and he had a limp at the time.'

'Who do you fancy as Hegan's police contact?'

'Dunno,' said Jacko honestly. He told him of the check-off list he carried in his mind. 'I'm a long way from a complete line of ticks yet.' He yawned. 'Connelly was just a diversion.'

'He certainly dissipated your efforts. You look knackered.' A mischievous smile now. 'What's this Shirley Thomas you kipped with last night like?'

'Hard-working, very efficient.'

'Has she got big tits?'

'Matter of fact, she has.'

'Slapped your truncheon in her hand last . . .'

'Christ . . .' Jacko spoke with an agonized twist on his face. 'She's a raging feminist. She'd hit anyone who tried.'

'Wouldn't do yours much harm. You're not exactly Cock of the North, are you?'

'Oh, I don't know.' Jacko filled his face with doubt. 'In my youth I could bend an iron bar over it. Can't any more, of course.' A headshake, very sad. 'When you get to my age your wrists go.' He held out his hands limply. They laughed.

13

Shirley Thomas unwrapped a thin brown parcel to show off a painting of the cathedral she had just bought for her mother's birthday from an uphill art shop.

Jacko, who had only come to appreciate the breathtaking beauties of his home town after he'd left, suitably oohed and aahed. Stan Young smiled quietly and nodded.

All three returned to their reading. Shirley to a new file which Stan had studied while she'd stolen an hour for shopping on a slow afternoon. He had left it on her desk to cross-check, the way the team operated.

Soon she was frowning over a statement the Met had forwarded from Hegan's solicitor in London. She got up and walked to a cabinet where she opened a drawer and fingered through to find a file marked 'Prison Staff'. She removed a statement Stan had taken from Senior Officer Downes, who'd been in charge of the cellblock detail, read it twice, standing up. Head over it, she walked back to Stan's desk and dragged the absent Ridgeback's chair alongside his.

Feet on desk, Jacko was vaguely aware of what sounded like a mild tiff and thought little of it.

'Tell him,' Stan whispered.

'No, you,' she said.

'No, you tell him. It's yours.'

Disturbed, Jacko dropped the file he was reading noisily on the desk. 'Tell me what?'

'Shirley's got a . . . er . . .' Stan decided on the polite version. '. . . a cor blimey.'

'Both of us, really.' Her apple cheeks reddened.

'No.' Stan shook his head. 'You spotted it.'

'Spotted what, for christsake?' Jacko gave them an impatient look.

'Hegan's solicitor couldn't stay at the White Hart, as Downes assumed in his statement,' she said. 'It was fully booked. He stopped at the Eastgate.' She paused, tantalizingly. 'So who sent in that smoked salmon sandwich for Hegan's lunch?'

Jacko felt his mouth sag open; surprise, certainly; but no joy, only suspicion. Why hadn't Stan spotted that? Was he being dozy? Or devious? He swung his feet off the desk and stood. 'Fancy tea and a toasted teacake?' he said. 'On exes, of course.'

Oh, yes, said the polite, fresh-faced young waiter in a spotlessly white jacket, who served them in the restful lounge, all deep sofas and chairs and richly decorated china in walnut display cabinets. It wasn't every day that he walked across the square up the long drive to the crown court with a sandwich kept fresh and cool between two plates of Royal Doulton.

He'd handed it over in the snack bar where they were preparing ham and cheese on pre-sliced white for the more plebeian prisoners and their guards.

Oh, yes, said the efficient blue-suited woman behind the panelled reception desk, looking up from a pad of carbon receipts. 'Cash. Mary in the cocktail bar took the order.'

They had to wait until Mary came on duty so they sat for almost an hour on the manicured castle lawn in the shade of the giant copper beech.

Shirley confessed a feeling of guilt at doing so little work all afternoon. Jacko told her not to worry, that he'd get more than forty hours out of her by the end of the week.

Without any preamble, she said, 'You like Stan, don't you?'

He dredged up an unconvincing laugh. 'We go back a bit. Known him from the month I joined. We've never had a cross word.'

'Ever meet his wife?'

'When we were all much younger.'

'His two children – are they boys or girls?'

'Dunno.' My God, he thought, she's falling for him. He inched away from domestic matters and told her of a junior rank escapade; how they'd been reported by the ever-keen Upjohn for catching a bus for four of the five miles of a cross-country run as new recruits. Then, with a serious face: 'And Stan was a good mate when my first marriage broke up.'

'What happened?'

'She ran off with a sergeant from the force's amateur dramatics society.'

'Stealing a colleague's wife!' An amateur dramatic exclamation. 'Unforgivable. Against the code.'

That's the way she sees me, he thought. Like a bloody old-time sheriff. Never shoot a man in the back. Never bed your deputy's girl. He was not in the least offended.

He'd spent his paper-round earnings at the pictures on a Saturday morning. 'We are the boys and girls well known of, minors of the ABC,' they sang to Uncle Arthur on the mighty Wurlitzer. Then they sat back in the dark and watched Randolph Scott playing by the rules.

The code had gone west with Randolph Scott. Jacko sometimes felt among a dying breed in a service with too many Rambos, Bronsons and Dirty Harrys.

He told her some of this, and about films he remembered. She told him of her family, her books, her music. She spoke of a Mozart opera she had seen with her ex-lover. 'I didn't understand half of it.'

'Just think of it as a Fred Astaire film,' he suggested expertly. 'The plot's tripe, the dialogue trite but you sit through it all for those half-a-dozen numbers that leave you spell-bound.'

She laughed affectionately. He had come to rate her highly and her obvious regard for him should have made it a magical little moment. Not so. He knew now that she fancied Stan and Jacko was coming to fancy Stan as Hegan's man. He felt awful, a Judas.

Both rose, he with a heavy heart, when the cathedral's Great Tom chimed five.

Mary was polishing glasses behind the cocktail bar. Oh, yes, she said, she remembered her because it was such an unusual request but they didn't take names with cash orders.

'Her?' asked Shirley.

'Blonde, about thirty, in a smart silky dress, very attractive. A small scar here.' Mary fingered the right-hand side of her jaw-bone.

Maureen Beckby, Jacko realized. Holden's bird. Gawfuckme.

He knew the plan had misfired as soon he drew his blue pool car on to the grass verge just short of their cottage, a snobby rural name for a damp red-brick two-up, two-down, built at the turn of the century.

Bryan Holden was at home at ten in the morning. His black Fiesta was parked at the green gate which hung precariously on one hinge. Ahead of it was Maureen Beckby's nearly new white, very dirty, Peugeot 205.

'Blast,' Jacko groaned.

Shirley knew his tactic had been to interview them separately. 'He was at work when I saw him,' she said, slightly flustered.

'Ah, well.' Jacko sighed. Both got out. Neither locked their door, a habit in the shires.

He used both hands to lift the gate and nudged it open with his right knee, transferring flakes of green paint on to his light blue trousers. He led the way up a short path of cracked concrete. A thorn on a climbing rose clinging to the brickwork pulled a thread from his deep blue sports jacket. Another flake of paint fell on to his clenched fist as he knocked on the door. The place is falling down, he thought.

Holden blinked through his spectacles at his first sight of that day's sun, already high and hot, when he opened the door. 'Oh,' he said with a hunted look.

Jacko felt as welcome as a milkman with a quarter's bill.

'I was going to contact you today,' Holden added.

'Saved you the bother, then,' said Jacko, pleasantly.

Holden seemed uncertain. 'I'm afraid I've had to call in sick.' His dull hazel eyes had matching lids and bags and looked like milk chocolate buttons on an iced cake. He seemed to have dressed for a spot of overdue gardening in khaki slacks sagging at the knees and a blood-red shirt that wasn't fresh off the ironing board. 'I've an abscess.'

He looked in search of sympathy at Shirley who stood slightly behind Jacko. 'At the base of the spine.' He smelt of last night's whisky.

'Sorry to hear that,' Shirley said.

Holden brightened a little. 'I've cleared it with my deputy director to tell you what you want to know.'

'Good.' Jacko switched off his smile. 'But, really, it's Miss Beckby we've come to see.' They looked at each other in long silence, which eventually Jacko broke. 'May we come in?'

'Just a minute.' He limped from view, closing the door. Jacko and Shirley looked at each other, their false doorstep smiles fading.

Holden returned, galvanized. 'What's this about?'

'About the events at the courthouse.'

'Now, look.' A sudden awakening. 'There's a perfectly reasonable explanation for my reluctance . . .'

'I'm sure there is.'

'. . . and I take great exception to this snooping.'

'What snooping?' Jacko gave him his innocent look.

'I know you and your officers have been pestering my colleagues . . .'

Jacko cut in again. 'This is a different aspect of the inquiry.' He hardened his voice. 'And we do need to speak to Miss Beckby.'

Holden vanished from their sight again. Mumbled conversation and music filtered through a gap in the door. Then it opened wide and he spoke from behind it, out of sight. 'You had better come in.'

Jacko went first.

J-e-e-e-sus. She took his breath away.

She was standing in a doorway which linked the small, cool lounge to a much smaller kitchen. She was wearing well-washed jeans that seemed to have shrunk and her flat stomach pushed at the zip. Her lacy white blouse, tucked in at the waist, was sleeveless, showing off the tan on her smooth shoulders. No make-up softened the scar on her chin or hid the faint lines, hinting at decadence, that spoked out from her ice-blue eyes.

Jacko felt his toes curl, even the left little one which had been in a coma, toe-dead, for years. From the radio in the kitchen came an old Abba number and he was reminded of the group's blonde singer he used to ogle on TV.

Head to one side, Maureen Beckby gave him a Veronica Lake peek-a-boo smile through strands of hair. 'How can I help?'

Jesus, he repeated under his breath, bewitched, Stan must be getting old not rating this bombshell.

'Just a loose end,' said Shirley in a leaf-patterned dress, greens and browns and golds, dressed, Jacko had told her, for undercover in a shrubbery.

Maureen stepped back – no, swayed back – into the kitchen to turn off the radio, then forward into the lounge. 'Let's sit down.'

She smiled again at Jacko, pointing him towards a brown three-piece, inviting him to take his pick. The seats had been packed so close together that he felt cold, real leather brush his legs as he slid sideways through a narrow gap. He chose an armchair in front of the badly fitted front window.

He surveyed the room as Maureen and Shirley followed through the gap. Patches of damp had browned the floral wallpaper at three corners and the woodwork was cheaply painted. They weren't spending money on property that wasn't their own, he decided.

The women sat together on a couch facing a black fireplace. Holden scooped up a newspaper before he sat down opposite Jacko. He put it on top of the TV set, an arm's stretch away.

The *Daily Express*, Jacko noted, a Tory tabloid, opened at the crossword page, not the *Guardian*, a radical broadsheet, which he always associated with social workers.

Shirley unzipped a black leather shoulder bag, withdrawing a notebook. She slipped off an elastic band and flipped back half a dozen pages to notes made at the White Hart. 'You know we are investigating the death of Andrew Heald, poisoned in the cells at the crown court.'

'So I gather.' Maureen's local accent had been lost listening in court to the mannered modulations of lawyers.

'Our inquiries have established that one sandwich eaten in the cellblock that lunchtime didn't come from the court snack bar, but was delivered from the White Hart Hotel.'

Maureen laughed, brittle, faked. 'Surely you're not suggesting it was poisoned?'

'No.' A single shake of Shirley's head. 'But we believe you ordered it.'

Holden's brow furrowed. He transferred his hostile look from Shirley to Maureen. She glanced down at her delicate hands, avoiding his eyes. She nodded, head down, coy.

'Why?' asked Shirley.

Maureen shrugged, head coming up. Her eyes sought out Jacko. 'A joke, really.' A stronger shrug, accompanied by a sigh as she faced up to Holden. 'It was for Michael.' She turned to Shirley. 'Hegan.' She hesitated. 'We went to his pub quite a lot, didn't we, Bryan?'

Holden nodded automatically.

'He was a bit, well, over-generous.' Maureen looked at Holden, urgently seeking support 'Embarrassingly so on occasions.' Back to Shirley. 'He often refused to let us have the tab after a snack at his pub. I told him more than once, "M-i-c-

97

h-a-e-l."' She strung out his name. "This is no way to run a business.' Isn't that right, Bryan?'

Holden gave an unhappy nod.

Maureen began to speak faster, gaining confidence. 'And he said, "Never mind. If I'm ever down on my uppers, stand me a smoked salmon sandwich." It's his favourite. I knew he was in court that day because Bryan told me. Didn't you?'

Another turn. Another nod.

'I still do my shopping around the Minster.' Maureen went on, looking at Shirley. 'I adore it there. So I just dropped into the White Hart and ordered a take-out for him. Just a bit of a joke, you see. Wasn't it, Bryan?'

'Yes.'

He's not seeing the funny side of it, Jacko detected.

'Really,' Maureen added, smiling brightly.

'Really?' said Jacko, acidly, no longer under her spell.

Holden snapped out of his torpor. 'Don't be so bloody sarcastic.'

Jacko didn't stir. 'Mr Holden, I have to remind you that you remain under caution from our previous interview.'

Maureen stiffened.

'What do you mean?' asked Holden.

'I'm bound to ask you why you didn't tell me this at our interview last week.'

'It's irrelevant.' He jerked his head towards Shirley. 'She's already said it was not the source of the poison.'

'You knew we were exploring every avenue . . .'

'And a few blind ones, if you ask me.' A grumbling aside directed at Maureen.

'. . . and with your court experience,' Jacko plodded on, 'both of you must have known every bit of information might be important.'

Maureen placed her hands on her knees, giving Holden that sexy sidelong look. 'I hope I haven't got you into trouble.'

'Of course not.' He answered without looking at her.

Jacko butted in. 'You've certainly delayed our inquiries. First you forgot to tell Miss Thomas you had spoken to Heald.'

Maureen rubbed her knees.

'Now this.' Jacko threw out a hand towards her.

'I've already apologized and cleared with my superiors what

I can say.' Holden pulled himself up, ready with his explanation.

Jacko sat back, unwilling to listen. 'That doesn't explain this omission. Did you know about that sandwich?'

'Neither of you ever mentioned contaminated food. You were suggesting it was turno-something.'

An evasive answer, Jacko noted. 'I did tell you that we believed Hegan may have been the target of a murder plot and young Heald died by mistake,' he said sternly.

Maureen stared away into the empty fireplace, in troubled thought.

'Anything eaten by anybody in the cellblock that lunchtime is important,' Jacko continued. 'Now.' Pause. 'Did you know about that sandwich?'

Holden eased forward. 'You are not seriously suggesting, are you, that Maureen or someone poisoned it?'

Jacko ignored him and turned to Maureen. 'Miss Beckby, have you had any recent contact with Hegan?'

'Now, see here . . .' Holden lent further forward.

'Mr Holden.' Jacko raised his voice slightly. 'We both know, with his background, that the main risk to Hegan comes from Ulster and we have, in fact, isolated and removed a possible threat.'

Holden tilted his head in interest. Maureen frowned, deeply.

'But,' Jacko continued, 'I have been frank with you. I told you that we can't rule out the robbery as a motive for an attempt on his life.'

'How's that going to lead any would-be murderer, if you're right, to the money?'

'Maybe the idea was to silence him.'

It silenced Holden. He sat back. Jacko looked at Maureen. 'When was your last contact with him?'

'My God . . .' Holden exploded, face enraged.

'It's all right, Bryan.' Maureen spoke tenderly. She paused, a calming look, smiling at him with those incredible eyes. 'I haven't seen or spoken to him, oh . . .' Another pause, pondering. '. . . Oh, not since about a month before he left his pub, so it must be all of two years.'

Holden broke in, face crimson now. 'I'm not having this. You won't be grilling your Sergeant Young like this, will you? Oh, no. And yet . . .'

'Bryan.' Maureen spoke like a stern mother to a petulant child, no tenderness now. 'He was no more involved than you were. He was miles from here, collecting his son, when Michael went away.'

She turned to Jacko. 'Sorry.' A shrug, sexy with those bare shoulders. 'He's in a lot of pain from his ailment.'

Jacko unclipped a biro from his breast pocket. 'I gather that you want to add to your statement.'

'Yes,' said Holden, still very tense.

His deputy director had given him permission to fill in the gap in his earlier interview, he said. He started talking at long-hand dictation speed . . .

During an adjournment, he said, he'd walked through the empty dock and down the stairs to the cells. A guard opened the door to him. He'd walked down the centre aisle. At the far end was another locked and guarded door leading to the car-park and the waiting bus.

Hegan was in the second cell from the dock door on the west side. He was still in conference with his solicitor. Holden wandered up the aisle and spoke to Senior Officer Downes, sitting at a desk with his back to the car-park door. He told Holden that as soon as Hegan's lawyer had finished the bus would be heading for prison. He realized there was no point in hanging around.

He walked back down the aisle towards the door to the dock steps. Heald called to him through the bars. 'Excuse me, sir. I was hoping my social worker might have popped in. Can you give him a message? I just want him to get in touch with my girl – he's got the address – and tell her, even with remission, it's a long time and if she wants to take off I'll understand.'

'Sleep on it,' said Holden, 'and see your own social worker in a day or two.'

Jacko looked up from note-taking, urging him on.

Holden appeared to have dried up. 'That's all there is to it. Prisoners often say things like that when they're in the shock of sentence. They nearly always change their minds next morning.'

'And you didn't pass that message on?' asked Jacko.

'I didn't even note his name so when I read the inquest report I didn't put two and two together. Even if I had, I couldn't have said anything without clearance.'

'Did you have any physical contact with Heald through the bars – a handshake or something like that?'

Holden smiled, bitterly. 'Still clutching at straws?' He shook his head. 'None.'

'Did you eventually see Hegan?'

'Last week in the remand wing.' Holden's smile had gone. 'Only to do with disposal of his personal assets. His premises are so dilapidated he can't find a buyer.'

Jacko pocketed his notebook and stuck his pen unretracted back into his top pocket. He rose sluggishly. Shirley followed him to his feet. She smiled and nodded from Maureen to Holden. 'Thank you.'

At the door, Jacko said, 'Inquest a week tomorrow. We'll let you know the venue and time.'

Holden and Maureen, eyes avoiding each other, watched him as he turned his back on them and closed the door.

Oh, Stan, you stupid sod, Jacko thought angrily. You've been screwing her. And Holden knows. Twice now he's tried to point me in your direction. And you tried to point me away from Maureen. Beauty that won't last. Bullshit. I don't know whether your kids are boys or girls. Shirl here who lunches with you nearly every day doesn't. But Maureen does. You're all in it. You, him, her and Hegan. You tipped them off about the bank, you bastard, and now I'm going to prove it.

Concentrate, you berk, he told himself sharply, after he'd almost missed a bend. Shirley, who'd complained on the way here that his driving was slow and careful to the point of being painful, looked at him in surprise.

'Bullshit,' he said, using the first word that came to his head to end a silence that had lasted more than a mile.

He gripped the steering wheel, looking straight ahead, concentrating like a Sunday driver. 'Did I cock it up? Should I have pulled him in and sweated him? Should I have waited until she was on her own?'

'Oh, no,' said Shirley, with absolute certainty. 'It was very revealing, seeing them together, wasn't it? She's got a thing for Hegan.'

'After two years of not seeing each other?'

Shirley smiled a secret smile. 'Women can carry a torch for a lifetime and no one need ever know. Not even her husband or live-in lover. Look at the way she drooled over his name.' She imitated Maureen's stretched out delivery. ' "M-i-c-h-a-e-l." She likes speaking it. Look at the way she said, "It's his favourite." She thinks of him in the present tense. There's something going on there and, if he's acquitted, it will be goodbye Bryan.'

And farewell Stan, Jacko thought, but he remained silent, happy to let her do the talking.

'What a wimp he is.' She pulled a face. 'Fancy him trying to land Stan in it.'

Oh, God. A panicky thought. She's spotted it, too. 'You're close to Stan, aren't you?'

Shirley gave him a curious look, half smile, half frown.

'In a matey way, I mean,' he added hurriedly. And then slowly, 'He could be in for a rough ride next week.'

Shirley asked how.

He reminded her of Stan's own briefing in which he described being lured to Sleaford on the day of the bank robbery. 'Hegan, I suspect, was setting him up. Next week at his trial he's going to stitch him up.' He told her what Scott had told him. 'Hegan's going to say Stan planted the fingerprint evidence on him.'

It was making sense now. Hegan knew that Stan was screwing Maureen. They were love rivals. Both Hegan and Stan wanted the other out of circulation.

'If Hegan's acquitted Upjohn might buy it,' Jacko went on. 'He's been wanting Stan out for years.'

'Have you told him?' Shirley's voice was dull.

'No – and neither must you.'

'Against your code, is it, breaking a boss's confidence to help out an old friend?' There was a sneer in it now.

Jacko looked at her with an understanding face. 'Why give him a week of sleepless nights? I . . .' emphasized '. . . will tell him when the time is right.'

'Sorry.' Her look matched her voice.

Jacko, eyes back on the road, nodded. He made a mental note not to team them up again. She could get badly hurt here, he thought gloomily.

'Surely there's something you can do?' she persisted.

'Let's chew it over.' He was prepared to play games, anything to stop her working out what he already knew.

He paused, gathering his thoughts. 'Holden didn't know, I'm

sure of it, about Maureen's gesture in sending in that sandwich for her M-i-c-h-a-e-l. He backed her up eventually but initially she caught him on the hop.'

Shirley nodded, enthused. 'And Holden didn't confide in her the full facts of your interview with him. She froze when you said Hegan was the real target. He's desperate to hang on to her. He'll say anything to keep her.'

So what had they got? they asked each other.

A triangle, emotional, if not proven sexually, they agreed, after hammering out the phrase by trial and error.

Jacko ventured that Holden could have been Hegan's accomplice on the raid. 'No alibi and he certainly needs the money. Look at that slum. And he's got a family to maintain.'

Or could Stan have been? he was asking himself privately. He's no alibi on the day of the raid and he walks with a limp.

'Maureen could have been in on it somewhere, either in the planning or the getaway,' Shirley suggested. 'Holden wants Hegan dead, either because he double-crossed him over the stolen money or because he's about to steal Maureen.' She considered it. 'But how's killing Hegan going to lead anyone to the missing money?'

Jacko didn't know. They lapsed into silence as the car climbed out of the fens on to the heath road that led to Lincoln.

'What was bullshit, by the way?' she asked.

'That crap Andy was supposed to have said in his cell. He and Tina were a pair, a couple. He'd never send her a message like that. It's like me getting six months for fiddling my exes . . .' Shirley laughed. '. . . and asking you to tell my missus, "Don't wait for me." She'd think we were both mad.'

Shirley smiled wistfully, and he knew she must long for a relationship like his, to draw strength on, and he was filled with pity for her.

'What now?' she asked.

His thoughts were ahead of hers. They needed to find out if Maureen had ever been away without Holden, he said, in case she'd linked up with Hegan while he was on the run in North Africa. 'Holden could have hung on to a few Turnotoxins after the death of his mother. He'd planned to slip them to Hegan, passing them off as tranquillizers. Hegan was busy with his lawyer so he asked Heald to hand them on. Instead Andy popped them himself.

'We'll have to see everyone again, seeking proof of physical contact between Holden and Heald through the cell bars. If we can prove possession and physical contact, we may have enough to sustain a charge.'

'On what?'

Good question, Jacko acknowledged. He had not addressed his mind to it before. 'Attempted murder of Hegan or manslaughter of Heald on the grounds of his recklessness with a lethal drug.'

Hit a weak character like Holden with a charge like either of them and he'll sing, experience was telling Jacko, and Stan's involvement and the whereabouts of the missing money would come tumbling out.

He was half-way home, all downhill from here.

14

The drink and drugs had combined to make him sleep, back towards her, on the leather couch. At last, Maureen Beckby could put aside the *Daily Express* and think.

One week and one day. Oh, Lord, make it pass quickly. She looked at Holden, breathing heavily, oblivious. Would he stay the course?

He'd believed her, hadn't hit her, and he'd passed the message on to Michael when he visited him in the remand wing. 'I'm doing it for you, not the money,' he'd said. And she'd believed him and hugged him and cooked him special dinners and gave him that look through the candle's flickering flame.

It had worked, too, like a charm, until that interview at the police station with that bastard Jackson. He came home that night in a worse state than when he'd watched his mother die. 'He's on to me.' He'd wring his hands. 'They've been asking colleagues at the office questions about me, looking into my past.'

He hadn't been to work since, couldn't face it. It wasn't the abscess. He was cracking up, drinking heavily; yet, she'd rather have him at home where she could watch over him than at work, confessing all to some fellow do-gooder.

If he'd told the truth straight away about his harmless conversation with that dead fire bomber, instead of standing on his high and mighty principles, Jackson wouldn't still be poking around.

That salmon sandwich proved nothing, other than confirm that they were all chums. That's what she'd told Holden when he'd questioned her after Jackson and the woman left. 'A chum's gesture.' He'd bought it and so would the police.

She thought she'd handled Jackson well. A cool, hard bastard, her police lover had called him, and he should know. He was one himself. He'd made a good show of attempting to capture Michael. No one could possibly accuse him of not trying. She'd wondered for a while if he had wanted Hegan out of the way, dead for preference, so he could have her to himself, instead of his pay-off, and it had been a thought that had flattered her. But he was desperate for the money now, with his commitments.

He wanted Michael out as badly as she did, so he couldn't be behind any plot to kill him. No escape, no pay-off.

Bryan can't be involved in that, either. No bottle.

So it must have been a terrorist plot, unconnected with the bank raid, and what had Jackson said? The risk has been removed.

Ed Layton had been paid his upfront money and had purchased the hideout. Michael was safe and the plan was in place. That's right, isn't it? She went through it all again and could find no flaws in her argument.

Maureen Beckby was feeling calm now. All she had to do was move the money, fly off, be patient for a week or two while Michael was holed-up and then he'd join her when he'd disposed of Layton.

Meantime, she would busy herself caring so, so tenderly for Holden. He'd have to go to that inquest on the day of the escape. That didn't matter. She and the money would be gone by then. He'll walk in and no me. What would he do? Report me missing? Didn't matter either. She'd be miles away. Anyway, he wouldn't want to explain all to Jackson. No, he was more likely to take some extra drugs and a full bottle of whisky and end it.

It was a thought that saddened her but only for a moment. Holden stirred on the couch, making the leather squeak, settled and began to snore raucously. Quiet, you useless bastard, Maureen sighed.

15

'What's up, doc?' Jacko gave the pathologist his normal, chirpy greeting. He was standing at his desk, buttoning his collar, about to pull up his old army tie and go to see the coroner to discuss the progress report he'd submitted.

'You can rule out Turnotoxin,' said the doctor.

His trouser seat plunged back on to his chair in pursuit of his plummeting spirits. 'What!'

'Three separate tests. All negative. The drug company ran their own. Same result.'

'What was it then?'

'Still can't say. Something rare. Any more bright ideas?'

None filtered into his scrambled mind on a slow drive up the hill and round the hairpin to the castle. He parked his pool car in the nearest space to the steps which he climbed heavy-legged, head down, chin on his chest. He walked on the footpath alongside the wall which overlooked the car-park, out of the bright sun, into the old jailhouse, through the empty courtroom and tapped on the door at the back of the raised bench.

Major Jarman was dressed to brighten the mournful proceedings he had just conducted into a road fatality on the A46, condemning it as 'an alley of death', ensuring another headline. His jacket was fawn and brown dog's tooth and his bow-tie was lemon. Not for him the black that most coroners wear.

Jacko stood until he nodded to a sturdy straight chair next to a round polished table where he sat, sipping sherry. 'We've just had a bit of a setback.'

The coroner cocked his head and listened without interruption to the pathologist's findings. 'Good lord, man. Nothing to worry about.' He waved his free hand regally. 'Right theory. Wrong drug. I'll get their GP to let us have the names of any drugs prescribed to Holden and his family in the last couple of years.'

The alternative for the GP, Jacko knew, was a summons to court. The major didn't mess about. Sometimes he wished he carried that clout.

The coroner had been out of the army for forty years but was still very much the commissioned officer. He seldom practised as a courtroom solicitor so, mercifully, he lacked an advocate's long-windedness. His questioning at inquests was short, often one-worded, his summing-ups brief, blunt and sometimes brutal. He was not a man to squander time or breath. 'Want to put back the inquest?'

'We might not have an answer by next Friday, sir.'

The coroner studied his pale sherry. 'I'm wondering, anyway, if we should hold it in the cellblock itself, instead of here. Hegan and the rapist will have to be present. It will save a security problem for the prison service.'

'What time?'

'Four thirty. When the judge rises.'

'What witnesses will you require?'

'All the duty guards and prisoners in their exact cells with a police stand-in for Heald. I'll excuse the child abuser. The prison MO says he's at death's door. His importance is diminished anyway by this elimination of Turnotoxin. Plus Mr Heald, the victim's girl Tina and Holden.'

'He's certainly holding something back,' said Jacko, his enthusiasm returning. 'I don't accept his explanation about his conversation with Heald. If he repeats that under oath, perhaps you'd consider allowing questions from the deceased's family. We could confront him with Tina.'

The coroner refilled his glass and offered the decanter with eyebrows raised towards Jacko who shook his head with grim determination. He sipped, glared at his glass, sipped again. 'Can't complete the inquest, of course, without a jury and without the exact cause of death.'

He seemed to be going off what Jacko had slowly come to recognize as a good tactic. 'But you could take all the sworn statements, adjourn again to empanel a jury when the doctor submits his final report, read them the fringe accounts and recall the important witnesses for them to hear in person.'

'Sort of sorting the sheep from the goats?'

Jacko nodded, sheepishly.

The coroner beamed. 'A reconstruction, in effect. All perfectly legal. Bloody brilliant, in fact. Pursue the truth whatever the cost. That must be our creed, Mr Jackson. Inform our witnesses.'

He made it sound as if it had all been Jacko's idea.

An incredible man, he acknowledged, retracing his steps, a spring in them now. He knew he needed the likes of Major Jarman and Scott behind him, urging him on. The truth, a terrible truth for a back-street boy of socialist stock to admit, was that the British officer class system worked for him. He knew he would have made a hopeless officer. Faced with the choice between advance and retreat, he would have opted to nip into the NAAFI and bounce it off the boys.

Coming up these steps he was ready for rest and recreation. Now he was happily going back down to the trenches.

'A blank,' said Philippe with an expressionless face at the debriefing which wrapped up their week. 'The district nurse swore she'd administered to Holden's dying mother all the Turnotoxin personally. She could account for every pill in her records.'

'We can forget that.' Jacko told them of the doctor's findings. Stan looked up in mild interest, Ridgeback in disappointment. Shirley shook her head dispiritedly.

Ridgeback reported on yet another interview with Carl Marsh who had been unfriendly at first, complaining, 'You're still trying to blame me. You even pulled in my brother last week.'

That was news to Ridgeback, so he'd asked, 'What for?'

'A supermarket job.' Eventually Carl accepted his brother's arrest had nothing to do with the Heald inquiry.

Ridgeback read out what he'd said. '"Come to think of it, Andy did talk to the social worker with both hands holding the cell bars at about face level and, yes, now I remember, the social worker did rest his right hand on a bar about a foot below Andy's left hand but, honest, I couldn't swear they touched."'

Shirley turned to Jacko. 'We're twelve inches from home.'

'Not without an ID on the fatal drug, we're not,' said Jacko moodily.

Stan shook his head. 'I can't make head nor tail of this. Rod

108

Daniels told me he heard some mention between Holden and Andy about a message but wasn't sure what was said. He was, however, adamant that the social worker stood a good yard from the bars.'

'But Holden had his back to him,' said Ridgeback, looking as confused as Stan. 'Carl had a much better view. Why should he lie to me?'

Stan shuffled through a file and spread a selection of statements on his desk. 'Carl's a dope peddler, right? But he doesn't smoke himself or mess with pills. A dealer, not a user. Right? He had a visitor before lunch.' He looked up at Jacko. 'Was it a girl?'

Jacko sorted out the ushers' statements. 'There was a bunch of them – five or six – at the back of court, a couple of girls among them. Why?'

Stan picked up another statement. 'Senior Officer Downes and Co. seemed to have been turning a blind eye to goodbye kisses in the cells. Andy's mother gave him one. Maybe a girl slipped Carl something during a French kiss.'

Ridgeback still struggled to make sense of it. 'But Andy and Carl were great mates.'

'Could have been an accident,' said Stan, animated for the first time. 'Maybe Andy asked Carl for some pills as a favour.'

Jacko's eyes had never left Stan's face. He's leading me away from Maureen Beckby again, the sneaky sod. 'So?'

'I'm duty man this weekend . . .' Jacko looked puzzled. '. . . I've swapped with Philippe, if that's OK. Next weekend I'm picking my kid up from college.'

Shirley hid her disappointment with a forced smile.

'I'll contact the drugs squad and see what they come up with,' said Stan eagerly.

'Sure,' Jacko said, couldn't-care-less.

He did not join them for the Friday night ther in the threatre bar that Philippe suggested. 'Got a meet,' he explained. At the end of the High Street and just beyond a roundabout he forked off the A46 which would have taken him home.

To his left golfers played on a hilly course in the showers that had brought in July. At a junction he pulled into the yard of a pub almost opposite Upjohn's sub-divisional headquarters.

Leaning against the bar was a dapper man in a sharp, striped suit and wearing tinted glasses, an Italian look.

They drank lagers as, at Jacko's request, Detective Inspector Jack Penson recalled events that were almost two years ago now . . .

It was four days after the raid on the bank wagon that Hegan's prints were found on a road map in a stolen van discovered in a lock-up garage near the scene.

'We knew he'd done a bunk because Stan Young had reported him missing. The prints positively tied him in.'

He had phoned Stan's home on Upjohn's instructions, to call him in from his day off. No reply.

'It turned out he was collecting one of his kids from university. Upjohn had his alibi carefully checked because of the limping man sighting but it was watertight for the day of the stake-out and getaway.'

So Penson had phoned Holden, Hegan's other minder. 'Out to lunch,' said the switchboard girl.

He thought he may have nipped home for a quick bite so he phoned there. 'I'm not expecting him,' said a classy female voice. 'Can I help?'

It was urgent so Penson said, 'We're anxious to find out if a client of his has been in touch in the last few days.'

'Who?' Maureen Beckby had asked.

'Michael Hegan.'

'He lives close by but I haven't seen or heard from him for some little time. Bryan may have. Try him at the office later.'

Penson added, 'I warned her Hegan was armed and dangerous and she promised she'd call if he did make contact.'

Jacko put on his poker face to hide his excitement. 'Was there a house-to-house canvas of New York after his getaway?'

'Yes, but it threw up nothing.'

'I'd still like to look.'

Penson slipped back across the road to collect a file which he handed to him over another drink.

Jacko drove back down the hill, pensive. So Maureen knew that Upjohn and his posse were after her M-i-c-h-a-e-l. So what would she do? Drive to his closed and empty pub and leave a pre-arranged warning? It would certainly explain why he scarpered at the door. No point, he decided, in pulling her in yet. All she would have to say was that she nipped round to

Michael's Pub out of curiosity or to save Holden a trip and I can't prove otherwise.

Alone in the office, he phoned Holden's cottage. He rather hoped Maureen would answer, not so he could chat her up, just to listen to that sexy voice. 'Hallo,' Holden slurred.

Disappointed, he gave him the time and venue of the resumed inquest, then idly asked, 'How's Miss Beckby?'

'Stop pestering us' – and the line went dead.

He looked down at the set of coloured photos Upjohn had ordered to be taken inside and outside Michael's Pub after Hegan fled. The answer had to be outside, as Hegan never set foot inside that night where Philippe lay in wait.

His tired eyes repeatedly ranged over the exterior shots. Wasn't much to look at. Not much bigger than a domestic house, grey slate roof whitened by birds resting on two chimneys. A bit of a dump then. God knows what it must look like after being unoccupied for two years.

The main door was half glass, its frame black. Above was the sign he couldn't read. He shuffled through the pile for a side view. MICHAEL'S PUB, it said, in black and white.

Each side of the door were bay windows, white frames round small panels of glass. The three upstairs windows had closed net curtains.

His eyes travelled downstairs again. The windows gave conflicting information to any passing customer. 'Closed', said a printed black-on-white notice inside the right window. In the left window was a Guinness advert which said 'Open at' and the hands of the clock showed 5.30. On the inside sill was a big glass vase without flowers. The heavy lined curtains behind it were fully closed; in the other window, a six-inch gap.

He studied the interior pictures. They were before and after pictures, showing the rooms the way they were before scenes of crime specialists ripped everything out searching for the missing two millions and the mess it looked when they'd finished in failure.

He went back to the outside scene. He took a magnifying glass out of his desk drawer. Somewhere in that photo, he told himself, is a clue. What had been the warning sign? The 'Closed' sign, the clock, the vase, the gap in the curtain? He didn't know. What would I give for a witness out and about that same day who'd seen Maureen, he sighed.

He flipped through the house-to-house file, remarkably thin. He soon discovered why. It was incomplete. When he checked the returns against the voters register, a dozen or so were missing. Jesus Christ, he thought, what a slipshod operation. Was it worth chasing up the uncanvassed residents? After a week witnesses' memories fade. No point after two years. Or was there? He ringed the names of residents who'd been missed and slipped the list in a pocket. He put the magnifying glass on top of the file in his in-tray.

All he could do was plod on. He started humming the Laurel and Hardy theme tune which youths whistle to bait policemen plodding on the beat.

Dum-de-dum, he hummed, dum-de-dum, de-de-de-dum, de-de-de-dum.

16

A super Saturday, no shopping, watching a lot of the Test match on TV. At close of play, he cut his lawn, a weekly twenty-minute chore, fantasizing to beat the boredom of trailing up and down behind his motor mower.

Just lately, without really realizing it, he had begun to invest his own failed boyhood dreams in his son. Here, on this green swath is where it will all start, he decided. Tomorrow. Not a day too soon.

He would coax him out of his habit of holding his tiny Made in Pakistan bat cack-handed, left below right, and teach him not to tee up their dog's chewed ball between his feet like a poncy golfer. He would lob slow underarms at him. He would not coach his lead elbow up or his head down but encourage him to belt the bloody thing out of the garden and when, oh, happy day, he broke a glass in next-door's greenhouse he would smuggle pop and chocolate up to his bedroom where his mother was bound to dispatch him.

This would be his nursery ground, his stepping stone to Old Trafford and Headingley and Edgbaston and Lords and, above all, Trent Bridge, that cathedral of cricket.

He looked back to inspect his work, expecting to see unbroken lines of sage and lime greens neatly alternating. He was horrified. Wiry stalks had escaped the blades and had sprung upwards, disfiguring the lawn and desecrating a turf that was to become hallowed.

Bents, they are called. The flowering stalks from bent grasses. It took another twenty minutes to pull them out, eradicating them to protect his dream.

England's future middle-order big hitter, aged three, was in bed. Their dog had been walked and was in a deep sleep behind the couch, grunting occasionally. His wife Jackie was beside him, legs curled up beneath her, concentrating on a crossword.

On the small, square coffee table Jacko spread out his checklist which he'd committed to paper and always kept at home. In the one-track way that his mind worked he was now seeking to eradicate the bent grass in the blue ranks of the police service.

Jackie dropped the *Guardian* on the patterned carpet, mainly maroon, serviceable with a kid and a dog. 'I just can't get on with this.' An irritated sigh. 'What are you up to?'

'A different sort of puzzle.'

She crawled, child-like, on her knees towards him, put a hand on his shoulder and looked down on this:

	Young	Marlowe	Cross
Bank-raid – opportunity to participate	✓	✓	✓
Access to info on money shipment	✓	✓	x
Access to armoury to obtain stolen gun	?	✓	x
Access to middleman in jail to plant lethal drug	x	x	✓
Opportunity to tamper with my car	✓	✓	✓
Necessary mechanical know-how	✓	x	✓
Access to tools	✓	?	?

Her eyes reached the bottom. 'So that car crash of yours wasn't an accident?'

He ran the tip of his tongue over his bottom lip. 'I don't think so.'

'Why didn't you tell me?' She spoke with real concern, no reprimand in her tone.

'I wasn't sure.' An unhappy shrug, caught out. 'I didn't want to worry you.'

Her hand moved behind his neck to his left ear. He stared down at his list. 'My trouble is that I've always worked with a sidekick before. Someone I can bounce ideas off. On this job I'm on my own. I can't talk it through.'

Gently, she pulled his head towards her and kissed his temple. 'Then we must catch him between us, mustn't we? I mean, I wouldn't want to lose you, would I? You're so useful about the house.'

He turned to kiss her then, softly, but for quite a long time. She broke away. 'Explain it to me.'

He went into great detail. She asked lots of questions. Example: 'Why hasn't Marlowe the mechanical know-how? Accepting his word for that isn't enough, surely?'

'I phoned his lady on some pretext while he was out and steered the conversation round to do-it-yourself. According to her, he can't even wire up a plug.'

When she was fully briefed, she considered in silence for some time. 'Is it possible that two of them are in it together?'

Bent grass? Or bent grasses? The notion didn't seem so fanciful to Jacko any more. He got up and talked on the phone to Scott. When he came back she had retrieved the newspaper and had resumed the crossword. She looked up. 'Well?'

'We're sending Stan Young up to Glasgow on some fictitious loose end to the Connelly inquiry, just to get him out the way, to put some distance between him and Marlowe and Maureen. He's having taps put on all their phones.'

'Not Cross?' she asked.

'We've ruled him out.'

Satisfied, Jackie returned to the crossword. Presently she asked, 'What's "Law enforcement officer on his metal" – six letters, second an O?'

He closed his eyes, then opened them, enlightened. 'Try Copper.'

'You're brilliant,' she said, delighted.

Sometimes, he concurred, privately but immodestly.

It was sunny and quite warm, but quiet outside and obviously early, when the upstairs phone ringing in his den dragged Jacko out of bed. 'Desk sergeant, Lincoln,' said a female voice. 'Mr Upjohn, the duty senior officer, asked me to alert you.'

Maybe he's getting his own back for that 3 a.m. 'Are you Upjohn?' call. Spectacle-less, Jacko focused with difficulty on his watch: half-six. 'What's the trouble?'

'Fire in your incident room.'

Jacko shook his head to clear it.

'Fairly minor,' she went on. 'One of my 6 a.m. starters saw the smoke coming from under the door.'

'What's the damage?'

'Confined to paperwork on your desk, we think.'

'What caused it?'

'The scenes specialist is on his way.'

Jacko was washed, dressed and there within an hour, ahead of the Monday morning rush. The forensic expert had easily beaten him to it. He was standing behind his desk wearing a white overall and plastic gloves, peering into the in tray where files and the photos of Michael's Pub had blackened and flaked. 'Come in. We've done the door and the floor. Come in.'

Jacko walked in cautiously. There was a raw, scorched smell, like a badly made garden bonfire that had suffocated from lack of air and died prematurely. The green paint on the steel desk had blistered but not peeled. A dark ring smeared the ceiling above it.

'Any of your team smoke?' asked the forensic man, routinely.

'Only Philippe Marlowe and he was off this weekend.'

'No desk lamp been shorting?'

Jacko shook his head.

The forensic man nodded towards the charred debris in the tray. 'Then this little chap may be the culprit.'

Jacko saw his magnifying glass, lense smoked over in several shades of grey. He frowned. 'Is that possible?'

The specialist looked behind him out of the window through which a low sun shone brightly. 'Do you suspect something else?'

'No.' Too firm. 'It's just that the angle has to be exactly right even to burn a hole through newspaper with one of them.'

'Experimented as a kid, did you?'

Jacko nodded.

'I'll run some tests for you. Whatever started it, you got away lightly. Anything important gone up?'

He had to think for a moment. There'd be duplicates of everything somewhere, surely, he decided. 'Nothing that can't be replaced.'

He breakfasted in the canteen, then organized an empty office as a temporary base. He phoned Scott. 'I dispatched Young on the first train yesterday,' he said. 'He travelled by warrant. It's easy to check if it was used.'

One phone call told him it had been.

Philippe arrived complaining of the boring weekend he'd spent at his bird's parents. Ridgeback enthused about a Sunday of solitary fishing. Jacko ruled him back in.

Between them two of them had tried to kill him in a sabotaged car. Now they had tried to destroy evidence. Two of them were in it. Must be. Two of them pretending to be workmates, drinking pals, friends. Evil bastards. But which two? And what have I stumbled across in the old paperwork that's so important? What do they know about that I don't?

No answers came.

What the fuck's going on here? he asked himself angrily, bewildered, and not without that familiar gut-contracting symptom of fear.

He still got no reply.

17

Only Michael Hegan, star turn, top-of-the-bill, was missing when the judge entered court No. 1 to much bowing as Great Tom chimed ten thirty.

Roger Haywood, bogus uniform newly pressed, sat in the dock next to an empty red leather chair. On the public benches were half a dozen spectators whose taxes were paying for this show.

Behind three reporters in their box sat three social workers. Bryan Holden was missing. The antibiotics must be working slowly, thought Jacko.

The judge looked down on the barristers at their horseshoe table. 'I've a short matter from Birmingham where I sat last week to dispose of first.' Jacko tutted to himself. Cases never seemed to start on time these days.

The short matter climbed the steps, nineteen with a pimply face, as tall as Haywood who rose to greet him. They stood at the rail shoulder to shoulder.

'I have given anxious consideration to your case over the weekend because, on first hearing, it troubled me greatly,' the judge began.

He recapped. As a baby the youth had been put up for adoption. At eighteen he decided to track down his real mum. She turned out to be thirty-five, three times married, ripe and randy. They'd been having intercourse, twice a week, until her third husband caught them at it and reported them to the police who had brought a charge of incest. The judge decided on probation on condition that he didn't call on mother dear again.

Oh, well, thought Jacko, fighting off a grin. That was worth waiting for. In a long career he had never before encountered a self-confessed, proven mother-fucker. He made a note to phone his great police mate, Blackie Le Grande, in New York soon to share it. Blackie loved stories liked that.

Hegan replaced the freed youth in the dock. Seven men and five women filed into the jury box when their names were called and were sworn in; a stirring, solemn moment at any trial.

The prosecutor rose. 'Almost two years ago,' he began, adjusting his wig, 'two armed men held up a bank vehicle and escaped with two million pounds leaving a child's pet dog dead in their wake.' Two women on the jury received the news with the doleful looks of dog lovers

'One of the raiders, the Crown alleges, was the man in the dock.' He half turned and met Hegan's steady gaze. 'The other man, who had a noticeable limp, has not been apprehended.'

He outlined the evidence against Hegan: first, his distinctive accent which the wagon's crew would describe to the jury. 'You will be able to hear it for yourselves if the prisoner exercises his right to go into the witness box.'

The defence QC rose to the bait and to his feet, flapping his black gown, a bat about to take off. 'Somewhat uncalled for at this stage.'

The prosecutor was unrepentant. 'I was going to add that, if not, the arresting officers would testify to his accent.'

'He will be giving evidence.' Defence counsel had shown his opponent an early card. All in the game, part of the gamble.

Second, the prosecutor continued, with a winning smile, the van used in the raid was found in lock-up garages a short walk from a pub where Hegan had been drinking within ten minutes of the robbery. A barmaid overheard him giving directions to Nottingham to a limping man.

Third, an empty, recently fired sawn-off shot gun was found in the garage along with two sets of overalls, transparent medical gloves, and trainers. On one of the soles of one pair, Hegan's size, were found traces of grit which matched in every detail samples from the car-park of Michael's Pub.

Four, the jury would recall mention of Nottingham. There, in the railway car-park, had been found a Fiat stolen before the raid. Its tyres matched exactly marks found in a garage next to the one where the getaway van had been hidden. In the boot, on a jack, were threads snagged from a bank bag.

Fifth – and most important – was the fact that Hegan's fingerprints were on a map in the getaway van.

Such is the consummate fairness of British justice, Jacko mused, that it is never explained to juries what the accused's fingerprints were doing on record in the first place. For all its warts, he respected British justice, felt fulfilled serving it.

'Naturally,' said the prosecutor, tossing down his brief on to the leather-topped table, 'police sought out Hegan to question him about these discoveries. They visited his premises and established, significantly, you may think, that he had vanished five days earlier, the day before this robbery.

'Observations were maintained. As darkness fell, a maroon Cortina, bought by Hegan earlier that day, pulled into the car park – the grit-covered car-park, you will recall. A man got out, approached the door, about-turned and drove off at high speed. An immediate search was launched in which two tracker dogs were used, one of which went missing. Soon afterwards, a shot was heard and that car was found in a barn two miles away.

Beside the car was a police dog, Winston, who had been shot to death.' The barrister's eyes dwelt on the two doggy jurors.

'Hegan was not at the barn. He fled the country and was only arrested on his return from North Africa eighteen months later. You must ask yourselves whether a totally innocent man would vacate his home and his business in such sudden circumstances.'

An audit of the public house accounts, he went on, showed he was in heavy debt and under pressure from creditors. 'And there, in a nutshell, you have it – a man turning to crime to stave off financial ruin.'

The ushers handed the jury the exhibits and they looked for a moment like passengers in a lifeboat going down under white waves of street maps and plans.

A strong case, Jacko judged, as he stole away.

'How's it going up there?' Jacko asked Haywood, out of uniform and in his casuals, in the theatre bar that evening.

'Like an express. Only the technical boys got a rough ride over what's so special about the car park surface.'

'How did Marlowe and Cross perform in the witness box?'

'Very sound. Marlowe was adamant that Hegan couldn't have spotted him lying in wait at Michael's Pub. Cross accepted that Hegan might not have seen him approaching the barn. Both came across as good reliable witnesses.'

Since Connelly's unmasking, Haywood had become almost redundant and he'd happily agreed to hold a watching brief in court, releasing Jacko to do other things, mainly double-checking to find a complete line of ticks against two names while all three of them were out of the office.

'How's it shaping up for the defence?' Jacko asked.

'Well.' A swift reply, ominous. The Crown QC, he explained, had sought to put Hegan's past before the jury, in view of his intention of blackening Young's reputation. Too prejudicial, the judge had ruled. 'And the case is a bit thin, apart from the fingerprints. Hegan should be in the box late tomorrow the way things are going. How's your inquiry going?'

'Slowly,' said Jacko. 'The local GP says Holden wasn't prescribed anything between painkillers after his car crash and the antibiotics for his abscess. Shirley's no nearer finding evidence that Maureen ever slipped away to see Hegan while he was on the run. Stan's similarly stymied on his Glasgow trip.

'The drugs squad in Nottingham reports that Carl Marsh's brother was lifted for a supermarket job where the chemist's counter had been the target a couple of weeks back, too late to be of any significance in Heald's death. They're cross-checking to see if the raid was on all fours with any earlier unsolved chemists job.' He sighed, frustrated. 'A big fat nothing.'

Philippe and Ridgeback joined them. Jacko bought himself out of the drinking school after two more halves to make and take a call in the temporary incident room.

'Nothing on the taps,' said Scott. 'Not a peep.'

A disgruntled Stan in Glasgow phoned. 'Sweet F.A.'

'Feared as much,' said Jacko, sounding sympathetic. 'Still, the Little Fat Man wants Connelly on conspiracy. He's asked the doc to check for Ricin.'

'What's that?'

'No therapeutic use for it, no known antidote.'

'How do you get hold of it, then?'

'With difficulty, but a terrorist might manage.'

Stan groaned. 'I'm wasting my time. All I'm doing up here is treading on Special Branch's toes.' An anxious pause. 'Can I come back?'

Now. Tell him now, Jacko told himself. Force his hand. 'Listen, Stan. I know you won't ask me where this came from but you ought to know that Hegan will say in the box that you planted those fingerprints in the getaway van.'

A long intake of breath, nothing said.

'I'm telling you this now so you don't have to read about it first in the papers.'

'Jesus.' A short outburst of breath.

'He's got to have some explanation and he's elected you the fall guy.'

'What's he going to claim?'

'Don't know the full details. His solicitor was in contact with the Yard and the Home Office trying to set up the same sort of deal that sprung him from Belfast. That's how it leaked. They wanted us to drop the charge completely but that was no-go.'

'Where does that leave me?' A plaintiveness in his voice now.

'Facing lousy publicity at the very least. Still, it's a fairly routine defence at the Old Bailey.' Jacko put on an encouraging tone.

'But not in the East Midlands. Will they call me in rebuttal?'

'The judge has ruled yet again that the jury can't be told his true identity or record. You can hardly go into the box and say you were minding him because he's a convicted terrorist hit man and supergrass, can you?'

'It's a bloody disgrace.'

'I know,' said Jacko. 'Really I'm only telling you this now to prepare you for the publicity. You can let your kids know before they read it, tell them that it's a load of old crap.'

'If the jury believes it so will Upjohn. He'll want a head on a platter if Hegan walks and it will be mine. Listen, I'd like to break this to them face to face. Can I come home?'

'Give it another day, Stan.' He put down the phone.

He didn't know whether to feel bad about it or not. These days he was having great difficulty in gauging his emotions. There was a numbness where his soul should have been and he had worried himself closer to eleven stone than twelve.

Nothing, not a word, was said in court next day about Hegan's first thirty-one years on this planet. It was as though some alien spaceship had descended and dumped him, fully grown, in the depths of Lincolnshire.

To a trained courtroom observer, like Jacko, back in his usual place earlier than expected to hear his evidence, it was a sure sign that a defendant had a record, but juries aren't trained. That is their beauty; along with full franchise, the finest gift a nation can possess.

Yes, Hegan confirmed, he was thirty-five. Four years earlier he took over, refurbished and renamed the public house. He was wearing his grey mohair, speaking with his transatlantic drawl, looking like a democrat from Boston, Mass.

And, yes, he agreed, he had difficulty in meeting the builder's bill for the kitchen extensions. 'I decided to put it up for sale to cut my losses. It's an offence to trade when you're technically insolvent, isn't it?'

A nice touch, Jacko granted.

Hegan claimed he drove to Sleaford, had a drink at a pub

where he often called, left his car there, went by train to Nottingham.

In a hotel near the station he met a man called Harris. 'He claimed to have connections with the brewery trade and promised to put out feelers for a loan with a view to buying.'

They spent the night at his flat. The next lunchtime both travelled to Sleaford by train. They walked round to the pub to collect his car and, yes, he agreed, Harris had a heavy limp. He couldn't recall discussing directions by road to Nottingham but he conceded they might have.

'I drove him to my pub but once he'd inspected the premises he went cold on the idea of purchase, though it was a bargain price.'

He drove him back to the station and carried on to the south coast searching in vain for an old friend from his American days who had once expressed an interest in coming into partnership with him. A few days later, in a different car acquired in a part-exchange deal, he drove home.

'As I approached the door I glimpsed a hidden intruder and fled.'

'Why?' asked his counsel.

'A few years ago I helped the authorities, including Scotland Yard, clear up some serious crime.' A practised answer, word-perfect. 'I'm an informer and vulnerable to revenge. I thought I was walking into an ambush. I just ran for my life.'

'Explain the events in the barn, if you will.'

'I rented it from a farmer as a sort of bolt-hole. I kept a change of car, clothes and a handgun there for self-defence. I knew I couldn't count on police protection all the time. I had to make my own contingency plans.'

'Explain the dog.'

Hegan looked down in contrition. 'There was no way of knowing it was a police dog. There wasn't a handler in sight. If there had been, I would have been relieved. I shot it because I feared its barking would attract the gang.'

A series of minor admissions followed to inform the doggy jurors that he would not get off scot-free if they acquitted. His passport was false. His gun was unlicensed. There was something decidedly dodgy about the car he bought on the south coast.

'I was desperate to get away.' Desperation in his face. 'There are people who want me dead.'

He was handed the police photos of the getaway van and the garage where it was found, said he'd seen neither.

'Then how do you explain your fingerprints on the map in the glove compartment?'

'A regular visitor to my pub was a policeman, Sergeant Young. He acted as a sort of liaison officer . . .' He was careful to avoid the underworld term 'minder'. '. . . for Scotland Yard. We sometimes travelled in each other's cars. I remember on one occasion thumbing through his road maps.' He was handed the map in a plastic folder. 'Looks like it.'

'That doesn't explain how that map got into that van.'

Hegan pulled his relaxed posture erect, gave his barrister a level look and said nothing.

'Well, Mr Hegan?'

The barrister smiled at him. There was no reply. He tried again. 'Is Sergeant Young a friend of yours?'

'I would hardly call him that. He was . . .' A pause to conjure up the right word. '. . . disillusioned with the assignment. He wanted to return to normal duties.'

There Hegan's QC left it, hanging in mid-air. A clever ploy, Jacko judged. If there was to be any dirt flying in the direction of the local constabulary, let the police's own mouthpiece dig for it, slowly and reluctantly, which is how it happened on the third day of the trial.

'You are not seriously suggesting that Sergeant Young framed you because he was bored?' asked the prosecutor.

A vigorous headshake.

'What then?'

'In his job he's bound to meet criminals. It's possible one of them took the map from his car.'

'A remarkable coincidence, wouldn't you say?' The prosecutor wore the icy smile of a headmaster who had heard every excuse before. 'What other explanation could there be?'

'It's not for me to say.'

'Just give us the benefit of your experience.' The prosecutor was pushing against the judge's ruling as hard as he dare. 'You have, after all, told us you are regarded as an informer among certain criminals. Tell us a bit about that.'

Hegan chose to misunderstand the question. 'Some police-men don't play by the rules.'

The prosecutor dropped his bundle of statements for dramatic effect. 'Are you suggesting Sergeant Young was bribed to implicate you?'

'It doesn't always work that way.'

'In what way does it work?'

'They incriminate people, then drop cases against them in return for information.'

'Blackmail, you mean. Fitting you up, I believe the phrase is. Not to jail you but to ensure your continuing co-operation. Is that what you're saying?'

A face of a schoolboy finally forced to snitch on his chum. 'Yes, sir.'

The QC gave him an open-mouthed look of amazement. 'It's nonsense, isn't it?'

'No, sir.'

'To explain the inexplicable?'

'No, sir.'

'And this missing mysterious Mr Harris is a figment of your imagination, is he not?'

'No, sir.'

Hegan, Jacko recognized, was doing now what the prosecut-ing authorities in Belfast had trained him to do. Speak up and shut up. No embroidered answers. Give them nothing to latch on to.

Yes, Hegan confirmed, he suspected Sergeant Young wanted him to act as an informer, an *agent provocateur*, taking part in criminal conspiracies and passing on tips. 'After I had shot one of their dogs I could hardly go to his superiors and report him, could I?'

Yes, it was a coincidence the real robber shot dead a dog four days earlier.

'No dog is safe within sight or sound of you, is it?' asked the prosecutor, eyes on the two doggy jurors.

'Not true, sir. I was brought up with them.'

He was sorry he hadn't noted the address of the mysterious Mr Harris or the man in the New Forest pub from whom he bought the Cortina. 'It was two years ago.'

The Crown QC ended where he begun. 'Are you suggesting it was an evil plot by Sergeant Young to convict you?'

Hegan reopened the options. 'Either that or, as I said before, his map got into the hands of the real robbers.'

Jacko didn't wait for the re-examination which only treads water. Not a bad defence, either, he conceded. It was total crap, of course, but well cooked and presented. He wouldn't like to bet on the verdict. The jury, after all, didn't know what he knew about Hegan. All any defence lawyer with a client like him can do is scatter the seeds of doubt, to confuse them, make them unsure, and he had done a good job.

He'd hate to be a juryman.

18

He had taken to his bed now, sweating, smelling rankly, looking so ghastly that he seemed to be on the doorstep of death.

Maureen Beckby was beginning to fantasize about him passing away quietly and naturally, but the phone had woken him up. 'Just popping out for ten minutes.' She smiled down at him. 'Olive's Malc has broken down the other side of the golf course.'

Bryan Holden grunted and turned on his side.

Heart too tight to flutter, she drove across Woodhall, past a row of shops with canopies, a long half-timbered hotel and Swiss-style clubhouse. She turned into a narrow lane beyond a wooded course with as many golden splashes of sand as a seaside links.

Layton, in clean white overalls, waited beside a blue van with white lettering which said 'Uptown Decorating'. A man in a paint-spotted boiler-suit sat in the passenger seat. Both had agitated faces. On a warm, windless evening, she felt a chill as she got out of the car.

'It's going too fucking fast.' Layton didn't even greet her. 'They're on closing speeches. It will be over by Friday midday, if not before.'

Maureen gritted her white teeth. Everyone had over estimated the length of the trial. 'Can't we bring it forward?'

Layton flicked his head at his passenger, who got out clumsily. She had not seen him before but, as soon as he spoke, she knew he was Mo Mercer, the Cockney crook who had partnered Michael on the bank robbery. Her police lover had given her his name and the club near London's Ludgate Circus where Michael hired him for a £100,000 share, still owed and never to be paid out.

She had phoned Mo Mercer at the club when her police lover smuggled the message out of jail. 'Hegan wants to come over the wall or he'll shop us all.' She'd relayed it to Mercer and told him, 'If you want your share, more on top, you'd better organize it.'

She could see why he must have called in Ed Layton to handle the financial negotiations with her and plan the operation. Mo Mercer looked a stupid little man with a limp brain and leg.

'You see, darling,' he was saying, 'the boys don't get here till Friday morning. We need a couple of hours at the racetrack on the tripod pulleys and platform, practising, see. We've got to get it down to under ten minutes.'

He deferred anxiously to Layton, much the senior partner, who said, 'Nobody's fault, so let's not fall out. All we need is a bit of a delay.'

'How, for God's sake?' Maureen just managed to avoid stamping a foot.

'Tell him.'

'Tell him?' Around narrowed eyes, her whole face wrinkled in ageing anger.

'Go to the court tomorrow and tell him to be ill for half a day,' said Layton evenly.

Impossible, she thought, close to panic.

'Friends and relations are allowed to see prisoners on trial,' Layton went on, still very patient.

'My missus saw me when I was done,' Mercer added with a lop-sided grin.

Possible but risky, she thought, calming. She couldn't dispatch Holden. He was a gibbering wreck. Her police lover had washed his hands of further involvement until he got them on his money, fat chance. She'd have to go herself and why not? They were right. Lawyers often took down visitors to the court cells. She accompanied some herself in her days at her old law firm.

She'd go, she decided, then move the cash, stay overnight near the airport and then . . . away. Right away. 'Right,' she said.

She got back into the car. 'By the way,' she said through the wound-down window, 'you ought to know that in addition to the crew in the police car with weapons in the boot, there's an armed warder. Actually he's an undercover detective. He's the one always handcuffed to Michael.'

'I'll take care of him.' Layton looked at ease, the completely confident professional again.

19

All day no one had looked up with the faintest whiff of a cor blimey (or whatever you want to call it). Jacko hadn't turned a wheel. The phone was so silent he thought it might be on the blink and he ought to report it but, to hell with it, it was peaceful this way. He was beginning to think about knocking off early, playing at bath-time with the kid, walking the dog and listening over a leisurely supper to his wife's riveting gossip.

So it was hard for him to stoke up a head of steam when the phone added strident accompaniment to the mellow melody of Great Tom striking quarter-past three.

'Hallo, guv.' Ridgeback's energy was beginning to grate. He'd been seeing the last two barristers who might have helped decide who was telling the truth – Carl Marsh or Daniels – about Holden's brief chat with Andy Heald in the cellblock. 'Neither could add to their original statements.'

Jacko yawned. 'Come back then.' Why he should be so tired puzzled him. He'd even zizzed for ten minutes at lunchtime.

'Seen the *Echo*?'

'Yes.' It was half-way down his new wire basket. 'POLICE FRAMED ME,' said the headline, and underneath in smaller type: 'Says Raid Case Man.'

'A bit rough, isn't it?'

Jacko didn't know about that. 'Why?'

'Stan's got a bigger headline than my poor Winston. Amazing, isn't it? Plastering him all over the front page on the say-so of a triple-killer. How's he taking it?'

'OK.' Jacko wasn't sure, really. Stan had disappeared with Shirley for a late lunch and a walk in the sun, they said. He suspected they had gone off to buy an early edition.

He'd been left with no one to drink with and he seldom drank alone. He'd stretched out his legs on the desk, shuffled low and comfortable in his chair and kipped. He stored sleep like a camel takes on water and his nights had been so disturbed recently that he was thirsty for it.

'See you soon.' Jacko replaced the phone and frowned at it. What was so big that was happening that day to knock the raid and its aftermath off the *Echo* front page? he asked himself. It wasn't every day that a quiet county had a huge robbery and a police dog shot dead.

He was beginning to wake up. He picked up the phone.

'The main story was the royal wedding,' said the woman clerk in the headquarters PR department after he'd heard the rustle of pages being turned in bound files. 'Fergie and Randy Andy got hitched on the day of the robbery.'

He said thanks, put down the phone and studied it. People often remember what they were doing on a day like that. Those villagers in New York missed in the house-to-house canvass just might, too. That same night there'd been a shooting. OK, it was only Ridgeback's poor old dog, not John Dillinger, but the combination of the two events made it a right royal dog's day in Little Apple.

He was engrossed in maps and the voters' register when Stan and Shirley returned, bringing with them the faint fumes of real ale and dry wine. He did not look up.

He walked to the cabinet and took out the replacement pictures of Michael's Pub. This time he studied the before and after interior photos. 'Did forensics put this place back into apple pie order?' He finally looked up.

'Don't ask me.' Stan had been off hand with him since his return from his abortive Glasgow trip and Jacko was beginning to worry that he had worked out the reason behind it. 'Upjohn had pulled me off by then.'

Jacko picked up the ringing phone. A private smile. Speak of the devil.

128

'We can't have publicity like this.' Jacko had a fresh mind's-eye view of Upjohn snorting over the *Echo*.

'We can't control what they write,' he replied languidly.

'We can control our own men.'

Jacko closed his eyes, sighing. Oh, Jumped-Up John, you may never know this but right now I could blow you a kiss. He needed to regain Stan's confidence and here it was, on a plate. 'It all evens itself out in the end.'

'That's your trouble. You've always been indisciplined. You don't give a shit for the force's reputation.'

'Oh, I don't know. I knocked off a couple of bent bobbies last year.'

Stan and Shirley listened, pretending not to.

'I want Young in my office when this trial ends,' Upjohn huffed.

'Why?' Jacko sat upright. 'I've got Mr Scott's authority . . .'

'Why? You talk about nicking bent cops and you ask me why. He's made a balls of Hegan from start to finish. First he's limping around a mile from a robbery being pulled by a villain he's supposed to be minding. Then he presents Hegan with a believable defence.'

'You don't surely believe Stan . . .'

Stan and Shirley had given up all pretence of not eavesdropping and were looking hard at him as Upjohn broke in again.

'I believe Hegan could get off. It's all down to Young. If it's a not guilty verdict, I shall be instituting an internal inquiry.'

'Let's wait for the verdict.' Jacko was waiting for the kill.

'I know your game. Defending your old mate, aren't you? Those days are over. There's a new mood in the force. Rooting out the rubbish. Young is a fucking liability. Time he went. You can't argue with that, eh? What have you got to say to that?'

Oh, Lordy, Lordy. Two sitting birds with one shot. He took aim. 'Get knotted.'

'*What?*' Upjohn was not believing what he was hearing and had to repeat it. 'What? What did you say?'

Jacko smiled into the mouthpiece. 'From the moment I first clapped eyes on you – and my view is unchanged with the passing of time – I have regarded you as an unmitigated moron.'

Stan shut his eyes. Shirley shook her head anxiously and mouthed, 'Easy.'

'Right.' A gasp for breath from the other end of the phone, winded, wounded. 'You, too. Tomorrow. Here. With Young.'

'Impossible.' Jacko still smiled.

'You bloody well will.'

'We've got the Heald inquest.' A glint shone from behind his spectacles. 'Unless you want me to tell the coroner you have ordered us not to attend.'

'Saturday then. First thing. You've done it this time. I've made a note of all you said. It will form the basis of a complaint to the deputy.'

'Oh, really. And what makes you think I haven't taped this whole conversation? First you use obscene language over the phone. Then you prejudge Stan's position before any inquiry has been launched. A terrific testament to police justice this.'

He was suddenly bored. The fun was over. There was work to do. 'Now we're very busy here so why don't you go and put your head in a helmet of horseshit?' He slammed down the phone and let go a roar of happy laughter.

Stan opened his eyes, reproachful. 'Upjohn?'

A bright grin.

Stan shook his head sadly. 'That was stupid, Jacko.'

'Why?' A hurt look now. 'He asked for my views and got them.'

'My days are numbered. I know that.' Stan shot a brief glance at Shirley who smiled weakly. He turned back to Jacko. 'There's no need for you to put your head on the block.'

'Bollocks. He won't institute an inquiry. If that tape goes before the deputy, it will be his head on the block.'

'You haven't got a tape.' Stan pecked out each word, exasperated.

'I know that. You know that. But he doesn't.'

He hooted more laughter. Shirley smiled cautiously.

'Look.' Jacko switched to his sermonizing tone. 'We've both got good pensions. Two or three more years will make it better but neither of us will ever starve. We don't have to take that shit from anybody. So let's enjoy that time we've got left. Otherwise we might as well take our tickets now.'

Shirley lent fully forward so her bosom, appetizingly full in her pink belted dress, touched the desk top. She was looking at Stan. 'His tactics are rash but you can't argue against the philosophy.'

Stan faked a smile, Jacko knew he was back in his good books. Stan trusted him again.

Soon Philippe returned and Jacko asked him the question Stan couldn't answer. 'Yes,' he said, 'forensics put Michael's Pub back the way they'd found it after completing their examination. Recovered nothing, though.'

Another phone call, Scott this time. He'd been listening to the tap tapes on Holden's line. 'Who's Olive and Malcolm?'

Jacko passed on the question round the room. Stan had that answer. 'Hegan's old barmaid and her husband.'

Jacko relayed it to Scott who expressed no interest.

It rang again as Ridgeback returned. Shirley answered. 'Someone called Jolly.' She placed the receiver in Jacko's outstretched hand.

He arched his back. 'Jolly.' He swung his legs off the desk and crouched over his pad, firing monosyllabic questions, asking twice for something to be spelt, making notes.

'Smashing. Will you push on with it?' A pause. 'I'll get back. Thanks.'

He put down the phone, clapped his hands and said quite sternly, 'Gather round, children.' It always got their full attention. It was the first team talk he'd called that week.

'Two items on the agenda,' he began. 'The Jolly Green Giant has been working hard.'

His real name, he explained, was Jim Astill, a detective in the Drugs Squad, a good mucker, a huge, happy man who perpetually wore a ghastly green golf society blazer in order to live up to his nickname.

Jacko flicked his head at Ridgeback but addressed the rest. 'You'll recall he discovered that Carl Marsh's brother had been questioned about a raid on a supermarket dispensary counter that happened after Andy Heald's death.' He looked at Stan. 'You were keen on this line, weren't you?'

He nodded at the phone. 'Jolly says entry was gained through a small transom window so a thin man is suspected. Carl Marsh has a brother, even thinner than him, but he'd denied it and was released because of lack of evidence.

'Jolly's been back through the files. Two chemist's shops had been entered the same way. One was broken into three nights before Andy and Carl appeared in court together for sentencing.

'Among the pills stolen was a small brown unmarked bottle

containing three Lynxipan tablets, a foreign drug, newly imported for use in limited trial amounts on acute arthritis sufferers.'

He broke off the briefing to phone the pathologist. 'One more bright idea for you, doc.' He passed on the drug's name, replaced the phone. 'Says he'll check.' He beamed from Ridgeback to Stan. 'Well done, you two.'

He shuffled the map of New York back on top of the pile of documents on his overflowing desk.

'Now . . .' Eyes back on Ridgeback. '. . .the day Winston died was royal wedding day. The combination of festivity and tragedy might be a sign-post down memory lane for locals. The house-to-house canvass was incomplete . . .'

'Eh?' Ridgeback's self-satisfied look dissolved into disbelief.

'It wasn't a complete canvass. A dozen or so were never seen.'

'We mopped it all up in a couple of days. Three of us.'

'Well, I saw the returns and there were some missing.'

'May I see?'

Ridgeback was grating on Jacko again. A month ago he would not have dared question anything any inspector said and Jacko suspected Philippe's devil-may-care style had corrupted him. 'They were lost in the fire and there are no photocopies. You are just going to have to take my word for it.' A twisted smile, unfriendly. 'But I made a note of the missing ones.'

Ridgeback sat back, looking baffled.

'So,' Jacko went on, 'which has top priority – Carl's brother in Nottingham or New York to complete the house-to-house? In my . . .'

This time Stan gatecrashed. 'Our assignment is to discover when, how and by what means Heald died. Hang on to that.' He clenched his fist lightly. 'You're not here to get me off the hook on Hegan. Holden lost his priority when Turnotoxin went down the pan. I say we go for Nottingham.'

He hung his left arm over the back of his chair and put his right hand flat on the desk, spreading the fingers, studying them. 'You've all worked hard on the Holden angle to square me with Upjohn. Thanks for that but it's up to the jury now.'

'Rubbish.' Shirley took a deep breath, pulling in her stomach, pushing out her breasts. Jacko at the top table got a breathtaking profile. 'Holden and Maureen Beckby have both been caught out on lies by omission. They are up to their necks. The doctor won't be able to tell us for a couple of days if Lynxipan killed Andy. Let's worry about it then.'

Jacko looked at Ridgeback. He was wearing a brand-new suit, well cut and fitted, olive green with a faint, thin orange check. It cried out for the coroner's lemon bow and brown brogues. He was wearing a tartan tie and scuffed black lace-ups.

His expression was still hangdog. 'Can't we split it – two in Nottingham, say, and three to New York?'

'No compromises,' said Jacko, uncompromisingly.

Cross nudged Philippe. 'What do you think?'

Philippe gave him a superior look, cool and disdainful, then his eyes roamed the room. 'Technically, Stan's right.' He paused. 'Operationally Shirley is. It will take more than a day to crack the Carl Marsh connection. It will take just an hour or so to crack Manhattan-in-the-Marshes. All the publicity Hegan's trial is getting helps. Everyone in that village will be recalling that day. Not last week. Not next week. Now.'

'I'm with Stan, too,' blurted Ridgeback.

'For Nottingham, you mean?' Jacko was teasing him.

'No. No.' He was flustered. 'You know what I mean. New York.'

Jacko looked at Stan, thinking: You've been trying to point me away from New York, away from Maureen Beckby again, you bastard. 'You're outvoted.'

Both looked down, Stan shaking his head, Jacko to the voters' register. The phone rang again.

'Inspector Haywood from the prison,' said Shirley as she handed it to Jacko.

Under sudden pressure, everything happening at once, he pulled an irritated face. It changed to puzzlement, then delight as he listened for a long time, making pages of notes.

'Gather round, children.' They listened again as Jacko read out his notes, the first bit mainly for Stan's benefit, leaving nothing out.

The court rose at four-thirty, Haywood had reported. The prosecutor had staged a spirited assault in his final address to the jury. 'Here is a man who has, on his own admission, murky connections with the underworld, seeking to escape his just deserts with unfounded allegations against the police. Don't fall for it.'

Hegan's QC, in his closing speech, played the bent bobby in the background theme fortissimo. 'You are men and women of the world. That is why you were chosen to sit there. Is what my client alleges beyond the bounds of possibility? If the answer is no, you will acquit.'

The judge, a firm old pro in his sixties with a razor-keen mind, cut right through all the bullshit to the heart of the matter. 'You didn't hang up your common sense with your raincoats in the foyer when you stepped into that box. Use it. Put yourself in Mr Hegan's position.

'You have been of some unspecified assistance to the police authorities; done your public duty. This has put your life at risk. In that time of crisis, Sergeant Young has been keeping a watchful eye on you.

'Late one night you arrive home. You suspect you have walked into an ambush staged by your enemies. You fear for your life. You flee. You shoot what you believe to be one of your would-be assassin's dogs to make good your escape. So far, so good, albeit tragic for the innocent dog, but put that from your mind.

'Wouldn't you have then made contact with the police who had protected you all those months and say, "Please come to my aid."? If not, why not? At that time, Mr Hegan wasn't to know that Sergeant Young had planted evidence on him, if what he claims is true. That map in that van wasn't found until four days later. At that time, as far as he knew, Sergeant Young was still his protector. These are the sort of questions you might address your minds to.'

The judge had risen with less than an hour's summing up left to complete. The verdict was expected before lunch tomorrow.

Jacko looked up from his notes. 'Good eh?' Stan nodded, non-committal.

Now, Jacko thought maliciously, let's see your reaction to this next bit. He went back to his notes . . .

Hegan descended the dock steps with Haywood at his heels. He was locked in a cell to await the prison transport.

His solicitor followed a few minutes later. Behind him, flip-flopping down the steps in flat, denim wedges, came Maureen

Beckby. She wore a formal smile and a casual blue towelling suit as though she had just come from tennis.

'A visitor for you,' said the solicitor.

Haywood stood to one side to let them talk with a view of each other, listening to every word, memorizing what was said, making notes as soon as he got back to prison. He'd read from those notes over the phone to Jacko.

At first Hegan ignored her, addressing the lawyer, harshly, angry. 'That beak is blowing a hole in my case.'

'Everyone on trial worries part-way through the summing up,' said the solicitor. 'I think it's going rather well. You could be out there by lunchtime tomorrow.'

The solicitor turned to Maureen. 'The guard will let you out when you're finished.' He left them to talk.

Maureen stood a good two feet from the bars. 'Bryan's ill.'

'So I've been told.' Hegan switched to his softer, Irish-American voice.

'He says any outstanding personal problems can be dealt with here tomorrow, four thirty.'

'I could be starting life by then.'

'Slow it down, Michael.'

'It's all right for you.'

'That was the arrangement he made when he last saw you, surely? Four thirtyish tomorrow?'

'Yeah. Right.' A pause, both smiling.

'You worry too much,' said Maureen. 'You could make yourself ill.'

'This judge has got me edgy.'

She tilted her head, just slightly, wafting freshly shampooed blonde hair. 'It's been a long road. You've just got to give it a bit more time. Then you'll be fine.'

'You're right.'

'So with a bit of luck we'll see you out and about tomorrow teatime.' She cocked her head deliberately to one side.

'With luck.' Hegan nodded, smiling.

'So let's make a date. I know you'll be busy for a couple of weeks but, afterwards, how about a celebration at Michael's Pub, New York?' Another smile. 'See you then.' She swayed away to the door which Officer Downes unlocked for her.

'Thanks,' Hegan called after her. She did not look back . . .

135

When Jacko had finished reading back his notes Philippe sucked air over his teeth into a reedy whistle.

'What does it mean?' asked Ridgeback, looking at him.

Philippe stood. He began pacing round the pushed-together desks, hands behind his back, head down.

Jacko lifted his legs on to the scorched desk, leaning back in his chair, hands clasped behind his head, thinking. So Holden was going to drag his aching arse to court to see him around four thirty tomorrow. Makes sense. Both would be there for the inquest. Nothing in that.

What outstanding personal problems? His unsold premises, perhaps.

'Could be a message of love,' Shirley ventured. 'If he's freed, they're going to walk hand-in-hand into the sunset.'

Stan shook his head, pessimistic again. 'Why tell him this evening? There's nothing to stop them doing that tomorrow when he walks.'

Jacko detected no hint of jealousy in Stan's tone.

He tried a new private theory. Maybe Maureen wasn't expecting him to walk. She was anticipating jail. She went to find out where the missing money is hidden. It's been a long road. Slow down. A slow sign on a long road?

'Shall I bring her in?' Ridgeback broke into his thoughts.

Philippe circled behind them again. He stopped at the cabinet, stooping to lower his chin on the steel top, staring blankly at the cream wall.

Ridgeback could be right this time, Jacko half decided. The tap had turned up nothing. She's got to be watched and followed.

'You don't think a breakout's on, do you?' Philippe spoke quietly with his hunched back towards them.

The phone rang again.

Shirley lifted it, listened briefly. Then: 'Oh shit.' It was the first time Jacko had heard her use an obscenity.

She turned her face away from the mouthpiece, still listening through the earpiece. 'Hegan's ill. Severe stomach pains. The MO wants him straight into hospital.'

'Who's that?'

'Senior Officer Downes.'

'Where's Haywood?'

Shirley repeated Jacko's question and relayed the answer. 'With Hegan.'

'Don't let them go.' Philippe swung round and upright. 'There is a break on. "You could make yourself ill." He's carrying out her orders.'

Shirley took the initiative. 'Tell them not to transfer him until Mr Haywood gets reinforcements.'

Jacko nodded at Philippe who turned, holding out his right hand to open the door three yards before he reached it. Ridgeback followed like a tracker dog.

Shirley debated with Downes. 'If the MO insists, muster as many guards as you can.'

The MO was bound to insist, Jacko knew. If he delayed and Hegan died, he'd be a dole queue doctor. Four weeks ago tomorrow he'd rushed Andy Heald straight into hospital and they still couldn't save him. What if Hegan were genuinely ill? What if he died? There could be a homicidal maniac running loose in that prison.

He picked up the internal line and asked the switchboard girl to find Superintendent Upjohn urgently. He hung on, re-reading his note.

Shirley stood. 'I'd better get up there.' She handed the phone to Stan, swept up her bulging canvas Gladstone from the desk and seemed to use its weight to propel herself to the opened door.

'What's this?' Upjohn was on the line. 'An abject apology?'

'I'm requesting a rapid response patrol to accompany the transfer of a sick prisoner from jail to hospital.'

'Who?'

'Hegan. We suspect a plot to spring him, maybe *en route*.'

Stan butted in. 'The MO says he must go.'

'It's urgent, sir – yes or no?'

Only a slight hesitation. 'Ten minutes.' Both slammed down their receivers.

Jacko repeated it to Stan. 'Can they wait that long?'

The answer finally came back: 'Yes.'

Jacko dialled Control Room and asked to be plugged in to the armed response car's calls. He heard all the orders being given.

Stan replaced the phone when Downes told him Hegan had left with a heavy police and prison escort. Jacko put his down within a couple of minutes when the crew reported: 'Arrival without incident.'

He heard Upjohn telling them to draw their weapons and stay as close to Hegan as medical staff would allow. More marksmen were detailed to strategic positions on the roof.

Jacko bent forward, massaging his brow, eyes shut. 'Jesus.'

'We're getting too old for this,' said Stan, wearily.

Speak for yourself, Jacko thought, offended.

20

She was almost finished now. It had been a dirty, dusty job, but she would dump this old jump-suit at the airport hotel. On her knees, Maureen Beckby was about to lock a second suitcase filled with banknotes.

A lane of light rolled across the dust-caked carpet towards her.

Holden, in his gardening clothes, stood in the sunlit doorway of Michael's Pub.

'Bryan.' A frightened voice, so she added, 'You frightened me.' She rose and smiled nervously.

He was squinting. She knew that when his eyes had focused in the shuttered gloom he would see the mess she had made ripping away the leading edges from all the inside doors where the money had been hidden in the cavities between the hard-board. 'I was just picking up our money.'

'You're running out on me.' A firm voice, positive.

'Nonsense.'

'To be with him.'

'Nonsense. I came for this.' She knelt again and took handfuls of notes which she offered up towards him.

He shook his head violently.

'No. No.' A smooth smile. 'You misunderstand.'

'You've packed.'

'Only for a day or two's break.' It was the best she could do, all she could think of.

'It's over for us, isn't it? After all I . . .'

'Wrong. You're wrong.' Her scolding tone. 'You don't understand . . .'

'Yes, I do,' Holden cut in, harshly. 'You're taking the money and joining him. Well, you're not going to get away . . .'

'Don't be silly. Please.' Pleading now.

'You've made a fool out of me. I've known it for a long time. I did my best to keep you out of it. I phoned them when he came back. If they'd caught him before . . .'

'Wait. Bryan.' She wafted a hand like a policeman's slow-down signal. No hope now, she knew. Too dangerous to let him live and talk. Too late. 'Let's think about this.' Then brightly. 'And have a drink.' She rose slowly and walked cautiously, looking at him, to the serving hatch. 'There's a bottle of . . .' She clicked it open. '. . . something old . . .' She felt along the ledge. '. . . in here.'

She'd found what she was feeling for – a black revolver she had hidden earlier beneath a towel.

She faced him, gun held in both hands in front of her stomach.

'You'll never use that.' He smiled, unafraid.

'Listen.' She was walking towards him, without caution now, smiling, too.

'Give it me.' She was close now. Close enough. He held out a hand. 'We can still . . .'

She wasn't sure which shocked her the most – the explosive ringing which deadened her ears or the jolt that made her almost step out of her denim wedges as Holden flew away from her, against the wall behind the door. His back slid down it. His head dropped towards the knees of his arched legs.

21

White and still he lay. Like a corpse. Two young doctors, both Asians, bent over him. 'Here?' One prodded with two brown fingers below his navel.

'Yes.' Hegan half moaned, half sighed.

Dead men don't talk, Jacko told himself. Driving up the hill, he'd felt cold, empty indifference. Now he wanted Hegan alive, but only for his secrets. Indifference had gone. Cold emptiness remained.

Hegan was face up on a trolley bed. His white T-shirt was tucked under his chin. His bright blue slacks were unzipped, Y-fronts pulled down, exposing pubic hairs several tones darker than his sandy public hairs.

Jacko looked down on a featherweight's torso. Only a gun made him a heavyweight. His indifference returned.

'Here?' Brown fingers prodded his rib cage.

'When you stretch the skin.' Hegan answered the ceiling.

'Or here?' The doctor ran his hands each side of his navel into his pubic hairs.

'No.'

His colleague in big round spectacles squeezed Hegan's jaw, forcing his mouth open and looked inside. A young black nurse handed him a tiny torch which he shone down.

Both medics straightened. 'We'll get you to X-ray,' said Big Specs.

They walked, white smocks unbuttoned, stethoscopes dangling, each side of the trolley. They elbowed a gap in the blue plastic curtains. Jacko followed into an ante-room. Haywood stayed by the bed between Hegan and a white worktop on which rested stainless steel instruments, sharp and sinister.

Jacko introduced himself.

'We've only just started,' said the doctor with a thin, shiny black moustache.

Here we go, fumed Jacko inwardly. The medical brick wall. Even if you're the patient, they say nothing until they are good and ready. Meantime they treat you as though you're brain dead.

'Did either of you tend Andy Heald?' No response. 'He was brought in from prison, too. Four weeks ago tomorrow.' Big Specs' face filled with interest but he still said nothing. 'He died soon after admission from toxic poisoning.'

'I did,' said Big Specs at last.

'You see, same prison, roughly the same time and a month ago.' Jacko shrugged. 'Are the symptoms the same?'

'Thank you,' said the other doctor, a thin smile running in parallel with his moustache. 'We'll check.'

Arseholes, thought Jacko, secretly seething. I'm telling them more than they're telling me. 'Will he survive?'

'There's every expectation.'

A set of doors swept silently open on black rubber skirting. Two constables, arms folded over navy-blue flak jackets, stood to one side. A tubby, balding porter in a white spacesuit and green galoshes sloshed to a halt. 'This one?'

Big Specs nodded and parted the curtains. Hegan came out, grey-stockinged feet first, on the trolley, then Haywood at the porter's side.

Jacko beckoned the two fresh-faced, flak-suited officers. 'Take over from Mr Haywood. I have to talk to him. If they won't let you into X-ray, guard the door.'

They went out the swing doors in a tight knot round the trolley, Big Specs bringing up the rear. 'As soon as we know, you'll know,' he said over his shoulder.

Pull the other one, thought Jacko, bitterly. A broken elbow playing Randolph Scott, a broken finger playing cricket, a broken hand chasing a burglar, a week in an isolation ward in the army with a fever, a couple of days last year when a mad dog attacked him. He knew hospitals well, hated them all.

He led Haywood through the lime-walled casualty department. Walking wounded stood at the glass-fronted reception desk, still more in a square of soft benches. One was in cricketing whites, a blood-stained pad held to a cut above his right eye. Happy days, thought Jacko.

They went into a cubbyhole of an office the night administrator had loaned him. Jacko fiddled through all his pockets to find a small contacts book with a disintegrating red cover and dialled a number.

'Not another bright idea,' groaned the pathologist.

'Of a different sort.' Jacko told him of his need for quick information, however scant, and the difficulty he anticipated in getting it. 'You can pull rank.'

'It's very unusual to consult the pathologist when there's every expectation of life.' The doctor gave a light laugh. He promised to get back.

Jacko hung up and looked at Haywood. 'Did he have those anti-depressants today?'

'Only one. After breakfast.'

Almost twelve hours ago, Jacko calculated. Andy Heald showed symptoms long before that. This is different. There has to be another explanation.

Haywood jerked his head towards the door which opened after a single tap. Shirley's blonde hair came in first. Her face was harassed, cheeks apple rosy. She rested her tight, trim bottom on a shelf in front of Haywood's swivel chair. She slid backwards, swinging her legs with their smooth calves.

Between them, they ran through Hegan's day and what he'd eaten. Here we go again, thought Jacko, depressed. Same scene. Only the name's changed.

'Maureen Beckby and his solicitor did not make contact with Hegan through the bars.' Haywood sounded sure; had to be. His job depended on it. 'Back at the prison, Downes fetched his tea on a tray while I phoned you about Maureen's visit.'

Shirley now. 'Downes says Hegan shouted through the cell door, "Not hungry." He peeped through the spy hole and saw him changing from suit to slacks and T-shirt.'

Back to Haywood. 'I unlocked when I got back. Hegan was lying on his bunk, holding his stomach, writhing in pain.'

Shirley said she had searched his clothing and cell after he'd gone to hospital. 'Nothing,' she said, glumly.

The door burst open without a knock. In its frame, like a black knight without charger, stood Upjohn. The entry of the Gladiator. He looked without recognition at Jacko, sitting behind a small desk.

He shone a warm smile at Shirley who was seeing him for the first time. He was everything that Jacko and Stan were not. Oozing power from every pore. Over six foot, dashingly handsome, barrel-chested as a sergeant-major. A black beret was tucked into the belt of his smooth, pressed uniform.

He beamed at Haywood as he pumped his hand and said, 'Hegan won't get out of here in one piece.'

Shirley's bosom wobbled with suppressed laughter at what was a funny thing to say about a hospital, a terrific advert for the NHS. Jacko, preoccupied, didn't spot it immediately, smiled belatedly.

Upjohn insisted on taking Haywood on a tour of inspection to show him where he had deployed his troops, still ignoring Jacko on his way out.

Within seconds, Philippe came in. 'I hid when I saw Jumped-Up – behind a pregnant woman this time.'

Shirley's bosom was wobbling again. Jacko was having deep trouble concentrating.

'Checked all the day's casualty and admission records,' said Philippe. 'Pegged everyone hanging around the waiting room. Ridgeback is prowling round the car-parks, checking out anyone sitting in vehicles for undue lengths of time. What now?'

'Wait,' Jacko mumbled, more or less to himself. 'What else is there to do in a bloody hospital?'

'Hallo, Stan.' Jacko snapped out his greeting as he snapped off his wandering thoughts.

Shirley, eyelids shiny, wilting at the end of a stint which had already lasted fourteen hours, straightened her shoulders.

'Neither the red Fiesta nor the white Peugeot are parked up,' Stan reported by car phone from outside Holden's cottage where Jacko had ordered him to keep watch while the rest of the team joined the hospital stake-out. 'No lights on. Haven't knocked. That's right, isn't it? That's what you want, right? Observation only?'

Jacko didn't know what he wanted or expected, was suddenly no longer sure of anything. He lowered the white mouthpiece below his chin, repeating the question, letting the team join in the decision-making.

'Maureen's part of an escape plot,' said Philippe.

'We've no evidence that there is one,' said Shirley, equally firm.

True, thought Jacko. This operation was beginning to have a false-alarm feel to it.

'We should at least knock on the door,' Philippe persisted.

Jacko spoke into the phone but looked round the room, 'Is there any point in talking to her yet? What's she done? Paid a courthouse visit to an old neighbour. Where's the crime in that? We've no arrestable cause unless something happens here.'

He called a vote. Ridgeback sided with Philippe. Stan went with Shirley. Jacko gave them his casting vote and changed the subject. 'So what's new in New York?'

'Nothing,' said Stan, sounding sad. 'There are eight million stories in the Naked City and I can't find one of the bastards.'

It was a distortion of the pay-off line used every week in a black-and-white American TV police series from their young days. Both laughed, Jacko warmly.

Shirley slid off the ledge, landing lightly on the grey carpet. 'May I?' She took the receiver. She said yes and no and ummm a few times, then, softly: 'Night, Stan-l-e-y.'

She handed the phone back with a teenager's secret smile, disturbing an unresolved debate Jacko was having with himself.

'OK,' he said, forcing himself to sound official. 'Book yourself into a guesthouse. And Stan . . .' He'd made up his mind and changed his voice to friendly. '. . . I'll see you at 7.45 a.m. outside that cottage.'

He replaced the receiver. A trickle of relief began to run through him but he didn't really know why yet; just that it was a good feeling. He looked at Shirley. 'Home and get some sleep.' They gave each other tired smiles.

Philippe opened the door, smirking as she passed him. 'Sweet dreams.' Her cheeks flushed ripe red.

He shut it and cocked his head to one side, impishly. 'You don't think she and Stan are up to some Gawf . . .'

'Hard to say,' said Jacko, grinning. 'But we'll have to remember to get him a bottle of Johnson's Baby Oil.'

Philippe's laughter left him doubled up, hands at his groin, a schoolboy in need of a pee. Ridgeback smiled half-heartedly.

Jacko's beam subsided into a smile. 'You all right, son?'

'Just a bit knackered.'

Jacko studied a forlorn face drained of all energy and enthusiasm. 'Off to bed, too.'

Ridgeback left after a muttered goodnight, awkward, almost embarrassed. Jacko nodded at the closed door, frowning.

Philippe gave a mournful headshake. 'While he was sniffing round the car-park, he saw his old canine partner, the one he was with when he lost his dog. He's got that old feeling. He wants to go back to Dogs Section.'

Jacko nodded, understandingly.

While Philippe fetched more machine coffee, Jacko phoned Control and passed on the numbers of Holden's Fiesta and Maureen's Peugeot. 'Locate but don't intercept,' he ordered. He asked, too, for the make and number of any car Maureen had owned before her nearly new Peugeot.

The pathologist phoned as they were sipping their plastic cups. 'Sorry it's taken so long. They're giving Hegan a thorough check after what happened to our boy Heald.'

He rattled through the hot out-of-the-stomach details: 'Virtually empty, contents normal. First blood tests negative. You can rule out an OD. Could be kidney obstruction, though he's a bit young for a stone. The scan found nothing. A bad dose of dyspepsia probably. He's been under a lot of strain.'

Haven't we all? Jacko wanted to say, but didn't.

'They're keeping him in a private side room overnight,' the doctor continued. 'Unless there are complications he could be released about 11 a.m. after morning rounds.'

'Could he be swinging the lead?'

'A possibility, I suppose,' said the doctor, unsure.

Jacko said goodnight and thanks and the same to Philippe, who promised to relieve him at 7.15 next morning.

He walked alone through a maze of corridors and up a flight of newly scrubbed steps. Two armed officers sat outside the side room. Each checked his warrant card, putting on a show for him.

Inside, the bed light was on. Head propped up on three pillows, Hegan lay listening to the radio through earphones. He looked beyond his raised knees, scowling as if irked by the intrusion. His right hand was cuffed to an invalid's rail bracketed to the cream wall, a black-framed bed pushed next to it.

Haywood sat inside the door on a chair with metal legs. His tunic top hung on the back of it. His pistol was holstered at his left armpit. His tie was down. His chin and cheeks were stubbled. 'Everything all right?'

'Fine.' Jacko turned to Hegan. 'How are you?'

He pulled the earphones down round his neck but didn't answer.

Jacko tried again. 'The doc says you'll be OK.'

Hegan chewed his tongue, digesting the information.

'Do you think you'll make court in the morning?'

He swallowed.

'Do you want me to cancel for you?'

'Let's wait and see.' A supercilious smile.

'I can always get the trial adjourned till Monday.'

'I should be able to make it.' Hegan lifted his bottom up, raising his head higher on his pillows.

'Then you'll be able to make the inquest, too.'

'What inquest?' Hegan was all attention now.

Jacko turned back to Haywood. 'Doesn't he know he's due at the Heald inquest?'

'I was going to tell him tomorrow. He's got to . . .'

'When?' Hegan was sitting up, full of urgent notice.

'Four thirty when . . .' said Jacko.

'Where?' Hegan's questions were coming out so fast that answers were left hanging.

'In the cellblock. Seems convenient.'

Hegan snaked his legs straight between the sheet and green top cover, his bottom sliding down, head lower, deeper in the pillows.

Jacko said goodnight from the door. Haywood winked. Hegan put the plugs in his ears.

Walking back down the stairs and the corridors, Jacko let his mind ramble again, going back over a month's work, mentally examining his check-list.

He found Upjohn's relief, a chief inspector, in a rapid response car half hidden in a row of ambulances. 'Full armed alert will be maintained,' the chief assured him.

Jacko was unassured. If Hegan's outlaws ever met up with Upjohn's posse, he knew for certain that the Randolph Scott rules would not apply and someone would wind up as dead as Ridgeback's poor old dog.

He walked towards his pool car to collect his toilet bag. He let his thoughts drift back to the questions floating around his head all night, continuing the debate, trying to make some sense of it, reach a decision.

Technically, he admitted, Stan's right about Heald's death. He wasn't pointing me away from New York and Maureen Beckby. He genuinely thinks the Carl Marsh lead is the strongest in solving the Heald mystery.

It was coming together. He's right. Heald's death had nothing to do with Hegan, his nark or his money. Stan's had his eye on a different ball, that's all, kicking towards a different goal. He's never guessed that Scott and me are really using Heald's death as a cover to find Hegan's police informant and cash.

Crash. The clues collided. A complete line of ticks. Housey-Housey. He'd hit the jackpot. He felt like a millionaire. All he had to do now was to work out a way of collecting his prize; of creeping out of the long grass unseen and make his killing.

22

Friday. D-Day.

What, Jacko sometimes idly wondered, does the D stand for in D-Day?

Decision? Departure? Disaster? Death?

Dawn on 4D-Day and the sun rose reluctantly with half-opened eye. Slowly it shed the dark blanket of night but stayed hidden beneath white cotton sheets.

It was not to be one of those spectacular Fenland sunrises, a sailor's sunrise, stretching as far as the eye can see.

The reeds in the creeks, the scrub willow in the dunes, the rushes in the long straight dykes tilted welcoming heads towards it, only to be cruelly rebuffed by a harsh breeze bringing rain clouds from the North Sea.

A gust picked up a rotting door to an outhouse at Michael's Pub, where Bryan Holden lay dead, crashing it against a brick wall, putting the gulls on the chimney stacks to frightened flight.

The sun found a gap in the clouds and the floral curtains of a guesthouse six miles away to nudge Stan Young awake to face the day his future would be decided.

Briefly, it looked in on Ridgeback clipping on a yellow bow tie to match his new suit and polished brown shoes. The dapper detective he'd look, for his final day in CID.

Across the valley Shirley had bathed with Oil of Orchid, a Boots special offer, and dabbed herself dry on a thick pink towel.

In a terraced house close to the castle Mo Mercer sat on the toilet, his second visit already, his underpants round his ankles. In the kitchen Layton snapped into place the final part of the rifle Mo would use from the top of the castle wall. He put it on the newspaper-covered table next to the revolver he would carry with him down the ladder.

At intervals of a mile or so two vans and a car brought six men up the Great North Road. In the back of each van was a sawn-off shot-gun.

On the shores of the Wash Rod Daniels ran through the dunes, effortlessly now, after a month of short, sharp, shock treatment.

In the roomy old vicarage that was home, the Little Fat Man was already on the phone. Jumped-Up John had showered after his jog and slowly ate his muesli. Major Jarman, the district coroner, wolfed streaky bacon and Lincolnshire pork sausage. He spooned another sugar into his second cup of coffee, lit his second cigarette and turned to the cricket page (never the law reports) in *The Times*.

After a boring night patrolling the hospital grounds, Corporal, a police alsatian, sniffed, cocked his leg up against the corner of a creosoted shed and growled happily to himself as he pawed more divots out of his handler's patchy lawn.

Roger Haywood stood, stretched and tugged the puffy pouches beneath his eyes with forefinger and thumb, running them down each side of his nose to rub his prickly chin with the palm of his hand. Hegan opened his eyes, looked at him, turned with a heave of his body, crooked his head on his right shoulder and went back to sleep.

Carl Marsh stood in the queue at the hotplate. The rapist had breakfast delivered to his cell. The child abuser raised his skeletal body on a sore elbow and took his Turnotoxin pill with a noisy gulp of tepid water.

Philippe's silver, super-charged Fiat flashed by the old country house headquarters of the East Midlands Combined Constabulary, devouring the A46 alley of death at a steady seventy, squinting as the sun burst out from behind the speeding clouds.

On a British Midlands plane Maureen Beckby was five minutes into her flight to Belfast, viewing an arctic scene, the sun shining, blindingly bright, reflecting on a lumpy carpet of virgin white, paining her eyes, so she closed them and thought of their future together. An apartment, overlooking Central Park, maybe, with all mod-cons, but no dog. Michael feared nothing apart from dogs.

Great Tom o' Lincoln gave residents, guests in the White Hart and the judge in his lodgings their seven o'clock call.

If you've just climbed between the sheets, like the two brown doctors and the black nurse after a gruelling hospital night shift, then tough-titty, Jacko grumbled to himself.

148

All night he had tossed and turned on a hard couch in the hospital cubbyhole office. Knowing, as every detective knows, is one thing. Proving is another. His neck was stiff. His lips were dry. He was desperate for a cigarette.

He'd just got off – or so it seemed – when the chimes awoke him in the sort of mood that, if he'd been a child, would have resulted in his teddy being tossed out of the cot.

He groped for his specs on the desk. He put on yesterday's shirt over yesterday's underpants, yawning loudly, drowning the seventh chime.

Bloody bells, sodding sun, he thought, exhausted already.

'Hop in,' said Jacko, pushing open the passenger door of his pool car.

Stan got out of his. 'Where are we going?'

'Door-knocking in Little Apple.'

Jacko watched the cottage and Stan's parked car getting smaller in his driving mirror. Then, eyes front, he gave his head a sorrowful shake. 'You've been bedding Maureen Beckby, haven't you, you randy little rabbit?'

'No.' Stan's reply came out with a jerk of his knees.

'Lying sod. Holden as good as told me.' It was an exaggeration he'd practised in his sleepless hours.

'When?'

'When Shirl and me saw him back there.' He jolted back his head in the direction of the cottage.

'Oh, shit. She knows.'

'No, she doesn't. I only spotted it because he also tried to drop you in it when I saw him with Ridgeback. He hasn't twigged either.'

'Who knows?'

'Only me.' A lie. Scott did. 'Come on, mate. I need to know.'

Stan threw his head back against the rest, 'It was a long time ago. Soon after Hegan opened Michael's Pub. All four of us used to meet up there. One night she threw me a look you wouldn't believe.' Jacko did. 'Three knife and fork jobs later, well . . .' He shrugged. 'Only lasted a month.'

'What went wrong?'

'Upjohn had me on the carpet. Said Holden had complained. Reckoned it was jeopardizing a security op. He warned me off.'

'Did she ever pump you for info?'

'Such as?'

'Movements of money, availability of weapons?'

'Never.' Sincere, shocked almost. 'Honest.'

'Spoken to her since?'

'Not for two years. Since I was taken off the case.'

They went through it all again in greater detail but it amounted to no more than a fling between two adult single people. 'OK,' said Jacko, satisfied. 'Mum's the word.' He gave him a snide smile. 'Did the earth move?'

'Like humping a bag of early potatoes,' said Stan, screwing his face.

Rush hour in New York, Lincs. A trailer-load of heaped and steaming manure blocks a minor road when its tractor breaks down, causing a two-car tailback. Both drivers fume.

Jacko latched the wooden gate of a flower-filled garden behind him and walked back towards the crossroads where Stan was to meet him outside the white-clad Post Office across from the chapel. They had split up the left-overs from the house-to-house canvass, Stan taking the car to the outlying ones, Jacko on foot round the crossroads.

Some of the omissions were logically explained. They'd either died or moved after the voters' register had been printed. Jacko was beginning to fret that he had misread it, was wasting his time. He had only one more call to make, a bungalow, where earlier there'd been no reply.

A man turned the corner from the main road, an alsatian at his side, heading towards the empty bungalow.

Jacko appraised the dog first. It walked low and slow, in the way his own dog did when she'd been scolded. Its black and tan coat was fine-haired, clean and shiny. Its gait, he realized, was due to age-stiffened joints and he recognized it as a bitch which had been cared for to beyond the normal life-span for its pedigree breed.

'Excuse me, sir.' Jacko called across the narrow lane.

'Morning.' Age had slowed his step. He seemed happy to rest. He'd be seventy, Jacko guessed, with most of those years spent outdoors. A black showerproof hung on a broad frame, his back tent-pole straight. An old soldier, if ever he saw one.

'You don't happen to be . . .' He looked down at his list. 'Mr Washington?'

Mr Washington nodded.

Jacko crossed the lane, introducing himself as he did so. The dog, untethered, strolled forward to smell his own pet's scent on his grey suit trousers. He looked down at her, clucking his tongue.

'I'm here inquiring into events on July the 23rd almost two years ago. I know it's a long time but it was Fergie's wedding day and . . .'

'The day the police alsatian was shot.'

'You do remember it?'

'Of course. I've been following the trial. Dreadful business.'

He cast his mind back, relating his movements, not to the royal wedding, but to walks with his dog. 'She's May, by the way.' Jacko, quite naturally, said hallo.

'I always take her out around eight in the morning, at lunchtime and before turning in, rain or shine. I saw a bit of the police activity but only found out what had happened via village gossip next day. We never go past Michael's Pub because May doesn't like the main road too much, do you, May?'

The dog did not deny or confirm it.

'And we've only ever been in once. The place was empty. Still wouldn't let me take her in. Said he didn't like dogs. Never been back, have we, May?'

'See any strangers about that day, any vehicles acting oddly?' asked Jacko.

He thought deeply, then shook his head severely. 'Nothing suspicious. I did have a friendly chat with a couple of Yanks. We get a few. One was taking lots of pictures. You know what they're like.' A shrugging delivery, long-suffering, non-complaining. 'He even took a couple of May and me outside the Post Office.'

He inclined his head in the direction of the shop. 'He promised to send us one but he didn't, did he, May?' Only his face registered disappointment.

'What else did he take?' asked Jacko, half-heartedly, losing interest.

'Anything and everything.'

'The pub?'

'Can't say. They'd have to pass it, though, on the road to

Boston. That's where they said they were bound. For tea, they said.'

Jacko laughed. 'When was this?'

'On our lunchtime walk.'

Jacko went over it again, got nothing extra. They were in a car but Mr Washington was one of those people who didn't know one make from another. 'On a golfing trip. Travelled miles all through Ireland and Scotland, they said.'

'Had they played Woodhall?'

'Yes.'

'That morning?'

'Yes. Very impressed, they were.' Mr Washington paused, puzzled. 'I've told the police all this before, you know.'

'When?'

'A few days later.'

'Who did you speak to?'

'Constable Cross.'

Jacko frowned deeply. 'How do you remember that after all this time?'

'He gave me his name at the time but I promptly forgot it. I only recalled it this week when I read his evidence in the *Echo*. He was that constable whose dog was shot. He told me that himself. Very upset, he was. It must be him. Quite young, reddish hair. Am I right?'

Jacko parked on the black asphalt approach to the chalet-style clubhouse with timber tiles and a backdrop of tall pines.

Humbler was a wooden cabin by the first tee which served as the professional's shop. He looked down the fairway as he walked from the car. It was lush green from the recent rain with drifts of purple heather each side and yellow gorse and broom. Behind them, spinneys of silver birch and woods of dark fir trees. Beyond the raised tee, the eighteenth green, like velvet, short, smooth; no bent grasses irritatingly sticking up to disfigure it.

He threaded his way through stands of clubs and huge, uncarriable bags to the counter.

Yes, sir, said the young assistant, they did keep records of visitors in their green fees book. He thumbed through a thick leather-bound ledger to the date Jacko gave.

'This must be them. They were second off.' He ran his finger further down that day's entries. 'They were our only visitors from American clubs that day.'

Jacko noted their names and the Long Island club they played at.

Now he had a reason for phoning his great police mate in Big Apple.

A great mystery in Jacko's life, though it never troubled him, was why they called Blackie Le Grande Blackie.

He wasn't black. Neither was he white. His big happy face was the olive colour of an overripe Conference pear, skin pitted by hailstones.

Just thinking about him brought a smile to his face. He was smiling now, as he drove alone back to Lincoln after dropping a fully-briefed Stan outside Holden's cottage.

They'd met ten years earlier. Jacko, between marriages, had taken a WPC to Venice. Blackie was doing Europe with his second wife.

They had booked into the same hotel, sandstone with green shutters, near the Rialto Bridge. In the bar, Blackie overheard Jacko and the policewoman talking about Newark, where he was then stationed as a sergeant.

The first words Jacko ever heard him slur were, 'Don't talk about that asshole of a place.'

The geographical misunderstanding sorted out, they each discovered the other was a policeman. From then on, in a place that seemed to go to sleep at eleven, they never got to bed till four.

The following year, with no one to take on holiday, Jacko went to New York to spend two weeks in Blackie's hovel of an apartment, recently vacated by his wife.

He was two inches taller than Jacko, three stones heavier, never wore a tie and his shirt often hung out of his straining waist-band. His black hair had thinned to the skin down the centre of his large round head. His eyes were black, always happy.

He was a detective sergeant with Robbery. His captain gave him permission to take Jacko out on a shift. It started at four on a Friday, the thirteenth, during a freezing February from a station as hot and as dirty as a steam train.

It ended just past midnight with a chase on the rooftop of a dingy hotel near Times Square whose receptionist had reported a guest held up at gunpoint. Blackie and his partner drew their weapons. Jacko, unarmed, lagged way behind, noting the positions of the chimney pots as places to hide if the shooting started. 'You can stuff this for a job,' said Jacko, shaking as he drank Jack Daniels afterwards.

The year after, Blackie visited Newark, Notts, and worked a shift with Jacko, questioning a gang of pros caught shop lifting. The sight and sound of a real New York cop secured full confessions and ten TICs, the biggest pinch of the week. 'Beats New Jersey,' Blackie declared.

They had not seen each other since. They passed on the news of their marriages in scribbled notes on the blank pages of Christmas cards. Blackie's came as a P.S. to a string of obscenities on the flip side of a picture of a robin red-breast.

On occasions, drunk at parties, they felt compelled to communicate on the host's phone in a set routine.

'This is your transatlantic operator,' the caller would begin. 'Testing. Testing. Please repeat after me. One, two, three, four.'

'One, two, three, four,' the solemn answer would come.

'I cannot eat my currant bun.'

'I cannot eat my currant bun.'

'Well, stick it up your arse then.'

It never failed to convulse them in long, happy laughter.

In the incident room, Jacko looked up his number in his little red book, dialled painstakingly. It rang for a full minute. He closed his eyes. Let him be in, dear Lord.

The ringing stopped. 'Errrrrrrrrr . . .'

'Mr Le Grande, this is your transatlantic operator . . .'

'Errrrrrrr.'

'Please repeat after . . .'

'Who the fuck?' He'd forgotten the routine.

'Blackie, it's me. Jacko. From Robinhoodsville.'

'What the fuck?'

'Blackie, I need your help.'

'Hold.'

Jacko visualized him rolling upright in bed, scratching his hairy belly under the white T-shirt he always wore. My Paul Newman vest, he called it. Women, he claimed, went crazy to see him in it.

'Have you any idea what time it is, you cock-sucking mother-fucker?'

Oh, good, Jacko thought, delighted. He remembers me. I must remember to tell that court story, but not now. 'Sorry.'

'I've only been in bed two hours, for christsake. Where are you?'

'In Lincoln, England, with a problem. I need you to track down two fellows who may have taken some pictures after a big robbery.'

'Where?'

'New York.'

'Are you pulling my pecker?'

Another geographical misunderstanding sorted out, he took down the names of the two touring golfers and their club, the dates and places of the bank robbery and Hegan's escape.

'What am I looking for?'

'Pictures of the village pub, if they took any.'

'Name?'

'Michael's Pub.'

'Certain to.'

'Why?'

'Two boys from here won't pass that by. They'd dine out on it. There's an in-place here with the same name. Woody Allen plays his liquorice stick there every Monday night.'

'Why didn't you take me, then?' asked Jacko, reproachfully.

'Why go listen to a white Jewish comic-cum-clarinettist play New Orleans when you can get genyouine grass down the road?'

He gave his throaty forty Lucky Strikes a day laugh. 'Leave it to me, shithead.'

23

Three police cars, lights blinking, swept into the castle car-park like limos bringing stars to collect their Oscars. The middle one drew up outside the cellblock entrance. Haywood jumped out, dragging Hegan in handcuffs with him, running inside, the doors slamming shut as they vanished from view.

Hands in pockets, Jacko sauntered down the stone steps from the terrace as Upjohn and Shirley got out of the lead car.

Upjohn pinched his shoulder blades together, throwing out his chest, a satisfied sort of stretch. 'I think we can record this as a false alarm.'

'With good intent,' said Shirley quickly.

He looked at Jacko, a small smile on his lips. 'Not having the best of luck, are you, Jackson?'

'We'll get there.' A carefree shrug.

'Why are you all so wrapped up in Hegan? He's my pinch.'

'He's also heavily involved in our inquiries into Andy Heald's death.' Jacko was certain now that he wasn't, was sure Stan had been right. He wasn't about to share these doubts with Jumped-Up.

'What made you think a break was on?'

'He had an unexpected visitor yesterday.'

'Put two and two together and made five, did you?' A gloating grin.

'What about the return trip?'

'If there is one,' said Upjohn, indifferently. 'My view is that he'll walk.' He paused. 'Thanks to your mate Young.'

Shirley bit the inside of her lower lip.

'The risk's gone,' Upjohn continued. 'If there ever was a plot, we'll have scared them away. We can't go on providing this level of protection.' He turned to Shirley, bowed slightly, touched his peaked cap with a finger. 'I'll see you again soon, I hope.'

They stood together and watched him strut back to his car, where the driver held open a back door.

'What a plonker.' Shirley hissed rather than sighed. 'You know, when we left the hospital in convoy, it was all he could do to stop himself winding down his window and hollering "Wagons Ho."'

From the rear car, Philippe joined them. 'What happened at the hospital?' Jacko asked him.

'Clean bill. He got a lecture about eating properly to avoid ulcers. Fish, the consultant recommended.'

'Maybe Maureen will drop by with some smoked salmon,' said Shirley, caustically. Then, softly, 'How's Stan?'

'Fine. Sends his love.' Jacko made that up, to please her. It worked. She smiled radiantly.

'Where's Ridgeback?' asked Philippe.

'At the station, typing up a statement. I've got to nip back there to take an important call.'

'And me?' asked Shirley.

He looked at her, still smiling at him.

She'd do it, he decided. It was dangerous, but he knew she'd do it. 'I'll have a little job for you soon.'

'You're half way there, Limey.' Blackie Le Grande didn't even say hallo.

The manager of the golf club had risen from bed and, Blackie claimed, obligingly tapped into his membership list after being told, 'You don't wanna visit from Vice, da'yer?'

The first home number was answered by a drowsy Wall Street high-flier, equally co-operative when told, 'You don't wanna a visit from Commercial Fraud, da'yer?'

Jacko was laughing again. New York detectives, he'd noted, strive to maintain and enhance their screen image. He only believed half Blackie ever told him but he told the other half well . . .

'Remember?' asked Bill O'Keefe. 'Will I ever forget?'

He'd taken several photos in New York, England, including Michael's Pub. 'Pity they weren't in black and white with a bit of Gershwin in the background. I'd have outdone Woody Allen. Haven't looked at them lately, though I know where they are, stored in a grocery box.'

He was bringing the box into his office where he'd meet Blackie at seven thirty, one thirty Jacko's time.

'What am I looking for?' asked Blackie.

Jacko looked down at the telex Control Room had sent overnight. 'An old Triumph sports car, blue, black soft top.' He gave the ten-year-old number of the car Maureen Beckby used to own and descriptions of both her and Holden.

'How am I going to get this stuff to you, if it's any use?'

Jacko never addressed his mind to technical problems. 'Dunno. Fax is a bit fudgy with photos.'

'How about wiring them?'

Jacko was technologically thick, hanging on, muddling through to retirement, praying people wouldn't discover just how thick. He played for time. 'It's possible, I suppose.'

'Course it's possible, you asshole. Does that one-horse town have a newspaper?'

'An evening.'

'Give 'em a call and ask 'em to use their receiver. I'll zip up to the *Daily News* with the negs. They'll transmit.'

'How long?'

Blackie calculated ten minutes to print, half an hour to open a line and then he'd have to get to 42nd Street in the rush hour. 'You should have them around two thirty.'

'Today?'

'J-e-e-sus. Da'yer still deliver by stagecoach over there? 'Course I fucking mean today. Call you from Swindle Street.' He didn't say goodbye.

Hegan was sitting in the dock when the jury filed in ninety minutes late. 'A technical hitch,' the judge told them in what passed for an apology for the delay.

He resumed his summing-up where he had left off the evening before and continued fluently without a break until just before half-past one. The judge told the jury that refreshments would be brought to them by ushers who took solemn oaths to keep them incommunicado. After they had trooped out, laden with bundles of documents and maps, the judge glanced up at the clock. 'I shall not be taking any verdict before two thirty at the earliest.'

Jacko walked slowly through the foyer. Lunchtime and knackered already, he thought. Sleep was more than a necessity to him. He had to average forty hours in a working week or he worried about collapsing from nervous exhaustion. He began working out how many hours the week owed him.

Ahead of him the reporter in the blazer who looked as though he should have been covering a rugby match collected a bag from the security desk. Jacko followed him in front of the ivy-clad building to the wall which overlooked the car-park where a black Austin van was stationed near the narrow exit.

By the terrace wall, he stopped and took out a portable phone which sang a synthetic song as he punched in a number.

Jacko walked past him down the steps.

*

Rush hour in New York, New York. Worker ants scramble out of their holes underground, a million on the move, busy, hungry. Between their streaming columns, yellow cabs, crawling like worker bees, secrete their fumes.

Thirty floors above, a mosaic of its namesake is scattered on one desk top; all there is to see and still desk space to spare. A Post Office with a brilliant white door that made its stucco look grey. A church with sharp lines softened by deep windows with rounded tops. A big house with one brown bay at the end of a curved drive with bushes, tall, thick and deep green either side. A proud old man and an adoring dog. Michael's Pub.

'Bingo, baby,' Blackie Le Grande sang into Jacko's ear as he described them, concentrating on the last in the set. 'Two straight-on shots, just windows, a door and a hedge. Nothing on the move. Next scene is side on. An English rose in a clapped-out blue sports car.'

A shudder of excitement ran through Jacko.

'The number you gave me,' Blackie went on. 'Above her, the pub sign. Same scene *sans* girl. Same scene *avec* girl again.' Jacko knew that Blackie regarded himself as a great linguist. 'Two more shots similar to the start of the sequence. That's it. What da'yer make of it?'

Jacko held the phone in his left hand, his chin in his right, looking down at the scenes of crime photos laid out in front of him.

Nothing. That's what he made of it. His excitement drained away.

It proves she went that lunchtime after she heard police were looking for Hegan. So what? She'd claim she had taken a quick look round and left. Nothing.

Depressed, Jacko described the ground-floor windows with the 'Closed' sign, the 'Open at 5.30' advert, the empty vase and the gap in the curtains. 'What's in yours?'

'I need a blow-up job for that.' A salacious laugh.

Incoherent coversation ended with him saying, 'Have a word with Bill while I find a magnifier.'

'Yes, sir,' said Bill as polite as a golf club assistant, 'these photos were definitely taken that lunchtime after our morning round. I've checked my score card souvenir. It's got the date on it.'

He remembered a sports car driving up to the pub while he

was taking shots with his new Nikon. 'A bit annoying, really. I wanted the pix to have that deserted Marie Celeste atmosphere, a sort of comparison scene with Manhattan. Big Apple v. Little Apple. She was in and out of the place in no time.'

He chatted amiably about his trip until he said, 'Here he comes.'

Sudden silence.

'Right,' said Blackie at last. Silence again. Then a long low whistle.

'You've done it, you old bastard. You have cracked it.' His sentences were finishing higher and faster than they started. 'That Guinness clock. In the last two pictures, I've got what you've got – five thirty. But in the first two it says eleven.'

'Are you sure?' Jacko closed his eyes to refocus them.

More mumbled conversation as he cross-checked the sequence in which the photos were taken. 'He's positive. The clock showed eleven before she arrived; five thirty after she left.'

'We've got her, Blackie.'

'She altered the clock.'

'We've got her, mate.' Jacko nearly sang the reprise.

'She went in and altered the clock. In Technicolor.'

'She altered the fucking clock.'

They yipped at each other, laughed with each other, a pair of rowdies on a spree. Jacko rattled off his requests for the photos he wanted on the wire.

'Do you want me to impound the camera?' asked Blackie mischievously. 'To exhibit in the Black Museum at Scotland Yard? This has got to be the greatest case of transatlantic detection since Crippen. Were you on that, by the way?'

They talked of their families for a few minutes, making promises to see each other soon that both knew would be hard to keep. Finally, Jacko said, 'Thanks, mate.'

'Go stick your prick in your ear,' said Blackie. A click cut short his raucous laughter.

'This job,' Jacko said, hesitantly. 'You can turn it down if you don't fancy it.' His eyes were downcast. He fingered his soiled shirt collar.

'What is it?' Shirley sat so close to him in the theatre bar that he could smell her Oil of Orchid.

From an inside pocket, he withdrew three warrants he had just sworn before a magistrate and handed them to her, still avoiding her inquisitive eyes.

She read them with a mild frown. They were for the arrest of Maureen Beckby and for searches of the cottage and Michael's Pub. She looked up at him and cocked her head, quizzically. 'What's going on?'

Out of a box file, he lifted a set of photos, ten by eight, in black and white, still warm and curved by the drying drum at the *Echo* building down by the marina. Heads close together, they studied them, Jacko explaining his theories and his plan in great detail, talking softly.

Her eyes glinted. Her cheeks glowed. 'Wonderful.' She gave him a wonderful smile. 'Why so glum?'

'If I'm right, it's not without risk. I can't be there myself. I'm committed to this inquest.' A genuine but lame-sounding excuse. 'I owe it to the coroner.'

'And to Andy's family,' she said, briskly.

He felt a cop-out and it must have shown.

'You must go,' she added, urgently. 'We've all worked so hard. You owe it to Stan, too, to prove him right.'

Jacko brightened just a little. 'You'd be watched over but, well, there may be blind spots. There's always a danger in an operation like this.'

'Will it help Stan?'

Don't play on their affection for each other, he ordered himself. 'It's too late to affect the outcome of Hegan's trial.'

'Will it help him?' She spoke impatiently.

'There's some risk to him, too. He's a professional policeman. He gets paid to take them. You're, well, not . . .'

'What do you take me for?' She looked at him, very crossly. 'Some typing pool bimbo? Will it help him?'

'Yes,' he was finally forced to say.

'Then, of course, I'll do it.'

24

Upjohn's blue BMW glided to a halt outside Holden's cottage. Shirley got out of a white pool car where she waited with Stan Young.

Upjohn wound down the window. 'Mr Scott arrived?'

'A major incident's cropped up,' said Shirley, pleasantly. 'We're to go ahead without him.'

'And do what?'

'Didn't he tell you?' She sounded surprised.

Upjohn shook his head, annoyed.

'We think your missing two million is in there.' Shirley nodded towards the cottage. 'Since it was your operation, Mr Scott thought you ought to be here. Out of courtesy.'

'Shouldn't we be armed?'

'No point. No one's in. Come on. We've got a warrant.' She walked away from him. Stan climbed out, opened the boot, removing a crowbar.

Upjohn, in full uniform, did not even acknowledge Stan's presence. He left his peaked cap sitting regally on the back seat of his car, got out, locked up and joined the procession up the garden path.

The whisky fumes hit them as soon as the Yale lock surrendered to the crowbar and the door shot back against the leather armchair in front of the lounge window.

'Good God,' Upjohn muttered. He stood motionless. Stan went ahead into the kitchen and then up the creaking stairs to the bedrooms.

Shirley pulled a face as she looked down at an empty bottle of Bells on its side in front of the fireplace. 'Someone's been knocking it back.'

She walked on into the kitchen where she started opening drawers while Upjohn's suspicious brown eyes circled the room. He picked up the crowbar Stan had abandoned on an arm of the chair in front of the window. Absently, he slapped it in the palm of his left hand.

A floorboard above groaned. 'Up here,' Stan called.

She ran up the stairs. Upjohn, taking two steps at a time, was right behind as she reached the tiny landing.

All three crowded into a cramped front bedroom with maroon curtains faded almost pink, wood-chip wallpaper, dusty cream, and women's clothing scattered on a double bed covered by a candy-striped duvet.

There were two low chests of drawers, pine veneer. On one stood a musical jewellery box, lid up and empty. Above, a long, narrow wall mirror. Below, two drawers fully out and rifled. The other chest looked undisturbed. 'Hope there's not been a break-in,' said Stan, examining the window.

Shirley crossed the landing to a smaller room, a storeroom really, where she found a big wardrobe that matched the chests. The door was opened. She parted the clothing which hung on hangers, wire for all of his, padded plastic and wood for what was left of hers.

'Whoever heard of a burglar who only took female stuff?' she said across the landing. 'And only summer stuff, too. She's off to warmer climes.'

Upjohn pulled hard on an ear.

'Come on.' Shirley spoke bossily with a little wave at Stan. 'He will take take care of this. We've another call to make.'

Jacko glanced at the clock on the wall: 3.55. The jury had been out for two and a half hours. A woman usher led them in procession from legally imposed purdah. They were sitting in their box when Hegan emerged into view.

He seemed to study their faces, desperately seeking a tell-tale glance in his direction, Jacko guessed. It is part of courtroom folklore that if the jury look at the defendant on their return from retirement they are about to bring in a not guilty verdict. It is a fallible guide. Nowadays, he'd noticed, some women jurors who have sat through sex cases bestial beyond their belief give the man in the dock a bold, unblinking stare which says, 'Now you're the one about to be stuffed, pervert.'

All twelve sat with eyes on their exhibits. The court stood as the judge entered and the jurors fixed their eyes on him as he bowed to them. In the course of the week, Jacko sensed, they had come to respect and admire him. Most juries do. Most juries are right.

Everyone sat, apart from Hegan and Haywood in the dock, and the clerk at his desk below the bench who said, 'Will the foreman please stand?'

He turned out to be a florid-faced, bulky man with a black bushy beard, more at home standing at a real-ale bar than by the bar of British justice.

'Has the jury reached a verdict on which you are all agreed?' asked the clerk.

'Yes,' said the foreman without a trace of nerves.

The clerk looked down at the indictment typed on paper so wide he had to hold it in both hands like a newspaper. 'And how say you to the charge – guilty or not?'

'Where now?' Upjohn asked as he trailed Shirley down the garden path.

'Michael's Pub.'

He slowed. 'We can't.'

'We've got a warrant.' Shirley spoke over her left shoulder which tilted slightly under the weight of the bag hanging at her hip.

'We can't go blundering into a man's home in the middle of his trial.' Upjohn caught her up at the pool car.

'A magistrate's warrant says we can.' Shirley addressed him over the roof as she opened the driver's door. She got in and opened the passenger door.

'What about mine?' He glanced towards his BMW.

'I've got to come back for Sergeant Young. I'll drop you off.'

He climbed in, leaning forward to put the crowbar on the car floor. 'Hegan's solicitors will play hell.'

Shirley turned the ignition. 'Jacko reckons once the jury's out it doesn't matter.'

'What the hell does he know?'

'And Chief Superintendent Scott, too,' she added. She smiled at his silence. 'Wonder if the jury's back?'

She lifted a handset phone from the rubber mat beside her feet and dumped it in his lap. A black wire ran from it to the cigarette lighter. 'Give Philippe – er, Marlowe a ring.'

He hugged the handset. 'What's this about?'

She lugged the shoulder bag which she had placed between

them on to her lap and opened it. She felt beyond a thick
address book and a thicker paperback book to find the warrant.

Upjohn released one hand to take it from her. 'Purpose of
search,' he read. 'Suspicion of stolen goods.'

She put the bag back between them, fastened her seat belt
and drove off the grass verge with a bump.

'What stolen goods?' he asked, nonplussed. 'No one has lived
there for two years.'

'That's the whole point. Jacko can't work out why Hegan was
prepared to sell it at below his own valuation two years ago but
hasn't put it on the market since.'

'He was abroad.'

'He's been back six months.' Shirley had worked smoothly
through the gears and settled for a steady forty. 'He's had
Bryan Holden looking after personal matters; yet he's done
nothing to cash his most valuable asset. Think about it.'

Upjohn thought about it, appearing to get nowhere.

'What better place for the money?' Shirley said in a prompting
way. 'Wait till forensics have turned it inside out, then go back
and hide it. No one would think of looking there again.'

'But he's been overseas or in jail ever since his getaway.'

'Not Maureen and Holden, though.' She glanced left and
smirked.

Upjohn hugged the handset closer to his stomach. 'Good
God.'

'Are you going to use that bloody thing?' she asked, sharply.
He gave her a dull, confused look. 'The phone.' She nodded
down. 'Hegan's your case. I'd like to know the verdict, too.
Besides, we ought to tell Marlowe that Maureen's done a bunk.'

He placed the phone on clamped-together knees, tapped out
the direct line number which Shirley dictated, gave a summary
of what they'd found at the cottage, then listened to what
Philippe had to say.

'What?' He contorted his face, bringing down his trimmed
black brows. 'His?' Finally, 'It doesn't make sense.'

Shirley detected the conversation was coming to an end.
'What was the verdict?'

Upjohn relayed her question and Philippe's answer. 'Not in
yet.' He clipped back the receiver and studied it.

'What doesn't make sense?' asked Shirley.

His mind seemed miles away, on another wavelength.

'What doesn't make sense?' Shirley repeated, sharper still.

'Traffic have located Holden's car at the airport hotel at East Midlands International.'

'Guilty,' said the foreman, firmly. Hegan shot him a stare of undisguised hostility.

The prosecutor called the sharp-suited Inspector Jack Penson to the witness box to give evidence of antecedents.

Jacko always found it fascinating to watch a jury in the moments that follow. In his time he had seen them clear a rapist who had to remain in the dock to be sentenced for lesser, admitted offences. When the police officer read his record which included two long sentences for sex crimes, one woman juror started to sob. Why was beyond him. She had done her sworn duty. She had adjudicated on the strength of the case against him, not his past, of which she knew nothing. The time to weep, he always thought, was when new evidence proved the convicted innocent.

Against that, overwhelming relief spreads across their faces, as it was sweeping over them now, when they find they were indisputably right.

Hegan, said Inspector Penson, reading from a thick file, was born William Roberts in Belfast. His record started with juvenile joyriding and ended in eighteen years on two charges of attempted murder following a Post Office robbery.

Relief turned to astonishment as the jurors worked out he should have been inside till the turn of the century.

The defence QC solved the puzzle for them. 'Is it correct that eighteen months into that sentence he was released as a result of assistance he was able to afford the authorities?'

Understanding faces now. A freed supergrass, a gunman whom the government had let loose on their streets.

His counsel did his well-paid best in his mitigation speech. 'Alone, friendless and at risk in an alien world . . . the only method he had known since boyhood of solving financial problems.' He pleaded with the judge not to make the sentence so long that he would be denied all hope of ever leading a normal life.

Judges have heard it all before. 'Despite your record,' he said, 'some four years ago, for what I'm sure were valid reasons, the authorities wiped the slate clean and gave you the chance to lead an honest and useful life. They even provided you with an experienced officer to oversee your well-being.

'And what did you do? You terrorized a peaceful town, its shoppers and bank staff and sought to shift the blame on to the policeman who protected you.

'I have not the slightest doubt that you would have dispatched anyone who got in your way with the same ruthlessness you displayed towards those two dogs. You are a violent criminal without mercy.

'It seems to me appropriate that you should start afresh the sentence that my fellow judge in your native province passed upon you. You will go to prison for eighteen years.'

Hegan turned from the bar of the dock, smiling.

'Sorry, Phil,' said the switchboard girl. 'Still ringing engaged. Maybe it's out of order.'

Or off the hook, Philippe concluded. Jacko had warned him that this old coroner didn't like his proceedings interrupted. No point in bleeping. He knew Jacko always switched off when he was in court.

'I'm going to have to nip up to the castle with a couple of important messages for my inspector. This office will be empty for twenty minutes. Cover me, will you?'

Senior Officer Downes hooked the phone back on its black base fixed to the wall next to the door to the dock.

'Keep that off.' Major Jarman used his commanding tone. He was standing behind an old desk unpacking his coffee-stained white Imperial portable from its battered black case. 'I don't want any interruptions.'

Downes removed the receiver, leaving it dangling by its cord.

'Everybody here?' The coroner turned to Jacko who looked up as Ridgeback, surprisingly smart in his bow-tie, sorted the papers into tidy piles on the desk.

Jacko walked slowly back the way he had come in. There were five cells on each side of the aisle, separated with white glazed brick walls. Each had grey bars running from ceiling to floor, a bunk on chains and a round wooden chair. The top two cells on either side were empty.

The first on the right was occupied by Connelly, lying on his bunk, eyes on the ceiling. Then came a vacant cell which had held the child abuser. Next came Marsh, sitting on the chair, legs wide apart, elbows on his knees, head hanging, like a soccer coach in a dug-out whose side was being thrashed. There were two more empty cells, the first of which had been occupied by Andrew Heald, deceased, and awaited Ridgeback as his stand-in.

On the left, the first two were empty; then the rapist, sitting on his chair, as close to the bars as he could get. Next was Hegan. He was sitting on his bunk, highly polished shoes firmly on the floor, head still, eyes constantly on the move. His neighbour was Rod Daniels, who had adopted Marsh's posture, apart from his head, held high, attentive, enjoying his day out.

He reached Haywood standing with Downes by the door. Beside them sat a girl reporter in a striped dress. 'Seen Holden today?' Jacko asked.

Both shook their heads. Jacko walked back. Above him mottled light was fighting its way through the filthy reinforced glass in long narrow windows just below the pale blue ceiling. He felt he was in the bowels of the earth.

Major Jarman was sitting now, setting the margins on his machine. He was wearing a flawless silvery-grey suit and a lemon bow-tie at a more rakish angle than Ridgeback's.

To his right was Tina Beaver in a colourfully embroidered black and gold waistcoat over a white cotton shirt and Mr Heald, pale and dark-suited. Both sat on wonky chairs with two guards standing behind them by the car-park door.

'Mr Holden is absent, sir,' Jacko reported.

The coroner looked at his gold wrist-watch. 'Does he know of the arrangements?'

'I informed him personally.'

'Better have a bloody good excuse.' A threatening pause, then, 'Carry on.'

Jacko turned again. 'All persons having anything to do at this inquest before Her Majesty's Coroner give your attendance.' He sat down beside the desk.

'This', the major began, 'is a resumption of the inquest opened three and half weeks ago. The object is to take depositions, then adjorn for a jury hearing when medical evidence will also be called. Witnesses I regarded as essential will be bound over to reappear before the jury. The rest will be released from further attendance.'

He read out aloud Mr Heald's evidence of identification from the opening of the inquest. 'Anything to add?'

'No, sir.'

He disposed of the four guards in similar brisk fashion. Mr Heald had no questions for them.

He turned to the prisoners, in cell order, beginning with Connelly, who stood at the bars while part of his statement was read to him. The coroner edited out all reference to his attack on Hegan and asked, 'Anything to add?'

'Yes, sir.'

Jacko walked to his cell, gave him a small black bible and administered the oath. The major looked up from rolling a statement form in his machine. 'Well?'

'There's been a conspiracy of silence.'

'Involving?' The coroner's fingers hovered over the keyboard, a concert pianist about to begin a recital.

'Him.' Connelly pointed across the aisle to Hegan, glaring menacingly.

'How?'

'He's Orange Billy Roberts, supergrass,' he said, triumphantly.

The coroner glared at him. 'The public in the court above were eventually informed of his past, isn't that so, Mr Jackson?'

Jacko nodded.

'How?' Connelly spluttered, deflating. 'When?'

'Now look here, young man.' Anyone under fifty was young when the major was losing his temper. 'I ask the questions in this court.'

'I tried to kill him and would have, if the police hadn't stopped me.'

'Who?' The major was confused and badly rattled. 'Andrew Heald?'

Connelly pointed at Hegan again. 'Him.'

'When?'

'In the exercise yard.'

'If and when you succeed in your mission, no doubt I shall

be required to conduct an inquest. In the mean time, did you kill your former cellmate Andrew Heald?'

'No, sir.' Connelly raised his voice. 'Most certainly not.'

'Then kindly sit down and keep quiet and don't pollute my proceedings with your tribal differences.'

'But . . .'

'Sit down, young man.' The coroner almost shouted. He ripped the statement form from his machine and ticked another name on his list of witnesses which he had already galloped half-way through.

25

So close did death await her, just a door's width away, that she missed it at first.

Shirley was standing among brown flakes of rotting wood which littered the front step when the door of Michael's Pub yielded to the crowbar. Two long shadows, hers and Upjohn's, lay along a sunlit avenue from the forced door across the bar floor, blackness on each side. No other light found its way through the boarded-up windows. The smell of decay, the odour of summer drains, made her nip her nostrils.

Upjohn, crowbar in hand, went first. Every footstep brought up grey puffs from the carpet on to his polished shoes.

To her left she could just make out ghostly silhouettes of sheets over tables piled high with upturned chairs and stools. To her right, a long bar, with a torn panel, empty shelves behind, and a serving hatch with a gap of less than an inch.

A stain, black, or so it seemed, spread from behind the door where she stood. It caught and held some of the dust Upjohn was kicking up, as tar does feathers. It looked like an oil spill, thick and sticky, with a river of rust running through it as though an old can had burst.

She took two paces inside. She pulled the door towards her, craning her neck behind it, narrowing the corridor of light, to find the source of the spill.

'Oh, my God.' Horror ran up from her toes, strangling stomach, heart, voice box, so she nearly screamed it.

'Shit,' shouted Upjohn. 'Shit. Shit. Shit.'

She hardly heard him. Her eyes weren't working, either. Her lids fluttered to bring them back to life.

She pulled the door another foot, held it with her left hand on the outside handle to steady it, lent her shoulder on the sharp edge to steady herself. She forced herself into a longer look.

Chin on his knees, Bryan Holden had slid sideways from a sitting position against the wall. He had departed this world the way he had waited in his late mother's womb to enter it.

Shirley held her breath and knelt. Her kneecaps had a sticky feeling. Acclimatized now, her eyes dwelt on his face. No restfulness there. No waxed whiteness. Matt grey. No shock, surprise even. Resignation, abdication.

She held a hand to his neck. For one stupid second she thought she felt something, then realized it was the irregular pumping of her own electrified system.

Through absorbent fingertips, his chill became her chill. His stiffness, her stiffness, freezing her, paralysing her.

In the semi-light, his red shirt seemed unsoiled but his khaki trousers had blackened. His blood had flowed out from his waistband.

'Oh, my God.' A gasp, more of a moan, really.

'Bitch.' Upjohn's voice, bitching, too distant to be directly behind her where she expected him to be.

She swivelled on her haunches. He was standing with his back to her in front of a door to the lounge. Same black door she had seen in the photos at the office but different somehow. Now she could see why. The long, leading vertical edge had been pulled away as though from a sardine tin. The hardboard panels remained intact to give the appearance of a long thin box, upright, gap facing her.

She looked at the doors from the bar to the toilets and kitchens. They had been peeled open, too.

Upjohn turned slowly from the door. 'She's taken the money. All of it.'

'Use the phone.'

'What?' Blunt, angry, powerful thoughts disturbed.

'The car. The phone. Call this in.' Her words came fast, urgent.

'Give me time to think.'

'Superintendent . . .' Patiently now. 'Holden has been shot dead. Murdered. We need forensics, police.'

'I am the bloody police.'

Two bags of potatoes rolled inside the boot of the silver Fiat as Philippe took the final hairpin. The early whites had been bought for his lady and Jacko from a farm shop off the A46. He got home so late last night that he forgot to take them out.

The vintage Rolls stood outside the Judge's lodgings which meant the trial was over. He drove at a crawl through the castle gates, past the foot of the observation tower and the entrance to the jailhouse chapel where tourists, heads up to view sights or down over guidebooks, tend to wander suicidally.

There was plenty of room in the car-park. On the left a black van pointed towards the narrow lane he had just driven down. Its young driver stood with door ajar, his back to a clump of elder bushes at the bottom of the bank on which stood the south wall. Out of the undergrowth a man's voice called, 'About twelve inches.' The van's back doors were wide apart. Standing before them was another man in overalls, his upper body bent inside the back of the van from which came the steady chip, chip, chip of a chisel working on stone.

In the far corner was the blue bus which had brought the prisoners and guards from jail for the inquest, empty, except for its driver, reading the *Mirror* spread out on his steering wheel. Ahead of the bus was a big white police car with a red flash down each side and a two-man crew.

A line of cars were parked with their noses towards the wall. He found a spot one row back. From a distance of thirty yards, he could see there was no handle or bell on the outer steel doors to the cellblock. He wasn't going to bother to knock.

He ran lightly up the steps and walked into the crown court via the side door. The foyer was empty except for a harassed agency reporter, his head out of the plastic hood above a public phone, arguing with someone. 'But I've still got to pick up this inquest from the *Echo* lass.'

Philippe shambled, soundless, over the sea-green carpet. The door to Court No. 1, which gave the only alternative access to the cellblock via the dock, was locked.

172

'No good,' called the agency man during a lull in his row. 'This coroner never lets people in or out while he's in session.'

Philippe sat on a bench and listened to the reporter lose his row and dictate a one-minute summary of Hegan's case, expertly cramming his past, present and future into less than two hundred words.

Carl Marsh stood at the bars, listening to the coroner read out his statement. 'Anything to add?'

'No, thanks.'

Major Jarman dug into a fresh file and read out extracts from Bryan Holden's interviews. 'You see, there's a discrepancy here. Holden clearly states he had no physical contact with Mr Heald. You say both had their hands on the cell bars.'

A startled look. 'I didn't say they touched.'

The major picked out Rod Daniels' statement. 'He says Mr Holden stood three feet from the bars. Explain that.'

Carl shot Daniels a dejected glance across the aisle. 'Don't know, sir.'

'Who's right – you or Mr Daniels?'

'Not sure, sir.'

'Think about it.'

Sullen silence.

'Well?'

'I mean, I suppose, well . . . I could have got mixed up,' said Carl, lamely. 'You can get confused in here.'

'You'll be in there a lot longer than anticipated if you mess about with me,' said the major sternly.

'Then I will.' Shirley pushed herself up with her fingertips in Holden's blood.

Six yards separated her from Upjohn. He stretched out his final strides. With the last one, he fly-kicked the outer door shut with the sole of his left shoe. 'I said *wait*.'

It hit its frame with such force that it bounced back ten inches so that the light in the broad avenue went out and came back as a narrow street, angled away from them.

'Please.' Shirley's voice was thin and frightened.

They stood face to face, a foot apart. She could feel his breath, his heat.

'They know, don't they?'

'Know what?' Brittle now, ready to break.

'Scott and Jackson. They know.'

'Know what?' Quieter, calmer, better, Shirley told herself. In the half-light, she stared at his face. His jaw tightened. His sallow cheeks twitched.

'Maureen and me.'

She lowered her head, closed her eyes. When she opened them they were on the crowbar gripped in his right hand. 'Oh, no. Poor you.'

'Very poor. She's taken the fucking money.' He swayed. He pulled back his shoulders to steady himself. 'What a mug, eh? What a total fool.' He shook his head. 'Me and you, she said, me and you.'

'Then count yourself lucky.' She looked towards Holden. 'She screwed you both.'

Wordless moments.

'It's over for me,' he said, lowly.

'Come on, sir.' Jollying him.

'They know I set it up for them. Greed's what fucked it.' His voice went astonishingly high. 'Everybody's.' Down a note. 'Everybody's.'

'Yours included.'

'I'd have settled for what was mine.'

'For selling confidential information.' Deep scorn.

'I don't want a lecture.' A sudden movement, frightening. She flinched, then saw it was his left hand raising a lecturing finger. 'How did they work it out?'

She said nothing.

'How?'

'It was Jacko.'

'How?'

No point in holding back, Shirley decided. He's trapped and being taped. String him along. Get more confessions. 'You know Hegan and Maureen. Your position gave you access to the bank's memo on the money and to the armoury for the gun. You saw Hegan in jail. You were around when Jacko's car was sabotaged and the files were set on fire.'

'Very clever,' he said sarcastically.

'It took some time to work out. We thought for a while that whoever killed Heald really aimed to kill Hegan.'

'Not so clever.'

'Once Stan Young . . .'

Upjohn snorted derisively.

'You underestimated him. He could see that Heald's death was an accident. Once Jacko bought that, he looked at your lifestyle. Three marriages, a big house, a big car, all the local dog-hangings. You need the money . . .'

Shirley trailed off, disappointed. Upjohn was not responding, not confirming anything. She tried again. 'What do you want to do?'

'Time to think.' Upjohn made another movement, away from her, less frightening. Clunk. Blackness told her he'd backed into the door. She took a pace back.

Gradually, like a badly focused print in a developing dish, his outline appeared, dark, murky. She addressed it, as casual as she could manage. 'How much was here?'

'The lot. And she knew. All the time, she knew.'

'And you didn't?'

'She conned me. Me. Conned.' He still couldn't believe it.

'I believe she did.'

'What the hell do you know about her?'

'I know it's Hegan for her. Her Michael. I just know, that's all.'

'How?' He moved, fractionally, but alarmingly.

'She lights up when she talks about him. A woman can tell. Wounded your ego, has it?'

'Shut up.' Upjohn was breathing deeply.

A long silence which she broke. 'Now what?'

'We wait. We can sit down and make ourselves comfortable, if you like, but we wait.'

'Wait for what?'

'You'll see.'

'And then what? Do I finish up like Holden?' She spoke without fear.

Rod Daniels listened listlessly to his statements being read. The major glowered over the top of his half-moons. 'Who's right?'

'I don't know.' Daniels flashed a distress signal towards Carl Marsh. 'He did have his back to me.'

175

The major looked down, re-reading Holden's statement. 'You say you heard mention of a message. You appear to be right about that.' He read an extract. "Tell her, even with remission, it's a long time and, if she wants to take off, I'll understand." He looked sideways at Tina. 'Can you throw any light on that?'

She spoke slowly, in thought. 'We had talked of doing some overseas work for Amnesty International, you know, leafleting and picketing jails where political prisoners are held. That sort of campaigning. When he was arrested I told him it could wait till he got out but it's possible he thought I ought to go ahead on my own. That's the only thing I can think of.'

So Stan's right. Jacko knew it. It was Carl. An accident. Had to be. He'd panicked, then coloured his account to get his burgling brother and his girlfriend courier off the hook.

He began wondering and worrying about how Stan and Shirl were making out.

'Anyway,' said Shirley, for something to say to end the long silence and to extract more confessions, 'she must love him. She's taken terrible risks for him.' She paused, teasing him. 'We've got photos. Came in on the wire today from New York. Some tourist took them. Here, outside this place, the day he got away. Very interesting.'

'I don't believe you.' Upjohn sounded like the voice of doom out of the gloom.

'Got a set in the boot if you'd like a look. One snap of her coming in here with the clock in the window showing eleven. One shot coming out and, lo, the clock's at five thirty. She changed the time to tip him your own men were lying in wait.'

'Bitch.' A wounded cry. 'The bitch. She's taken the money to *him*.' Two cracks, almost together, the back of his head on the door, the door in its frame.

Fearful now, she backed away towards the sheeted-down tables.

'Now. She's with him *now*.' A bitter laugh. 'That's one thing clever-dick Jackson didn't work out.'

'She's flown off,' said Shirley dismissively.

'To wait for him.'

'Rubbish. She's . . .'

'Now they've sprung him. That's where he'll go. He won't come here. To her. He'll join her.'

'We took care of that at the hospital last night. You're talking . . .'

'You took care of nothing.' A misty figure, bigger than she'd ever seen him, loomed towards her. 'He's coming over the castle wall, not the hospital . . .'

'*Bastard*.' Her right hand ripped the strap from her left shoulder. Legs apart, feet anchored, she extended her right arm beyond her left hip and swung the bag forward.

'Bitch.' The shadow in front of her gasped, twisted, shrunk, but still came forward. The weight of the bag pitched her involuntarily towards the strangled sound. One forward step and, with the second, she jerked up her knee.

Lower still was the shadow, groaning, winded. A head was at her stomach. She felt for the hair. Hands, boiling hot, weakly palmed the back of her knees. She grabbed a greasy handful, yanked it back and pushed her left hand into the face.

'Arhh.' The shortened shadow fell away. A hand found and held her left ankle. She kicked her leg away, then lashed out with her foot. A pained, pleading voice moaned something inaudible from the floor.

The door burst open, flooding her with light. '*Armed police*.' Stan Young was framed in classic pose – knees flexed, arms extended towards her, gun hand rock steady.

She looked down to see Upjohn roll over, face down, in Holden's blood.

'Did you hear that?'

'Not all of it,' said Stan.

She ran towards him. He moved to one side without losing his view and aim. She darted past, on to her car, tugged open the passenger door, pulled the handset on to the seat. Kneeling on the cinders, she tapped out a number. It rang six times while she counted. 'Sergeant Marlowe, please '

'Out, I'm afraid.'

She drew a deep breath and identified herself. 'I need Mr Scott very, very urgently. It's life or death.'

'Hold on tight, dear,' said the switchboard operator, calmly.

A clipped, cool voice, 'Yes, Miss Thomas.'

*

Tiny yellow bulbs flashed like lights on a Christmas tree as Scott entered the Control Room. A row of six held a steady red glow on the console they had cleared for him. They had made most of the calls he had ordered when he was transferring Shirley across from his office extension.

'Who first?' said an inspector pulling out a grey swivel chair on its castors.

'The armed escort car.' Scott sat down and wheeled himself back in front of the console. A WPC handed him light black earphones with a mouthpiece no bigger than a match stick.

He introduced himself when the inspector nodded. 'What are your names?'

'Taylor, sir, and my partner's Slade,' came the nervous reply.

'First names?'

'I'm John, sir, and he's Gerry.'

'Now, John. I want you and Gerry to look happy and laugh and joke together while I tell you the score. You two are sitting on a time bomb that's about to go off. There's going to be a breakout attempt at the castle at any second. They're bound to be armed. Are you still smiling?'

'Trying to, sir,' said Taylor, gamely.

'Good. Take a very casual look about you and tell me what you see. Very casual, mind.'

A very brief pause. 'The prison bus in the mirror, a line and a half of cars near the wall to my left and a gang of masons in a van near the exit.'

'Hold,' said Scott. The WPC flicked a switch. 'Do you have any stonemasons working in the car-park?'

'Not staff, no,' said the castle custodian in a voice from the Welsh valleys.

'Any outside contractors?'

'Not on my list.'

'John.' All lines to the console had been linked and the patrolman had heard the conversation. 'Keep an eye on that van. The problem we have is this. We have a coroner, several civvies, half a dozen prisoners, including Michael Hegan, the target for the escape, and some of our own men in that cellblock and out of touch. One is a Met undercover man dressed as a prison guard. Shirley, describe Inspector Haywood.'

Shirley was on her bloodstained knees, frightened that her legs would give way if she stood. A patrol car ground the grit as it skidded to a halt in front of the pub door. Upjohn was being bundled into the back, handcuffed to Stan.

'Six foot. Short, fair hair. Pale skin. And he's armed.'

'Got that, John? So if a warder produces a gun don't shoot him. He's one of ours. Also there is Sergeant Frank Marlowe who is weapon-trained but unaware of the situation until he answers his bleep.'

'Just seen him, sir, going up the steps.'

'He's not in the cellblock then? Good. When we raise him, he'll take charge. He knows who's who.'

'Right,' said Taylor, sounding relieved.

'How long will it take to give them back-up?' asked Scott.

The Control Room inspector answered. 'Nearest armed response is *en route* from the A1. Twenty minutes at best.'

'Direct them to the outside of the west wall. No sirens on the final approach. We don't want hostages taken. What other patrol is nearest?'

'A dog handler's van, east side of the cathedral,' said the WPC.

'Tell him to get to the castle. Straight up the drive to the court building. Not the car-park.'

The inspector butted in. 'Sergeant Marlowe is responding to his bleep.'

'Philippe,' said Scott, cheerfully. 'Thank Christ. Where are you?'

'Up at the castle.'

'Where?'

'In a public phone box in the court foyer.' Philippe lowered his voice.

Scott briefed him in staccato sentences.

'Oh, Jesus,' Philippe whispered gruffly. 'I can't get in. Both entrances are locked. What about the phone?'

'Engaged still.' Scott gave it only a few seconds' thought and spoke to the driver of the armed response car. 'Sergeant Marlowe will be with you in a tick. Now, you two, how can you make contact without being spotted?'

The coroner turned to Jacko after Hegan and the rapist told him they had nothing to add. 'And you, inspector?'

'Yes, sir.' His eyes found Carl's, imprisoning them. 'We are working on a promising line of inquiry with the Drugs Squad. The results of more tests are expected very shortly.'

'You?' The major addressed Mr Heald, but it was Tina who answered, quietly. 'We appreciate the efforts being made to find the reason for Andrew's death. We don't want retribution, just an explanation. If we understood it, then we might be better able to accept it.' She looked down at her hands, clenched on her lap. Carl's head dropped.

Major Jarman rested his elbows on either side of his typewriter and formed a rest for his chin with the backs of his hands. 'Be assured that I will find that reason. There is undoubtedly a conspiracy of silence, though not in the context that has been mentioned. It is unacceptable that drugs, in this case a lethal dose, should be so freely available in penal establishments.'

The *Echo* girl's pen was speeding across the page.

'I trust the authorities will take immediate action to stamp out their circulation.' He formally adjourned.

Mr Heald and Tina stood and walked down the aisle. Jacko saw her smile sideways at Carl who looked away. They reached the door to the dock steps, waiting for it to be unlocked.

The coroner glanced up when he had fitted his machine back in its case. 'I'd like to observe the order in which the witnesses left here for the bus.'

He saw Mr Heald and Tina had stopped to listen. 'Don't let me detain you. I mean the prisoners and their escorts. You're free to go.'

Officer Downes unlocked the door and relocked it behind them. He walked up the aisle, a big bunch of keys in his hand.

'What's his name?' asked Philippe.

'Corporal,' said the handler.

Philippe, unembarrassed, let the dog sniff at the crutch of his trousers.

He began to talk softly to avoid being overheard by the agency man studying Monday's list on the notice-board. He finished his briefing with, 'As soon as that door to the court opens, go in, through the dock and down the stairs. There's another security door at the bottom and that may be locked. Warn them any way you can.'

He looked down at the bored dog, then up at its handler, a fifty-year-old whose tracking duties had kept him lean and fit. 'Good luck, mate.'

'You, too, sarge.' They gave each other soldiers' smiles.

Philippe walked swiftly out the side entrance, doubling back in front of the closed oak doors, slowing as he approached the terrace wall.

He leant on it, looking down. 'Got you them spuds, Johnny,' he called a little too loudly.

PC Taylor climbed out of the patrol car below him. 'Smashing.' It came out in a numbed sort of mumble.

'Want them now?'

'Why not?'

Philippe took the steps down at an easy, even pace, eyes ranging the car-park, resting on the two men in overalls standing with their heads inside the back of the black van.

He walked to his car, opened the boot and lifted out a big brown paper bag, fastened at the top with strong wire. He carried it with obvious effort in both hands towards the patrol car when PC Taylor stood with his boot open. From fifteen yards away, he called again, still too loud, 'Three quid. All right?'

'Smashing.' The constable bent forward under the boot lid and unlocked a heavy silver box. He unclipped a black .38 Special, checked it was loaded and handed it to Philippe as soon as he had dropped the potato bag at his feet. He took out a second gun.

They stood up straight, arms extended, pistols pointing to the ground at knee-height.

'OK, mate?' Philippe breathed in, expanding his chest to relieve a weight, heavier than that bag of potatoes, round his heart.

'Smashing.' PC Taylor was barely able to get the word out.

26

'*Arm* . . .' Philippe started to shout when he reached the van. An explosion blew away the rest; a blast so loud the walls of the car-park seemed to tremble and close in on him.

The van jumped crazily up and down, sides expanding outwards. A man was shaken out of the back. He fell in front of Philippe who dropped on his knees, deafened.

'Arrrrr.' A pitiful scream from the cab. The van shot forward, back doors flapping.

Another man dived forward in desperation. He fell face first. A shot gun clattered on the asphalt.

Almost simultaneously, Jacko heard a scream from the other side of the castle wall. '*Now.*'

What the f . . .? he thought, totally bewildered.

Major Jarman swept him in both arms towards the foot of the steps. 'Gunfire,' he said with astonishing calmness.

Three or four chained-together men who had walked out the cellblock behind them tried to drop to the ground. Only one guard made it. Haywood and the rapist were held half-way, suspended, neither up nor down. Hegan, feet wide apart, threw back his shoulder, stiffened his arms and legs. '*Here. I'm here.*'

From the top of the wall a squatting man fired a short horizontal burst that sounded like r's rasped over a short tongue. Philippe and his partner fell flat.

Major Jarman took command. 'Shut that bloody door,' he called, urgently, but without panic. Downes pulled from the inside, slamming it on frightened faces.

Outside, stranded and handcuffed together, stood Ridgeback and Carl Marsh, looking more than lost, petrified.

'Take cover,' boomed Major Jarman, hunched up in a ball next to Jacko. They ran, getting lower with every stride, and slid, legs outstretched in front of them, beneath the bus.

Another man, masked, heavier than the first, was heaving a ladder over the top of the wall. He rammed its feet hard into the grass bank and tossed down yellow-handled cutters.

'There's an escape on,' said Major Jarman, unflustered.

'We were a day too early.' Jacko's voice was almost soprano. He looked across the car-park. The van, engine running, blocked the driveway. Philippe and his partner lay face down, the soles of their shoes towards him. He saw their revolvers. Ahead of them two unarmed men in overalls lay prone. 'That end's under control, well covered.' A croak, contralto, getting better.

'This end's the problem,' said the major, matter-of-fact.

'Here,' screamed Hegan, the only person in the car-park standing completely upright. 'Here.'

The masked man slid down the ladder, ankles and knees gripping the outer struts. He landed with a stumble and picked the cutters out of the damp grass. He tobogganed down the bank on his back.

'Here,' screamed Hegan. 'Here.'

The masked man ran towards him. Haywood rose from one knee. The man held the cutters out in front of him, a sort of bayonet charge, stainless steel end first. In his last stride, he swung his right shoulder across his chest and smashed the long yellow handles against Haywood's left arm. He slumped back, crying out in agony.

The warder at the other end of the chain-gang darted in front of the kneeling rapist and grabbed the cutter head with his free hand. He was elbowed hard and repeatedly in the face and fell, mouth oozing blood.

'It's over-the-top time, Mr Jackson,' said the major.

Oh, shit, thought Jacko. My moment's come. Oh, shit. In all his life, he'd never felt more shit-scared than now. Right now.

Snap. The cutter separated Hegan and the rapist who collapsed on his back, looking up, begging. 'No. Please. No.'

The officer handcuffed to him, a big blob of blood for a mouth, staggered up, grabbed the cutter head again, twisting it. The masked man smashed a fist, crunchingly, into his face.

Haywood threw out his useless left arm, missed his target. The effort exhausted him. He pulled down hard on the handcuff which held Hegan to him. His right hand was an inch from the boiler suited man's testicles. The cutter, blunt end first, chopped down on his wrist. His fingers made a claw squeezing nothing but unbearable pain.

Snap. The cuff was cut. Hegan was free.

'Go,' said Major Jarman, quite quietly. Jacko pushed down on tips of toes and fingers. He was off and running, low, rising higher every step, the major at his elbow.

The tea-cosy black hair of Carl Marsh and the ginger of Ridgeback's were just visible beneath the bus. 'Let's go, men,' the major yelled. 'Go.'

Ridgeback crawled out first, turning, bending, to pull Carl. Bullets were bursting alongside the bus over their heads. All four reached the grass bank. Jacko threw himself on to the long wet stalks, wishing they would swallow him, cover him, hide him. He tried to lie still but shuddered too much.

Hegan was crawling up the bank on hands and knees, the masked man close behind.

A fresh burst skipped like flat stones on water along car boot lids towards an approaching Philippe, leaving a trail of jagged holes. He ducked, ran, crouching, past a line of cars.

Jacko scrambled sideways, on all fours, like a crab. He caught the masked man's ankle cleanly. A second's elation. He pulled it towards his stomach, a wicketkeeper's catch. Disaster. He dropped his catch as a heel rammed his balls together. Again and again and again. Judders shot and stung right through his body.

He fell, groin bursting, on the man's arched back. A second's glimpse of a rounded handle of a black gun. Frozen horror was followed by numbness as it flattened itself on his temple. His head rang like Great Tom. He swayed, fell sideways, a leg trapped under a heavy body.

In muzzy outline, he could just make out Hegan as he reached the foot of the ladder and stepped on the first rung.

The gunman on the wall above limped into a fresh position, looking down on the masked man, shouting instructions, screaming. Things that had happened on fast-forward were now in slow motion and he could no longer distinguish each word, every face.

He lay there, trapped, a spectator, seeing everything through a lace curtain, understanding nothing.

Black and red heads crawling up the grass each side of the masked man . . . The cellblock door opening outwards . . . An alsatian emerging, tail straight as a ramrod, glistening nose twitching . . . Men in a cursing pile on the grass next to him.

Surrealistically, a yellow bow-tie dropped in front of him among the blades of grass. Wet plugs of earth hit his right cheek. Hysterical voices called above and around.

Philippe reached the end car in the row. The gunman fired a burst which whitened the rear window of the car.

The dog lengthened his stride under the gunfire, then shortened it to climb the bank.

Hegan reached the top of the ladder.

Ridgeback, right-handed, and Carl, left-handed, hooked their chain over the masked man's forehead. Major Jarman knelt on his gun hand, swearing. With his free hand the masked man tried to tug the chain away. They pushed him down. He pressed up with head and stomach. Push, pull, push. Jacko's leg was suddenly released. Pull, push, pull. Over his nose. His slit mouth opened, gasping for air. They bridled him. His face fell on the grass.

The dog's front legs hooked a rung at a time. His hind legs danced together four rungs behind.

'Shoot the fokker,' Hegan screamed at the gunman, standing next to him.

Jacko rolled away, free from the mêlée, never saw the gun trained on him, never saw Philippe suddenly stand upright, legs apart, arms extended in front of him.

Thwack. A bullet found its target. It didn't whine or sing. Thwack. No death rattle. No piercing scream. No lazy Hollywood-style fall.

One moment the gunman had been there on top of the wall. Now he was gone.

The dog bounded on to the parapet.

'Fokker.' Hegan, alone, was screaming louder still.

The dog sprang four feet through the air towards him. Hegan twisted away, covering his face with his right arm. 'Fok . . .' The dog sank its teeth in just below an elbow. They fell outwards and backwards, the dog locked on. It let go as it landed lightly on both front paws on the outside grass bank.

Crack. A different sound, dull, nauseating, paralysing.

Hegan rolled over and over, out of control. He came to rest next to the gunman, hanging face up over a low garden wall. Blood and white splinters of bone were pouring out of him on to chalky soil in which a wigwam of French beans grew. From beneath them both came pungent ammonia. Humus began to feed the beans.

'Shall I crank you up?' A girl's voice, warm and mischievous.

I bet private patients don't get offered personal services like this, Jacko thought. He opened his eyes and saw a vague outline of a black face and a white nurse's cap.

He thought of saying something like, 'Will it jerk me off?', decided against it until he got to know her better. He was pleased he'd kept silent when the back of the bed rose slowly and Jackie and Scott came into blurred view.

Jackie took his hand, stood, bent and kissed his nose. The Little Fat Man sat beaming.

Jacko had the sort of dull headache he always associated with oversleeping. She gave him his old Buddy Holly specs with heavy black frames. His eyes focused on a newspaper on the bed. The *Sunday Times*. Jesus. I've missed a day.

They teamed up as a double act to tell him his injuries. 'A hairline skull fracture,' said Jackie. 'But no additional brain damage,' added Scott maliciously. 'Contusions in the nether regions,' said Jackie. 'Black balls, she means. You'll never make the Masons now,' he chortled.

Jacko gave him a weak smile as he felt himself beneath the sheet. Still there but unclad. Oh, God, those underpants were a day old. He felt a pang of deep shame.

Scott nodded to a bowl of mixed flowers on the bedside cabinet. 'Shirl and Stan brought them but you were asleep. They've gone off to collect one of his kids. Staying in Bath overnight.' He smirked, knowingly.

Jacko thought of Johnson's Baby Oil again and smiled.

'Haywood's been discharged to the care of his steady, an army nurse,' Scott went on. 'Ridgeback got shot in the bum but he's back home flat on his stomach watching "One Man and his Dog" on TV. Just a flesh wound; horizontal so it looks like a hot cross bun. Hot cross bum, get it?'

Jacko chuckled, rattling his aching testicles.

Scott, serious-faced now, told him the dead gunman was called Mo Mercer, a small-time Cockney crook, the accomplice on the bank raid. Hegan and the getaway driver might never walk again. The van driver's crippling hip and thigh wounds had been caused by one of the shooters. Just as he was taking a sawn-off shot-gun out of the back, he pulled the trigger as Philippe surprised him with the shouted challenge. The gang leader, called Edward Layton, and the two shooters were in custody.

'The rest are on the run, including Maureen. We traced her to Belfast where she vanished,' he said, gloom setting in.

'And the money?'

'She's moved it. She won't have taken it through all that security. Just enough to get by on. She'll have tucked it away in a new place until it can be laundered through a bookie or a shelf company.'

Jacko had never served in Fraud and didn't really know how such financial transactions worked. He did know where Maureen would be, though. An idea was beginning to form. He decided not to share it yet. 'Upjohn?'

'On remand, round the corner, saying nothing. We won't get him for fixing your car or for the fire.' Scott shrugged. 'But Shirley's got him bang to rights on conspiracy.'

'And Philippe?'

Scott's face shadowed. 'I ran him home. Hardly said a word. I've called his lady. He isn't sleeping.'

They chatted for a while. Then Scott stood. 'Your pool car's a write-off.' He turned to Jackie with a grave face. 'And I'm afraid your potatoes are goners. Slugs got 'em.'

Jacko laughed through the pain. Even if they were unplugging the life support, the Little Fat Man would want him to go happy. They winked affectionate goodbyes.

Jackie stayed another hour. The Buddy Hollys were tight and obsolete and he couldn't concentrate to read. He took them off. 'I'll let you rest.' She kissed his nose goodnight.

He dozed and awoke to find Major Jarman standing over him, dressed in country tweeds. '*En route* home from the prison,' he said. 'I'm not sure if it was conscience or the fact they were strip-searching every cell, but Carl Marsh asked to see me. He's admitted giving Andy Heald three pills he thought were brown bombers. He claims he brought them into jail with him.'

There was no way, Jacko realized, Marsh was going to shop his brother and girlfriend who'd passed them to him with a kiss in the cellblock.

'So it amounts to misadventure,' said the coroner, rehearsing his summing-up.

Jacko knew he'd publicly condemn indiscriminate use of drugs but privately he'd petition for Carl's early release, a reward for his courage under fire. Carl was one of his men now.

'Sleep well,' he said, patting his hand.

Jacko called him back. 'Tell me. What does the D in D-day stand for?'

'Determined.' Jacko gave him a puzzled frown. 'As in decide. It's the day planners have determined for an operation before they know the exact date it will take place. Everything is planned forward and back from the day determined. A bit clumsy.' He shrugged. 'You know the military. Why?'

'I was just thinking. That's all.'

'Good man. That's what I like to hear.' He waved goodbye.

Man, thought Jacko, smiling to himself. In his world of officers and men, the major had put him in his place and he was one of the men, one of the boys, and he was happy there.

Soon Philippe replaced him at the bedside. He pulled up a chair as close as he could get. His face was haggard. His frame seemed wizened.

Jacko did most of the talking. 'Sorry I couldn't cut you in. Scotty was pulling the strings. He just used Andy Heald's death as a cover to find the two million and who tipped Hegan off. We thought it was Stan at first. He didn't perform well on that sandwich clue.' A forgiving shrug. 'Still, he was falling in love.'

'How did you rumble Upjohn?' A mechanical tone, not really interested, too much on his mind.

'When he made a big fuss of Haywood with that tour of inspection round here, the creep. To him, he should have been just another buckshee warder. Only Scott and us knew his identity. What was a great womanizer like Upjohn doing ignoring a classy bird like Shirl for a rank-and-file guard?

'Hegan could have told him who Haywood was when he saw him in the remand wing. He put on a good show of protecting Hegan here. He could afford to. He knew we'd got the wrong day and place. Same as he put on a show of catching him at the pub. Ridgeback submitted that house-to-house return from New York but Upjohn binned it instead of following it up. That's about it, really.'

188

They were silent. Jacko knew the time had come. 'Thanks, son.'

Philippe gave a helpless, hopeless shake of his head.

'How are you?' Jacko spoke gently.

'Hard to tell, really. It's like watching a film. I see him vanished over the wall but I can't bring myself to accept it was me who did it.'

Work, Jacko decided, was the cure for that. And a smoke. He sat up. 'Give us a fag.'

'I thought you'd . . .'

Jacko flicked his fingers impatiently.

Drawing in, surreptitiously but contentedly, he reached in the cabinet, got out his old red contacts book.

'Put yourself in the perp's size five wedges,' ordered Blackie Le Grande.

"Some shoes to fill,' Philippe agreed over a second Jack Daniels. 'She'd been living with Holden while screwing Stan, Upjohn and Hegan on the side.'

Upjohn, he theorized, wanted her exclusively so he fed her the inside info on the bank job. He suggested that Hegan con both Stan and Holden to the scene in the hope that one or other would be implicated. He planted the fingerprints to make sure police knew Hegan, his other rival, was on the robbery.

'Leaving him a clear field to Maureen,' suggested Blackie, getting the picture.

'Yeah, but Maureen just used Upjohn. All the time it was really her M-i-c-h-a-e-l for her. She strung along Upjohn with a story that she didn't know where the money was hidden. He advised on the escape plot so he could finally get his hands on his share. He didn't want Hegan inside, anyway, talking to Special Branch.

'Holden suspected what was going on. He called me with that anonymous tip to try to put an end to it. But he only knew how badly he had been taken when he trailed Maureen to Michael's Pub and found her recovering the money and got himself killed.'

Much of this, Philippe had to admit, was guesswork. Holden was dead. Hegan was too ill to talk and Layton too smart. So was Upjohn.

'Now you put yourself in Maureen's place,' Philippe said.

'Well,' said Blackie contemplatively, 'you'd have sense enough not to book into a room under your own name or use your Amex.

'But you're going to be a mite interested in finding out what's going on back home. You'd buy the papers and turn on TV.'

They checked but the deaths of a social worker and a small-time crook in a jailbreak had not made the New York press. They had, Blackie pointed out, almost two thousand killings a year of their own to report plus 30,000 firearms deaths nationally, thanks all the same.

'So you'd buy a Brit paper, right, preferably one that you knew your way round,' Blackie ventured.

There were, he discovered, lots of outlets for day-old London *Daily Express*es in New York but only a handful at each.

They worked down the list. 'Why, yes,' one vendor finally said. 'A real English rose. Last three lunchtimes.'

Maureen Beckby had settled into a routine now. A few drinks at night with out-of-towners, never giving that look to any men in the company.

A morning lie-in during which she'd rationalized Bryan Holden's death as a sad accident and had almost dismissed him from her mind. Then the first of three showers a day, a stroll down to pick up a paper so she could do the crossword over brunch.

For a few days she'd immersed herself in TV and fat local papers but none carried any stories about a British shooting or a jailbreak. Walking back from Central Park she'd spotted a shop that sold English papers, including the *Express*, but found nothing in it. By now, she realized, the jailbreak would be old news and maybe they hadn't found Bryan yet. She decided to go on buying it, just to keep an eye on developments and, besides, she liked its crosswords.

In a new, cool silk paisley dress, she walked out of the store just off 3rd Avenue. She scanned the front page through tinted glasses that had steamed over in the heat. She slipped the paper in her new leather shoulder bag.

She did not see a huge untidy man and a tall lumbering man appraising her, comparing what they saw with a photo. They began to follow ten yards but twenty-five people behind her on the crowded sidewalk.

Love this place, she thought. The shops, the shows, the sights, the eating places we'll be visiting. Not one little bit did she miss the open spaces and the cooling breezes of the other New York.

She turned into 42nd, past the towering News building, with frontage of marble and stainless steel. She crossed 2nd Avenue. She walked into a red-brick hotel: thirties, looking older.

She crossed the foyer (more marble, very plush) to the reception desk and noticed the men for the first time as she asked for her tenth-floor key.

'You English?' the big American asked, matily.

'Yes,' she said coldly, looking into an olive face with amused black eyes fixed on the little scar on her chin.

'Maybe you know this buddy of mine?' He cocked a thumb over his shoulder. 'Phil Marlowe.'

She gave both the wan smile of a woman who had heard all the best chat-up lines in her time and this wasn't one of them. 'I'm afraid not.'

'Think you know his partner, though. Name of Jackson. He's from Robinhoodsville, Sheriff's department.' He pulled his badge from his pen pocket.

'And on his behalf I'm arresting you in da name of da Queen.'